Drunk With Passion...

"Are you real?" she asked haltingly, barely able to breathe, much less speak. "Or are you a dream?"

A smile transformed his dark, shadowed features. The flash of white teeth gave him a look of boyish recklessness. "If it's a dream, I'm having it, too."

He touched her hair, pushing the golden tresses over her shoulders so that she lay bare to his gaze and to the kiss of the sun. Apollo, the sun god, in the sky and here beside her, the two somehow mixed in her dazzled mind. She no longer knew—or cared—where one left off and the other began.

She watched, mesmerized, as his head lowered toward hers. She had waited all her life for this very moment, and her life would be altered by it forever.

Dear Reader:

Romance offers us all so much. It makes us "walk on sunshine." It gives us hope. It takes us out of our own lives, encouraging us to reach out to others. Janet Dailey is fond of saying that romance is a state of mind, that it could happen anywhere. Yet nowhere does romance seem to be as good as when it happens *here*.

Starting in February 1986, Silhouette Special Edition will feature the AMERICAN TRIBUTE—a tribute to America, where romance has never been so wonderful. For six consecutive months, one out of every six Special Editions will be an episode in the AMERICAN TRIBUTE, a portrait of the lives of six women, all from Oklahoma. Look for the first book, *Love's Haunting Refrain* by Ada Steward, as well as stories by other favorites—Jeanne Stephens, Gena Dalton, Elaine Camp and Renee Roszel. You'll know the AMERICAN TRIBUTE by its patriotic stripe under the Silhouette Special Edition border.

AMERICAN TRIBUTE—six women, six stories, starting in February.

AMERICAN TRIBUTE—one of the reasons Silhouette Special Edition is just that—Special.

The Editors at Silhouette Books

FREDA VASILOS
Summer
Wine

Silhouette Special Edition

Published by Silhouette Books New York

America's Publisher of Contemporary Romance

With love to John,
for his unfailing support and practical advice.
Also thanks to Tara,
for nursing "the new girl on the block."

SILHOUETTE BOOKS
300 E. 42nd St., New York, N.Y. 10017

Copyright © 1986 by Freda Vasilopoulos

Distributed by Pocket Books

ISBN: 0-373-09286-5

First Silhouette Books printing January 1986

10 9 8 7 6 5 4 3 2 1

America's Publisher of Contemporary Romance

Printed in the U.S.A.

Books by Freda Vasilos

Silhouette Desire
Moon Madness #231

Silhouette Special Edition
Summer Wine #286

FREDA VASILOS

has been married for fifteen years to a genuine Greek who
bears little resemblance to the heroes of early romance
novels set in Greece. She decided to write a book that
would change readers' misconceptions about Greek
heroes. Greek men are gorgeous!

Chapter One

She lay in the sea, cradled by the silken deep. Closing her eyes against the intense blue of the sky, she floated, lulled by the friendly lap of tiny waves. The faraway chirring of cicadas wove a gentle serenade through the somnolent heat of the summer afternoon.

Greece. Sun, sand and sea, and air the sweet lucid gold of summer wine. Everything about the country struck a responsive chord deep within her, as if in a former life she'd walked its sere hills and fertile valleys.

Why hadn't she come here before this? She'd written her Ph.D. thesis on the early inhabitants of this land, those who had built civilizations centuries before Pericles, but she'd never seen where they'd lived. Now she was here, and the sense of walking where those ancient wise men had walked was overwhelming, a dream come to vivid life. Even after four days in Greece, Sara couldn't shake the feeling that she might meet Agamemnon striding through a lemon orchard, or see powerful Zeus on one of the treeless crags in the distance, braced to unleash a handful of thunderbolts on a slumbering world.

The smile on her face turned into a quiet chuckle of contentment as she stretched her legs sensuously in the liquid warmth of the sea. Its saline buoyancy made swimming effortless. Her long hair fanned out behind her as she moved her arms only enough to let her body slide through the water with languid grace. She could lie here forever, floating mindlessly, an elemental return to the warm fluid of the womb.

Her own departure from Athens yesterday and the grueling drive to reach Sparta the same day had been worth the effort. This morning she'd driven the remaining distance south to the village her father had mentioned in his letter, and checked into the small hotel. After lunch at a taverna she'd driven into the hills to locate the house of Dr. Andreas Stamoulis, who was to arrange the final lap of her journey to join her father.

By the time she'd found the house in a tangled skein of roads, the siesta hour was well under way. She drove on, tracking along a winding road through olive and citrus orchards, drawn by tantalizing glimpses of a sea the rich blue color of robes painted in a Raphael masterpiece.

At last, when she was aching to feel its cool ripples against her skin, the road had twisted and brought her to a beach with sand the color of pale cream. It was as deserted as an unexplored planet, she realized with delight, remembering the overcrowded beach she'd visited near Athens her first day there.

With a feeling of bold exhilaration she jumped out of the little Renault. She threw off the sundress that concealed her turquoise bikini. The carefree gesture with which she tossed it into the car said she was stripping off more than just her clothes; she was shedding all the restraints of civilization.

Without thought of tides or currents she flung herself into the water, swimming out with vigorous strokes until her breath labored in her chest and her arms ached.

Now she floated, inhaling the heady air as the water enfolded her with silken arms, warm and alive as a human embrace.

Time passed until the sting of heat on her skin reminded her that this sun was not forgiving of those who spent too long under its rays. She shifted her weight and let her feet touch bottom. For a moment she stood, stretching her arms high in a silent tribute to good health, lucent air and that glorious sun. The disturbed sand under her feet settled, and she could see a little school of minnows darting through the water, so close they brushed her knees.

Tiny ripples surged around her shins, then her ankles, as she waded to the shore. They lapped on the hard-packed sand with soft kissing noises, sea mating with land.

Picking up her towel Sara briskly rubbed the salt residue from her skin. In the heat her swimsuit would dry in no time. Her watch, lying in the sand where she'd dropped the towel, told her it would be another two hours before social custom allowed her to present herself at Dr. Stamoulis's house.

Sara smiled. Who was she to go against the custom of the country? After her swim a nap was just what she needed. With a carefree grin at a tiny lizard sunning itself on a rock nearby, Sara spread her towel on the sand and followed its example. The sand was as soft as talc and as resilient as a bed. The sun's rays seeped into her, turning her limbs into boneless languor. Her eyelids fluttered closed. She would rest for a few minutes, then find her way back to the hotel to shower and change for her meeting with her father's colleague.

A faint breeze ruffled the leaves of the olive tree over her head, shifting the pattern of dappled shade that covered her. No danger of sunburn here out of the full glare of midafternoon. She already had the beginning of a tan and, in spite of her golden hair, rarely burned.

Feeling drowsy, she let her eyes close. So peaceful—the whisper of the leaves, the sleepy music of cicadas, the gentle suck and lap of the sea...

A shadow fell across her, cutting the sunlight. She stirred restlessly, then opened her eyes. A man stood over her, a black outline against the vivid blue sky. She froze, her muscles paralyzed as several emotions ripped through her at once: fear at her isolated vulnerability and chagrin at having slept so long and deeply—the sun had moved and she was fully exposed to its rays.

Her arms and legs were flaccid with heat and sleep. She couldn't move as her eyes devoured the powerful shape of the man before her.

Tall and straight, water flattening the hair on his body and legs, he was the epitome of maleness, a bronzed god dressed only in the minutest nylon swimming trunks. A strange breathlessness assailed her and her heart did a curious lurch in her chest. This was what early maidens must have felt when the gods descended from Olympus to mingle with mortal men.

She couldn't take her eyes from him, and her thoughts formed into involuntary speech. "Apollo," she whispered, all her habitual reticence drowning in the black depths of his eyes. Dazzled by the sun behind him she couldn't make out his features, but his eyes seemed to shine and hold all the secrets of the cosmos.

"Aphrodite," he breathed, kneeling at her side. His brown fingers tentatively stroked her shoulder, as if to ensure that she was flesh and blood. Sara felt his eyes caressing her and watched in fascination as her nipples tingled and stood erect, hard buds under the thin stretch fabric of her bikini top. Some part of her mind told her she shouldn't feel this way with a stranger, that she should run from his arousing eyes and hands, but a breathless excitement held her in thrall.

With astonishment she realized she wanted him to see her. More, she wanted those brown hands to touch her. She wanted him to hold her breasts, to weigh them in his hands and ease the tingling that was rapidly becoming an electric throbbing.

"Are you real?" she asked haltingly, barely able to breathe, much less speak. "Or are you a dream?"

A smile transformed his dark shadowed features, the flash of white teeth giving him a look of boyish recklessness. "If it's a dream, I'm having it too."

He touched her hair, pushing the golden tresses over her shoulders so that she lay bared to his gaze and to the kiss of the sun. Apollo, the sun god, in the sky and here beside her—the two somehow mixed in her dazzled mind. She no longer knew, or cared, where one left off and the other began.

She watched, mesmerized, as his head lowered toward hers. Without thought of turning away she felt his mouth touch her lips, soft and gently tasting, asking without demanding. She answered it from the buried depths of sensuality within her, not questioning the rightness of it, not even wondering at the mystery of her willing response. In her subconscious mind she knew. She had waited all her life for this very moment and her life would be altered by it forever.

Delicately, with consummate gentleness, he teased her with tiny kisses, then slid his mouth over her flushed cheeks. He barely nipped her tender earlobe before slowly tracing a path over her temple, her forehead, down her straight nose back to her eagerly parted lips. She would have pressed her mouth against his but he ignored her invitation. He played lightly, tantalizing her with his mouth, giving her only lightning-quick flicks with the tip of his tongue.

She was on fire. She wanted to lift herself to meet his touch. She yearned to throw her arms around him and pull him close so that she could feel all of him against her, but her body was heavy with a mystical lassitude. She couldn't move; he had bewitched her, his will holding her captive.

He lay beside her now, thighs against hers, rough with hair in contrast to her golden smoothness. When his muscles contracted under the skin, she felt the abrasiveness of his body hair and a shiver of pleasure went through her. He was so clearly male, the antithesis of her femininity, and she gloried in the knowledge.

One of her feet lay on top of his, and her toes curled against his instep. His hands were tangled in her hair, threading through its glossy curls and arranging them in a fan over her head. Sara opened her mouth with a tiny whimper as his tongue ran around the inside of her lower lip, rubbing over her teeth. She wanted to scream at him to stop playing this tormenting game. She needed him to deepen the kiss, to increase the delicious pressure of his hands. She needed him with a hunger that would have frightened her, if she could have thought beyond the pleasure of his touch.

She shifted her thigh, gratified as she heard the sharp intake of his breath. His hand slid down to grip her head and at last his tongue came into her mouth, joining with hers, sliding over it with hot sensuality. As if energized by this small invasion of her body, her arms lost their lethargy and wrapped themselves around his head, fingers weaving into silky black curls.

Kissing could fill a whole world, she found, drinking his sweetness as his tongue probed the depths of her mouth, now deep, now gentle. If this was a dream, she hoped she never woke up. She moved her hands down to his shoulders, golden satin skin over hard muscles, absorbing the texture of him through her palms.

As she felt the hot wetness of his tongue trace the shallow valley between her breasts, her arms lost their strength and fell back over her head. She closed her eyes, arching her back in an effort to soothe the fiery throbbing that started at her breasts and flashed through her, to her stomach and restlessly shifting thighs. His mouth moved lower, tongue examining with minute attention the small indentation of her navel, then lower still until it lapped at the edge of her bikini bottom.

Sara waited, tense with anticipation, her breath trapped in her throat. All her nerves seemed exposed on the surface of her skin, and his next caress would send her shooting off into space. Without opening her eyes she reached up to bring him to her.

To her astonishment, her arms embraced empty air. Only then did she realize that nothing but the sun's burning rays touched her. Her bemused eyes flew open and she sat up, fighting the lethargy that stole her will. The beach was deserted, an expanse of pale yellow sand shimmering with heat waves.

She laughed unsteadily, shaking her golden head. She had slept and it had been a dream, the most blatantly erotic dream she'd ever had. That was what came from falling asleep in the sun, she thought ruefully, amazed at the boundless and fanciful extent of her subconscious imagination. Apollo, indeed!

She squinted at the sun, a copper globe well past its zenith, and reached for her watch. Her groping hand found the edge of the towel, and warm powdery sand slipped through her fingers. She twisted around to look at the spot where she'd left it. Nothing.

Her straight brows drew together in a frown. A dream?

Then she heard a rhythmic pounding, which was magnified through the ground. A horse's hooves, their sound fading into the distance and leaving only a residual vibration under her that matched the suddenly urgent thud of her heart.

Apollo? The man who had kissed her, who in a moment of time had not only touched her lips but had left his imprint upon her soul? It had to be. Horses didn't roam free in these vast, unfenced orchards.

A dream? A figment of her imagination, conjured up by the heat of the sun and a suppressed inner yearning?

She sat up, biting her bottom lip in consternation. If he'd been real—and she had a sinking feeling that he had—then she might meet him again. Would she know him? With the sun behind him, all she'd seen was his powerful, provocative silhouette. She'd been left with only the impression of leashed strength and masculinity.

And felt those hands and that magical mouth that had the power with only a kiss to transport her to a nirvana that surpassed fantasy.

Skin burning with a heat that owed nothing to the sun, Sara wrapped the towel around her body and walked up the beach to her car. It was still locked, apparently undisturbed, a tiny rented Renault that looked like a cute, snub-nosed boy. She found her keys in the fork of the orange tree that shaded the vehicle, exactly where she'd left them.

Unlocking the door she took her sundress from the seat and pulled it on over her bikini. "Damn," she muttered as she started the engine and turned the car in the direction of her hotel. Her watch couldn't have evaporated into the limpid air....

The setting sun was a golden sphere on the horizon when Sara pulled up in Dr. Stamoulis's front drive. As she got out of the car she paused for a moment, taking in the clean lines of the white stucco house. The architect had designed it so that the various levels clung to the undulations of the land, as if the house had grown there rather than been built. Tall cypresses edged the raked gravel driveway and a lush trumpet vine enhanced the entry porch. If this was an indication of how Dr. Andreas Stamoulis lived, they must pay university professors more here than they did in the United States, Sara mused.

Birds twittered in the orchard that ran along the side of the house, and a muted roar came to her ears as she skipped lightly up the low flight of steps leading to the front door.

The doorbell echoed through the house with the mellow sound of chimes. After a moment the paneled door was opened by a young girl dressed in a crisp black uniform with a cap set at a perky angle on her dark hair. Sara suppressed a smile. A uniformed maid out here? Dr. Stamoulis must harbor yearnings for the past in more than his archaeological work.

"I'm Sara Morgan," Sara said, hoping the girl understood English. "Dr. Stamoulis is expecting me."

The girl smiled, dark eyes sparkling with welcome and good humor. "Come in, Dr. Morgan."

Sara grimaced wryly as she followed the girl down a narrow hall. She had earned the title, but it still struck her as pretentious when anyone addressed her by it outside of her classes. It made her feel as if she should be wearing tweeds and sensible shoes instead of a bare-shouldered sundress covered by a brief little jacket. She pushed her hands into her pockets, letting her shoulder bag swing back against her hip. Besides, her father was Dr. Morgan, Dr. Daniel Morgan, a professor of archaeology like Stamoulis. Her own degree was in ancient history, the period she specialized in matching her father's interests, Greece before the Golden Age of Pericles.

The maid opened the door at the end of the hall and Sara walked past her into a large room. Some of the windows that made up the entire far wall stood open. The roar she'd noted earlier was more pronounced. Of course. The house overlooked the sea, a fact not apparent from the road, which wound through the orchards in a haphazard fashion. With an uneasy premonition she realized she wasn't far from the beach where a stranger had touched her soul.

Had it been someone from this house who had so disturbingly introduced himself to her? No, it couldn't have been, if it was only a dream. Still, she hadn't dreamed the galloping horse.

She pushed the disconcerting thoughts into the back of her mind and slammed the door on them as an elderly man rose from a chair and shambled toward her. He was shorter than her own five feet eight inches, slightly stooped but radiating vitality. His face was brown and deeply wrinkled, his wide smile and prominent teeth giving him the appearance of a good-natured monkey.

"Ah, Dr. Morgan," he said warmly, his voice surprisingly resonant for his slight frame. "I'm happy to meet you at last. Your father has talked about you so often that I feel I know you already."

"Dr. Stamoulis." Sara smiled as she shook his hand. His palm was dry and impersonal, his fingers barely gripping hers before letting go. Odd, she thought, since his smile seemed so welcoming.

She gave a mental shrug as he added, "Andreas, please. We can't have formality between us." The accent in his English was more British than Greek, and Sara remembered Daniel saying that Andreas had lived in London. "Come into the library and have a drink."

"This is a marvelous house," Sara said, following him through an open door on the side of the room. "Did you design it?"

He laughed, as he led her into the next room, the sound harsh as if he didn't laugh often despite his look of good humor. "Not me. I'm only interested in old buildings. A friend of mine planned it and supervised the building," Dr. Stamoulis explained as he moved with his peculiar graceless walk to a side cabinet.

This room was smaller than the living room but again unconventional. Here, also, wide windows framed a view of the sea. The remaining walls were covered with pictures and photographs, with bookshelves jutting at right angles out from the walls, forming alcoves furnished with deep armchairs. A cozy place to sit and read, thought Sara, whose idea of paradise was an unlimited supply of books.

The bar was cleverly concealed in an antique armoire. "What will you have, Dr. Morgan?" Stamoulis asked, glasses clinking on the glossy wood.

Sara had gone to the windows, which opened onto a narrow balcony. "Some wine, if you have it, please," she said over her shoulder. "And please call me Sara." He had been the one to suggest informality, yet he wasn't reciprocating. Was this his normal manner, closing a distance and then creating another? She wondered how it would be to work in close proximity with such a man.

Never mind, she was sure she could adapt to his vagaries of character.

"How about white wine and soda?" he suggested, his voice warmer.

"Yes, that sounds fine," she said absently, focusing on the limitless blue of the sea. The wind had picked up, and whitecaps gilded by the setting sun ruffled the surface. A fresh scent of salt and residual heat came through the open window and she inhaled deeply, closing her eyes in sheer enjoyment.

She jumped slightly and took her hand from her pocket as Dr. Stamoulis came up to her. The glass he handed her was cold, tinkling with ice.

"To your good health," Andreas said, lifting his own glass, which contained a dark amber liquid. "And to a successful summer."

"Episis," Sara said, dredging up the correct response from her meager fund of Greek words. Andreas remained close to her, so close he began to crowd her personal space. Forcing down her nervous discomfort, she moved away from him and sat in a nearby armchair.

Andreas sat in a chair opposite hers, the light from the window falling across his face. Sara noticed his features were never still, as if a restless current of energy drove him. Not the most relaxing person to be with.

"Now, Sara," Stamoulis said, "what can I do for you?"

Sara started at the totally unexpected question. She set her glass carefully on the table beside her chair. "Didn't my father make arrangements for you or one of your assistants to take me to the excavation site?"

Andreas's bright eyes flickered for an instant, not quite meeting hers. He started to speak, then seemed to change his mind. When he finally spoke she had the distinct impression he'd reconsidered whatever he'd been about to say. "Oh, yes, how stupid of me. I'd forgotten for the moment." He paused, then added in a tone that seemed hurried and nervous, "Daniel was to meet you here, but he thought he was on to something in the area where we're digging and decided not to take time off."

Sara was disappointed that her long-awaited chance to work on an archaeological dig in progress might be delayed. "Then when will I be able to join him?"

Andreas lifted his glass and took a long swallow, making a vague gesture with his free hand. Sara was about to speak again when an indefinable sound made her sit up and turn her head. She glanced at Andreas, but he was staring at the titles on a row of books near his head, apparently hearing nothing out of the ordinary.

A shiver touched her spine, as though a door had opened and let in a draft. She had the oddest sensation of being watched, and chided herself for her imagination. This afternoon's encounter, dream or whatever it was, must have unsettled her more than she'd realized. She wasn't usually nervous in any circumstances.

Stamoulis put down his glass next to hers. "It might be difficult for you to get to the site," he said hesitantly. "I'm not going back for a couple of days. Supplies coming..." He trailed off in indecision.

"Then can you get someone else to take me?" Sara asked, frustration giving her voice a sharp edge. "I don't want to waste any more time than I have to. I've only got until the end of August."

Before the archaeologist could reply, another voice spoke from the twilight shadows that had crept into the room, "I'll take you to the site, Dr. Morgan."

Chapter Two

"Nick, you're back," Andreas cried with every evidence of surprise. He reached for a lamp switch, flooding the alcove with light.

"Yes, I'm back." His voice slid over Sara's senses like a caress of heavy silk. Moving with the fluid grace of a jaguar he seated himself on the arm of a chair at a right angle to Sara's. The position pulled the tan material of his trousers snugly over his thighs, and for a moment Sara found herself staring at his body. No man had a right to wear pants that tight, nor to look so good in them.

She dragged her eyes up to his face and found it no less disconcerting. His strongly molded features were handsome, marked by lines of humor at odds with the shrewdness with which he watched her. Plenty of character in that face, she thought, and an unmistakable hint of cynicism. She guessed there wasn't much he hadn't seen or done, and that there was nothing left on earth that still had the power to shock him.

His eyes appeared black in this light but with a depth and sparkle that made her speculate that in daylight they might well be another color. They were fringed with long, curling lashes that emphasized rather than detracted from his tough masculinity. She saw at once that he used them to advantage, lowering them to hide the kindling interest in his eyes as he returned her gaze.

He sat quietly, cool under her scrutiny, but his mind was far from calm. He'd seen her enter the room with Andreas and had moved back into the shadows, somewhat shaken that the golden mermaid of this afternoon had walked into his life. He'd anticipated a search to find her again. Now here she was, still golden but decorously clothed and very businesslike.

And he knew her. That nagging sense of familiarity hadn't been his imagination, although the woman before him was a far cry from the image he'd carried of a carefree girl in a picture hat. That photo her father kept on his desk at the site must have been taken several years ago.

In the photo she was young, laughing. The woman she had become was serious, mature and awesomely sure of herself and her place in life. That graceful walk of hers as she'd crossed the room to the windows, the way she had stood with her hands pushed deep into the pockets of her dress, the tilt of her head as she'd quickly recovered from the surprise of learning her father's arrangements had been altered. She was obviously used to analyzing a situation and quickly making her own decisions.

He was suddenly glad he hadn't pressed his advantage on the beach. He wanted to get to know this woman before their relationship went in a physical direction. Of course if he'd realized this afternoon that she was Daniel's daughter he would never have intruded on her privacy.

Unobtrusively he wiped his damp palms. Damn his own arrogance this afternoon. If she never spoke to him at all, it was what he deserved.

"I'm Nick Angelopoulos," he said with what he hoped was a disarming smile. Humor glinted in his dark eyes as he looked at Andreas. "Since Andreas seems to be tongue-tied."

"I'm Sara Morgan." She shook his hand, the brief contact firm and matter-of-fact. With a start Nick realized she didn't recognize him. Had the sun dazzled her to that extent? Maybe it *had* been a dream....

Andreas gave a laugh that sounded to Sara's ears too studiedly offhand. "Just surprised to see you, my boy. I thought you were out for the evening."

"Changed my mind," Nick said, his lashes shadowing his eyes. "Besides, I wanted to see Dr. Morgan." He laid the faintest emphasis on her title, and Sara glanced up. Then his voice softened, sending a shiver up her spine that was no longer uneasiness. Was it her overactive imagination or did he put a deliberately seductive note in his deep, rich voice? "Your father talked about you so much I had to see if the reality lived up to his words."

For a wild instant Sara seemed to hear again a whisper. "Aphrodite." She shook her head to get rid of the image of a nearly naked man with a sexy voice that still echoed in her brain. Throwing Nick a bright social smile, she asked, "Well, does it?"

"And more," Nick said so coolly that Sara was sure she'd imagined the overtones before. "Have you had dinner?"

"No, I haven't." To her dismay, her pulse accelerated.

"Then will you have it with me? We can discuss the drive to the site. It's rough country and it's better if you're prepared."

His eyes were roving over her slender figure in its light dress, and Sara bristled at the implication that she wasn't up to the trip. "I've camped, Mr. Angelopoulos," she said crisply. "And gone on plenty of hikes. I can make it if you can."

He had trouble controlling a grin. He liked the way she stood up to him. "We'll see," he said calmly, pushing his hands into his pockets as he rose to his feet.

Andreas also stood up, looking smaller and more simian than ever beside the tall, lean Angelopoulos. "Well, then," he said with the air of a man disposing of an annoying problem. "I'll leave you in Nick's competent hands."

"Thank you, Dr. Stamoulis," Sara said, holding out a hand, which he politely shook. "I'll look forward to seeing you again." She bent and picked up her purse from the floor, straightening to find her eyes on a level with Nick's square, cleanly shaved chin. The fragrance of lime teased at her senses.

"Shall we go?" he said softly, and with a little start she turned. He didn't crowd her, but she was very aware of his closeness as he followed her across the room.

At the door he leaned forward to hold it open for her. Again Sara caught the warm scent of him, that citrus lotion and the indefinable smell of clean skin overlaid with a faint muskiness as if he had recently been in the sun. His pale blue shirt, only an inch or two away from her, was open a couple of buttons, revealing a darkly bronzed chest covered with black curls. Half hidden in the dense forest a gold cross glinted in the lamplight, the delicacy of the thin chain oddly emphasizing his masculinity.

Head high, determined not to reveal that his nearness could affect her at a primitive, female level, Sara went through the doorway. Dangerous, she thought, dangerous and much too sure of himself. That untamed, stalking jaguar quality he had might attract some women, but thank heavens she was immune, thoroughly inoculated by her experience with Eric. He'd been jealous of her ambition, and that had spelled the death warrant to their relationship. She needed another chauvinist like she needed a fur coat in July.

Still, he had a certain charm, she mused with a faint smile as she cast a sidelong glance at his aristocratic profile. Angelopoulos meant angel's son. In her studies last winter she had come across a list of the roots of Greek surnames. Nick's, while appearing cumbersome to Anglo-Saxon eyes, was one of the easy ones.

Angel's son? He looked more like Lucifer's son. The innocence of angels didn't live in that face. But maybe the name wasn't so inappropriate after all. Hadn't Lucifer, the beautiful son of morning, been tossed out of heaven because of his ambition and pride? She had no doubt that Nick also possessed those qualities in abundance.

"D'you want to drive your car to the village?" Nick asked as they went down the wide steps to the driveway. "I suppose you're staying at the hotel?"

"Yes," Sara answered. "Do you have your own car here?" She hadn't seen one, but there might be another parking area around the side of the house. She had gained the impression that Nick was staying with Dr. Stamoulis. She wondered what his connection was with the dig. Her father had intermittently mentioned Nick in his letters, as though he showed up only now and then. His letters had been full of Dr. Stamoulis and his work.

Full of admiration for his fellow archaeologist—until lately.

"I'll ride with you," Nick said with a grin before her thoughts could progress further. "I can walk back."

"Walk?" Sara exclaimed. "But it was a fifteen-minute drive."

"By road," he said, opening the driver's door and handing her in. He got in at the passenger side, folding his long legs into the tiny car. "It's not a long walk through the orchards."

"Okay," she said, turning the ignition key, faintly surprised that he hadn't offered to drive. A man of his ego letting a woman drive—maybe she had pegged him as a chauvinist too hastily. "Where to?" she asked.

"That little taverna on the waterfront in the village is quite good," Nick said, making no comment as she let out the clutch too quickly and nearly stalled the engine. Woman driver, that supercilious half smile seemed to be saying. Why did he make her so nervous? Well, she would show him. To save face for womanhood, she turned with admirable smoothness and perfect control onto the road.

"Yes, it is good," she said, taking refuge in social chitchat as she steered expertly along the twisting road, braking, shifting and accelerating with a skill learned through years of navigating the complex roads of the New England countryside. She'd been driving on the sly since she was ten, had her license the day she turned sixteen. "I had lunch there."

His smile deepened, as if he knew a secret and was debating whether to let her in on it. The look on his face increased her annoyance and again jarred some memory that hovered just out of reach. Before she could grasp it, he broke her train of thought. "We've met before, you know."

Her heart lurched and she almost missed a turn, the headlights slanting across whitewashed tree trunks. This afternoon on the beach? No, that was a dream. It couldn't have been him. "Oh?" she asked coolly, giving nothing away.

"Yes, you probably don't remember. We weren't introduced. It was at your father's house, about ten years ago. You were in a hurry, carrying a tennis racket and wearing white shorts and a halter top." Over the years the image had surfaced now and then, the coltish young girl with her long hair flying as she ran into the room, kissed her father, then ran out, barely sparing her father's visitor a nod in passing. He'd never forgotten, yet he hadn't recognized her immediately. This Sara was far removed from the girl whose laughing eyes seemed to hold the essence of joy. "You must have been in high school."

Sara exhaled, absurdly relieved that their meeting had been in the innocent past. Frowning, she searched the far corners of her memory. If they had met, how could she have forgotten? His was a commanding presence, the kind of man any girl of seventeen, as she had been then, would have drooled over. Any girl but her. Her mind remained blank. "No, I was already in college," she said. "I skipped a couple of grades in school. I was ahead of my age group." Her frown deepened, furrowing her brow. "I don't remember you at all."

Nick smiled. "Since I was about twenty and I've grown some since, I don't wonder. Besides, you came and went so fast I wondered afterward if I'd only dreamed you."

Dream. There it was again, that sense of unreality. Maybe she was dreaming this entire day, like Alice in Wonderland.

"Did you enjoy your swim?" Nick said suddenly in a smoky drawl that sent a tingling heat into her stomach and thighs.

"Swim? What swim?" she bluffed, still clinging to her dream theory but losing ground fast, sinking into quicksand.

"This afternoon." His voice was silky as cat's fur. The heat pooled in her lower abdomen and she gulped to stabilize her breathing. From his pocket he produced her watch, dangling it in front of her. She jerked back suddenly, moist palms sliding on the steering wheel. Slamming her foot on the brake she brought the car to an abrupt halt at the edge of the road, raising a cloud of dust that shimmered before the headlights. Red dash lights glared accusingly at her.

"You—you bastard," she exploded, her head against the steering wheel. "You took advantage of me."

His eyes widened in innocence. "Me? I stopped before things got out of hand. And I only took your watch as an introduction for our next meeting. Anyway, from what I saw you weren't exactly fighting me off."

"I was sleeping," she muttered with a scowl as she lifted her head. Her hand darted out and snatched the watch from his hand. With deft efficiency she strapped it on her wrist.

"And so delightfully, too. All soft and golden in the sun. I didn't recognize you then. For a moment I thought you were a mermaid."

His low words wove a spell that dissolved her anger. "Okay," she conceded grudgingly, restarting the stalled car. "You didn't do anything."

She engaged the gear and let out the clutch without the smallest jerk, belying the turmoil inside her. Wasn't this what she'd half expected and tried to deny? Yet, to have her Apollo on the beach turn into this man with his cynical smile sent a hot rush of embarrassment through her that made her hands clumsy and colored her cheeks with fiery pink. He would never let her hear the end of it. And they had to spend the summer together.

Maybe he wouldn't stay at the site. Maybe he'd go back to Athens or wherever he'd come from. She tried to convince herself of this, but her wits scattered again as he added softly, "No, I didn't do anything. I only took a taste." The confident sensuality in his low voice was unmistakable. Her color deepened to scarlet and she tightened her lips into a severe line, pretending that driving required all her concentration.

Mercifully the village lights appeared before them, a necklace of diamonds reflected in the little harbor. She stole a glance at Nick. His face wore a smug look. Anger cancelled Sara's embarrassment. She glared at him, eyes shooting stilettos. The smug look changed to open amusement, infuriating her further, and she ground the gears as she downshifted into the narrow village street.

His arm lay across the back of the seat, and he lowered his hand until it brushed her bare shoulder. She shrugged it off but not before a charge of electricity flashed between them. He didn't touch her again, but she was aware of his hand an inch away from her skin.

"Was that really a horse I heard?" she asked to stop the erratic racing of her pulse.

"Yes, I was riding him," Nick said coolly, as if discussing the weather.

"Like that? Practically naked?" she asked disbelievingly.

Nick shrugged. "Sure, why not?"

The image of his unclothed body flashed through her mind with relentless heat. She made a sound as if she couldn't get her breath.

"You ought to try it sometime," Nick went on conversationally. "Totally naked is even better."

Sara found her voice with difficulty. "No, thanks."

"Why not?" he asked offhandedly, and Sara had a curious sensation that he was enjoying her discomfort even though his face remained carefully neutral.

She stopped the car in front of the little hotel. "Why should I?" she said disdainfully. "Not everyone goes in for public nudity."

"It was hardly public. And you weren't exactly dressed in a burnoose." He got out of the car and looked at her over its roof. "Besides, that dream you thought you were having must have been pretty hot stuff."

Sara colored again. She was glad the business of locking the car and putting away the key kept her from having to face him. "But it wasn't a dream," she said faintly.

"Exactly." The word held a weight of promise and satisfaction.

Before Sara could organize a suitably quelling retaliation they were among the evening strollers on the waterfront. Now and then someone would call out a greeting to Nick and stare at Sara in open curiosity. Nick answered politely but showed no sign of stopping for conversation. The villagers seemed to respect him, Sara thought, and to accept him. He wasn't a stranger, yet their greetings lacked the familiarity they would accord a close friend. Another side of a complex man.

She could find no fault with his manner as he led the way into the taverna and pulled out her chair, politcly waiting for her to be seated. He had thrown her off balance but now she was firmly in control once more. Their first meeting might have been provocative, but Sara had no doubt that she could keep that near intimacy from recurring. She would keep things strictly business between them from now on.

Nick's eyes were narrowed as he studied her across the table. She was beautiful, her features classically pure: straight nose, firm chin with a hint of a dimple and clear, guileless eyes. Her eyes were a golden hazel fringed by sooty lashes, the irises pale when she was calm, darkening to copper when she was thoughtful or disturbed. They were dark now.

She wore what he was beginning to think of as her imperious look, the cool reticence that shut him out more effectively than a fence of thorns. Damn it, he didn't want her to shut him out. He wanted her to talk to him, to tell him about her accomplishments, her work and her leisure activities, what she ate for breakfast, what books she read, whether she liked Mozart or Michael Jackson. He wanted her to share her feelings and her dreams. He wanted to know all of her.

He wasn't sure what he'd do with this knowledge, but the desire to know her mind was an aching hunger in him, greater than his hunger to know her body. Now that he knew who she was he couldn't be the impulsive hunter he'd been this afternoon.

He didn't blame her for being suspicious of him. After the way he'd behaved, all the talking in the world wouldn't convince her he was honorable, that he didn't seduce helpless women on lonely beaches for a living. So he had to show her in other ways.

But how, when her lips were parted so sweetly and he remembered their taste, heady as summer wine?

Her perfume drifted to his nostrils. Gardenia. Odd; gardenias seemed more suited to a sultry dark beauty. Yet on Sara the scent was right, the fragrance sensual as her skin chemistry gave it a complexity that called to him at a deep masculine level.

Tonight her hair was coiled around her head. It suited her reserve, but the severity of the style made him want to tear out the pins so that he would see again the responsive woman of this afternoon. That woman he could relate to; this one puzzled him. He smiled to himself.

He'd always liked puzzles and they had the whole summer to find a solution.

And he was going to stick around to find it.

Sara sighed as she imagined what he was thinking. She could practically see the little wheels going around in his head. Men with their one-track minds.

Then she looked at his face and wondered if she'd been too hasty in her assumptions. He looked serious and thoughtful, not at all a predator. Maybe she should give him another chance.

"You've changed since the first time I saw you, Sara," Nick said contemplatively.

"I should hope so," she said tartly. "I was only seventeen then, just a child."

"Not so much a child as I recall." He smiled in a secretive way that made Sara wish she could remember that occasion. So many students had passed through their house during her childhood and adolescence that they had all faded into a blur. "You still move the same way," Nick added. "You still have that graceful, free walk. And those long legs so sleek and brown."

Sara's face burned. Did he have to keep reminding her? She had taken her body for granted, after getting over a teenage dissatisfaction with the size of her breasts. She rarely considered how men might perceive her. With only a few words and those significant glances Nick had awakened yearnings she'd thought dormant or nonexistent. And she wasn't sure she liked it. She'd been content with her life the way it was and now Nick threatened her peace of mind.

"And you blush so delightfully," he went on. "I thought ladies had lost the ability to blush like Victorian maidens." Damn, he was doing it again. He couldn't seem to stop himself from needling her where he was sure she would react.

"I'm not a Victorian maiden," Sara retorted.

Nick's smile was lazy and provocative, his voice dropping to a near whisper that caressed her vibrant nerve endings. "No, just a mermaid washed up on the beach for me to find. Victorian maidens didn't suntan in bikinis."

"They didn't suntan at all. They protected their complexions."

Nick raised his hands in mock surrender at her acerbic tone. "I apologize. I forgot your specialty is history. You know all about Victorian maidens."

Sara smiled. She couldn't remain annoyed with him. "More about Minoan ones. And I suppose you know all about modern ones."

"Not maidens," Nick said with a chuckle.

Sara was saved a reply by the arrival of the waiter with menus and the coffee Nick had ordered earlier. "Shall I?" Nick asked, indicating the menus.

"Please do," Sara told him. He would know what was good.

Barely glancing at the list, he gave the order in rapid Greek and the waiter left. Nick lifted his coffee cup and took a sip, then drank from the glass of ice water. "You're young for a Ph.D., aren't you, Sara?"

Sara shrugged. She'd always been young for her accomplishments, but learning had come easily to her. "I suppose so, but don't forget I graduated from high school two years early, which put me that much ahead before I even entered college."

"And in the fall you'll be teaching at one of the most prestigious universities in New England, if not the whole U.S. Quite a feat."

"Why? Because I'm young?" Her eyes hardened as she reached for her coffee. "Or because I'm a woman?"

Nick threw up his hands. "Whoa! Did I say anything about that? I wasn't trying to insult you. You don't have to get your hackles up."

Sara knew she'd overreacted. "Sorry," she muttered, hiding her face behind her water glass.

"I wasn't being patronizing," Nick said. "But I can imagine you've often had to put up with that kind of idiocy. No wonder feminists are so militant in North America. People are still judged by their sex rather than by what they've done. Here there've always been women doctors, lawyers, judges and so forth, and no one seems to treat them any differently than the males in the same line of work."

Sara raised candid eyes to his. "At least in the work I do, it's only been my youth which is questioned—not my sex." She smiled suddenly, her face transformed into an open friendliness that took his breath away. "And that will remedy itself in a few years."

But when she began to look older would she also lose that youthful zest for life that he found so charming? It was so much a part of her, the impression that had remained strongest in his memory since that summer day in Daniel's study. "Does your father still have that house?" he asked to cover the faintly disconcerting sensation that from this day his life would never regain its formerly even tenor.

"Yes, he still lives there. It's convenient to his work. I live in an apartment just outside of Boston, but I like the old house. I'm glad he kept it although it's big for one person. He has a housekeeper, of course, and it's handy to have large rooms for student gatherings."

"So he still takes a personal interest in his students, as he did in me."

Sara's straight brows lifted in a quizzical arc. "You were one of his students? He never mentioned that."

Nick finished his coffee and set down the cup. "Only for one term. I'd come to say goodbye that summer I saw you. I was going back to Greece to take over parts of the family business."

"But you grew up in the States. Wasn't it difficult to go back?"

"In many ways," he agreed. "But I felt I had to. I haven't regretted it."

"What about your parents? Do they still live over there?"

"They died, my mother when I was small and my father later. My sister married an American, and she more or less brought me up. I'm the baby of the family. Stephanie is the only mother I remember. They live near Manchester, New Hampshire."

"I've been there," Sara said. "The Greek community had an archaeologist over to speak on Santorini and its connection to ancient Atlantis. Since that's one of my interests I attended his lecture."

"And that's why you're here, isn't it? To explore the possibility that Andreas's dig will give us something on the Minoans."

"Or Mycenae," Sara said. "There's a theory that the two civilizations traded with each another but it hasn't been proved."

"And you hope to prove it?" Nick asked, more fascinated with the intelligence and enthusiasm that lit her eyes than with the topic.

"I'd like to do some work in that direction. This may be a start."

Nick drummed his fingers on the table as he looked around for the waiter. "If they find anything. They haven't up to now, but Paul, a friend of mine who's also working at the dig, phoned to tell me they think they're coming close. They've dug up some earrings and other trinkets, but of course everything has to be cleaned and catalogued."

"So I may be in on a major find," Sara said, barely able to contain her eagerness.

Nick shook his head. "Don't get too fired up. Even if they discover something important it may not mean anything. There was a lot of looting going on over the centuries, and there's no hard evidence that the excavation site is the location of a settlement."

Sara's enthusiasm deflated. "Then why are they digging there?"

"A few years ago a shepherd found stone fragments inscribed with strange writing." He grinned briefly. "Things move very slowly in archaeology, getting funding, permits, miles of red tape. The writing turned out to be Linear A, which may prove the Minoans came here. But nothing further was found that substantiates this. Unless—" He paused, frowning thoughtfully. "Unless Paul's message meant they've found something now."

Sara nodded as she tried to stem her rising excitement. To be on hand at a major find would enhance her academic prospects as nothing else could. And Daniel must be beside himself. It had been his dream since his student days. "How did you get involved in this, Nick?" she asked. "You're not an archaeologist."

He laughed. "No, I'm not. My business provided some of the funding for this dig. I'm the go-between. We like to keep an eye on our investments."

"What kind of business are you in?" Sara asked.

He gestured vaguely. "Architecture, construction, a couple of hotels, that kind of thing. I got involved in archaeology because of my interest in architecture. That was one of the reasons I returned to Greece. I wanted to design buildings that relate to the landscape and reflect the light and clarity of the air, buildings that complement the country rather than serve only as the easiest possible means of housing the tourists.''

"You designed Dr. Stamoulis's house," Sara exclaimed in sudden comprehension. "I love it. It fits so perfectly into the site; those spare lines and wide cool rooms are exactly suited to this climate."

"Yes, I'd originally intended it for myself." He stopped abruptly, staring into the grounds at the bottom of his coffee cup as if he read some dark secret there.

"Then why—" Sara asked in bewilderment at his change of mood. She broke off as his frown deepened. It read No Trespassing as clearly as if he'd erected a sign. So he had items in his past that were taboo. She added, a little awkwardly, forcing a bright smile, "I wonder what's taking so long. Maybe they're still chasing the meat?"

"It's fish," Nick said shortly, then his face relaxed as if he'd pushed a distasteful memory back into a closed corner of his mind. "Ah, here it comes, and it looks as if it was worth the wait."

The tiny fish were fried to a brown crispness and were meant to be eaten whole, bones and all. With them was a salad of tomatoes, onions and cucumbers, as well as a bowl of *tsiziki*, cucumbers chopped into yogurt flavored with dill and garlic.

Nick dipped a chunk of bread into the mixture and chewed with relish. "I hope you don't mind a little garlic."

"I don't if you don't," Sara said easily. "We're not going to be that close. We're not even riding home together."

His eyes crinkled at the corners as he grinned. "True, but there's still the walk back to your hotel."

Sara glanced at the building, only fifty yards down the well-lit street. "I doubt I'd have trouble finding it."

"I always deliver my dates to the door," Nick said firmly.

"And farther if they let you, I'm sure," Sara said dryly. She concentrated on her fish for a moment, ignoring the wickedly humorous gleam that came into his eyes. "How soon will we go to the excavation site?"

His grin told her he saw through her ploy. "We're expecting a shipment of supplies tonight or tomorrow. Probably tomorrow since it hasn't arrived yet. Some of it has to go up to the site. So we'll leave the day after tomorrow—Monday. You don't mind waiting a day, do you?"

"I don't have much choice, do I?" Sara took a sip from her wineglass, savoring the dry tangy taste. "This isn't retsina, is it?"

Nick smiled. "No, it isn't retsina. Even Greeks don't drink retsina with every meal, no matter what the tourist guides tell you. And no, you don't have a choice. I could give you directions, but I doubt if that cracker box you're driving could make it."

"I'll have you know that 'cracker box' regularly wins car rallies." Sara defended the car indignantly even though it was hers only temporarily.

"Okay, okay, I won't insult your toy. You can leave it here or at Andreas's. We'll go in my car, which is better equipped to handle that rocky mule-track of a road. As it is we have to walk the last couple of kilometers."

"How far is it?" Sara asked, envisioning a safari into the densely treed mountains she'd driven through near Sparta.

"If we start early we can be there by lunchtime or early afternoon. It's not that far, just rough." He reached across the table and speared the last chunk of tomato out of the communal salad bowl and offered it to Sara. She chewed it with enjoyment.

"Delicious," she pronounced, leaning back in her chair. "I love the food here." She twirled the stem of her wineglass between her fingers, then drank the last of the wine. Nick grinned at her with uncomplicated warmth, and she returned his smile with none of her previous defensiveness. When he dropped that predatory male act, he was a companion she couldn't fault. In fact she was beginning to like him. A lot.

"Do you ride?" Nick asked.

"I used to," she said. "I haven't in a good many years."

"Will you come riding with me tomorrow?" Nick asked with an engaging little-boy grin. His mercurial changes of mood were so intriguing, any objection she might have made fled from her mind.

"I'd like that," Sara said. "I presume I get my own horse."

"Of course." His eyes gleamed in sudden mischief. "Unless you want to ride double."

"No," she said slowly. "I think not. Besides, the horse might not like the extra weight."

"You can ride Andreas's horse. It needs the exercise, since he only uses it for trips into the mountains where a car or jeep won't go. I'll show you some of the countryside around here. Once you're up at the dig you won't have much time."

The afternoon's dream-reality came back to her and Sara had a sudden vision of Nick sitting astride a golden horse, his tanned body merging with the horse's until they became one being, a centaur, untamed creature of myths. She shook her head, chasing away the image that caused a flush to heat her skin.

"Don't you want to spend the day with me?" Nick asked in disappointment, mistaking the movement of her head.

"What?" she stammered. "Oh. Yes, I do. I was thinking of something else."

"It must have been pretty interesting to cause that blush," Nick observed dryly. "A penny?" He dug in his pocket, coming up with a coin that he dropped on the table. "A drachma will do. It's not worth much more than a penny."

Sara pushed the coin back to him. "None of your business, Nick." The severity of her tone sent his brows up, and his expression was so comically hurt that she couldn't stop her peal of laughter. "You'll have to take up mind reading."

He pulled a face. "Now that would be interesting." His eyes, no longer humorous, seemed to pierce her brain, then he dropped them. "Come by Andreas's house about eight in the morning. I'll even supply your breakfast. And a picnic for our lunch. Don't forget your swimsuit."

Again he flashed that infectious grin.

"Don't forget yours," Sara said, her severe look spoiled by another bubble of laughter. Suddenly she was looking forward to the day with him. The excavation site had been there for thousands of years; it would wait another day.

Chapter Three

The hotel must have acquired several new guests," Sara remarked later as they walked past the parking area into the garden courtyard. One of the cars was conspicuous, a large red Pontiac with New York license plates.

Nick glanced at the car. "Far from home, isn't he?" he commented. "But not so strange. A lot of people emigrated to the United States. Some of them come back occasionally to visit relatives."

"And bring a car all that way?" Sara said skeptically, although the evidence was before her eyes.

"Why not?" Nick shrugged. "If it makes the returning native son feel like a success."

It was close to midnight, and only a faint light glowed in the entrance of the hotel. The garden was dark, warm in the night air, and filled with the scent of roses and honeysuckle. A row of squat palms edged the path, creating deep shadows.

"Wait a minute," Nick said softly, pulling Sara off the path into an even denser shadow. The clean citrus aroma of his after-shave mingled with the scent of the flowers around them, teasing her and making her want to be close to him. His easy companionship at dinner had done much to ease her initial antagonism toward him.

The shadows wrapped around them, as intimate as a boudoir. Nick stood in front of her, his hands resting lightly on her shoulders. "You're so beautiful, sweet Sara," he murmured. "Let me kiss you again."

Sara knew she could move away, but mesmerized by the soft night and the tender light in his eyes, she no longer wanted to. It seemed right that he should kiss her. She sighed, her lips parting in anticipation.

Nick bent his head and brushed her lips with his, a light teasing caress that made her sway toward him. Never had she felt this open and receptive to a man so quickly.

Of course she had dated. She'd had several relationships in the past couple of years that might have become serious, but she'd always been in command. After her one affair, which she'd honestly expected to be more than that, she hadn't given her heart. She'd always maintained a distance, building an invisible wall around her heart. Now all thought of barriers dissolved, melted by this intriguing stranger who had kissed her with such erotic sweetness in the sunshine.

She fell back into that dream as he kissed her again, more firmly yet questioningly, as if he were feeling his way to a fresh start. His mouth was soft and warm, tasting of wine and a deep sensual appreciation of her as a woman.

Sara trembled in his arms. Nothing had prepared her for the seduction and sheer art Nick brought to the simple act of kissing. Total concentration—it was as if his whole being was centered on her pleasure.

He asked and Sara gave, willingly. Her senses were spinning out of control as his restless hands molded her against his body and she welcomed the hard feel of him. His arousal was all too evident through their light summer clothes, and he made no effort to hide it.

"Sara," he said raggedly, lifting his head to drag air into his lungs. "Sara, sweet Sara."

Sara stared at him, at the desire in his face, awed by the tenderness she also saw there. She ducked her face into the hollow of his throat and he held her, resting his chin on her bowed head. She could feel his rapid heartbeat under her palm. Somehow she had managed to insert her hand into the open front of his shirt. His skin was faintly, tantalizing damp. For a long moment she indulged herself, breathing in the scent of him, lime, warm skin and the elusive scent of aroused passion.

It would be easy to invite him up to her room, to let him—to take from him. He would be a marvelous lover; no selfish taker kissed like that.

But sanity and her innate caution were reasserting themselves as Nick made no further moves. No, she told herself sternly, it was too soon. No matter what impression she'd given him on the beach, he had to realize that her easy compliance then was not her usual behavior. Yes, she liked him, enjoyed his kisses, but that was as far as she could allow it to go. She was not in the market for a short summer affair, a little bonus to fill her leisure hours.

As if he sensed her mental and emotional withdrawal, Nick tightened his arms. "Sara, don't pull away. You know you want me."

Again that weak feeling invaded her limbs. Thinking she was cooperating, he bent his head. He ran his tongue over her lower lip, requesting entrance. Struggling for coherent thought, Sara clamped her teeth together.

Nick drew back a fraction. Her eyes were closed, her face a pale oval in the dim light. "Sara," he murmured. "Let me kiss you one last time before I go."

Her eyes flew open. "No," she said clearly, closing them again to shut out the passion in his dark eyes. Her voice grew stronger. "Yes, I want you. But I don't *want* to want you. Not so soon."

"Just one more," Nick whispered. "One more and I'll go."

Yes, said the wanton part of her that he'd awakened. One more. She relaxed imperceptibly and he must have understood. His mouth came down again, without force but infinitely seductive. A wave of heat swept up her body as his long fingers skillfully fastened themselves over her breast, finding the betraying hardness of her nipple through her dress.

Her inner restraints vanished like tissue paper in a bonfire. Her mouth opened under his and his tongue easily breached the token barrier of her teeth. With a low moan she welcomed him as he probed the sweet inner regions of her mouth. She wrapped her arms about his head, her fingers sinking into the soft thickness of his hair. The heady scent of him filled her nostrils until he became her whole world as he molded her closer to his hard man's body.

Then, abruptly, he let her go and she had to forcibly restrain the cry of disappointment that rose to her lips. "You're right," he said thickly. "It is too soon." Sara stared up at him, her eyes wide and bewildered, but his face, spare and lean in the darkness, gave nothing away.

After a small pause during which their eyes remained locked in an embrace as strong as their arms had been, he added, "I'd like nothing better than to come in with you but there will be time for that later. We have the whole summer ahead of us." He flicked a fingertip across her rosy mouth, swollen from his kisses. "So not tonight." He sighed pensively, his light humor fading. "But when I feel you in my arms it's as if I've waited all my life for you, and I find my control slipping."

Sara stared at him. "What are you saying?" she managed to stammer. The very air between them was charged with hidden currents.

Nick touched her lips again. "Shh, Sara. Enough for tonight."

On this baffling note he led her into the hotel and up the stairs to her room. Common sense took hold in Sara's mind, shot with dismay that she had allowed herself to be so thoroughly carried away by Nick's kisses. He wanted her and she'd let him believe she was his for the taking, another conquest—probably one of many.

She was here to work. A summer affair, no matter how pleasant, was not on her agenda. Especially not one with a man like Nick, who had just amply demonstrated that he had the power not only to possess her body but to subvert her heart and soul as well.

At her door she braced herself for another assault on her senses, but he neither touched her nor made an attempt to come in. "Good night, Sara," he said as formally as if they were two strangers who had shared no more than a meal. "I'll see you in the morning."

He turned away from her, walking with his graceful, loose stride toward the stairs. He had taken only half a dozen steps when he swung around. Sara was still standing outside her open door. Seizing her with ungentle fingers he dropped a hard, almost bruising kiss on her surprised mouth, then whirled and ran down the stairs with the haste of a man escaping from overwhelming temptation.

Sara prepared for bed, half in a daze. She chided herself for her fancies. She hadn't felt this fluttery since her first high school dance when the class playboy had kissed her in a dark hallway. She thought she'd grown up since then but now, only a few hours after meeting Nick, she was imagining herself more than a little in love with him. Chemistry, that's all it was, she scoffed. And love certainly was the farthest thing from Nick's mind, despite his intense and puzzling words. Lust, more likely; he hadn't learned that devastating expertise at lovemaking by practicing celibacy.

Well, she wasn't taken in. She was not going to fall headlong in love with any man and let him lead her around by the nose. Her mother's example had shown her all too graphically where that could lead.

In the bathroom she squeezed toothpaste onto her toothbrush. Just as well there hadn't been anyone downstairs when she came in, she thought with a grimace at her reflection in the mirror. There was no mistaking that wanton look, hair all over the place, her eyes heavy-lidded and slumberous, her mouth soft with a stung look that shouted it had been expertly kissed.

A blush heated her face as she recalled her abandoned response. She had done everything to lead him on, completely out of character for her. If her students saw her now, they would never recognize the cool, rather formal woman who taught them every day.

She uttered a short vulgar word that also would have shocked them, coming from her, and stuck the toothbrush in her mouth, scrubbing away the taste of Nick's mouth.

But her eyes softened. He had been delicious.

It was a long time before she slept, and her dreams were haunted by a naked golden Apollo who urged her closer and closer to the fiery heart of the sun, until she woke in the darkness drenched with perspiration. The early summer dawn was lighting the room before she slept again.

Nick walked home through the olive and orange groves. Home. His mouth twisted. It would have been his home if events had cooperated, if he'd married Irene. Women! Too often they were creatures of caprice, tempting a man and then letting him down.

Was Sara different? She seemed to be. She was more direct than any woman he'd ever met, with no use for sophisticated games of attraction and rejection. And she certainly wasn't afraid to stand up to him.

She was intelligent and challenging and she intrigued him. He had just left her and he was already anticipating their next meeting.

The house was quiet and dark except for night-lights along the hallways. The walk had caused his passion to subside, but even so a cold shower seemed like a good idea. Afterward he slid naked between crisp linen sheets that smelled of lavender and sunshine.

But sleep was elusive. He tossed for some time, his mind going back to Sara. For all her directness in other matters, her responses to his kisses had been ambiguous. He admitted that he had pushed her a little, that his own passion had begun to control him rather than the other way around.

He'd meant to backtrack after coming on so strong at the beach, but somehow that resolution hadn't been fulfilled. In her arms he'd lost himself.

What was it? What was it in Sara that made him lose the controlled finesse he usually practiced with women?

Hell. Go to sleep, Angelopoulos, he snarled at his busy, nitpicking brain. Save the analysis for business. He gave his pillow a vicious punch, then smiled craftily as a thought crept into his mind.

Her mouth had been delectable.

Desire began to reawaken in him and he turned over on his stomach, rebuking his body with its inconvenient demands. Tomorrow. He would see her tomorrow and he would be in total command of himself.

On that thought he slept.

They were just finishing their breakfast the next morning when Eva, the maid, called Nick into the house to the telephone. With a muttered excuse Nick left the table. Sara leaned back in her chair, enjoying the heat of the early-morning sun on her face. Andreas was affable and expansive this morning, talking about the excavation and what progress they'd made, his face more animated than usual.

Eva began to clear away the breakfast dishes, fine china that Sara recognized as antiques, probably heirlooms handed down from Stamoulis's grandparents or great-grandparents. She wondered why someone as obviously formal as Stamoulis would use these for everyday. Her assessment of his character indicated that it was more likely he would lock away the good dishes and use plainer ones. She shrugged and moved aside as Eva took her cup and plate. Perhaps Andreas wasn't as easy to read as she'd thought.

Then disaster struck, a minor disaster but one that stuck in Sara's mind for a long time afterward.

As she reached across the table, Eva's elbow knocked against the empty cup at Nick's place. It teetered for a breathless instant, then toppled from the table to smash on the tiled floor.

Both Sara and Eva reached down to pick up the broken pieces, only to freeze as Dr. Stamoulis exploded.

"You stupid, clumsy girl. Can't you be more careful? That china has been in our family for a hundred years and now you've ruined the value of the set."

Eva dropped the piece she'd picked up, breaking it into even smaller sections. Sara knew it was irreparable and she placed the bits in her hand carefully on the table, wishing she could disappear rather than be a witness to poor Eva's humiliation. The girl's face was scarlet as she tried to stammer an apology in the face of her employer's ungoverned rage.

Stamoulis cut off the incoherent flow of words. "Get a broom," he snarled. "A replacement will come out of your salary. If it's possible to find one."

Wringing her hands, Eva scuttled into the house, still muttering apologies.

"Stupid, careless girls," Stamoulis growled. "Always with their heads in the clouds."

Sara had been stunned by his vehement reaction to the accident. She bent and picked up another piece of the broken cup, turning it over in her hands. The delicate shard seemed to let the sunlight through, turning it into translucent pearl. "Perhaps it can be mended," she suggested without much confidence.

She broke off as she heard a subservient note that was an echo of Eva's in her own voice. What was the matter with her? She hadn't broken the cup, yet the inordinate fury Stamoulis had shown over a minor incident had shaken her, as if the man's civilized veneer had cracked and shown her something dark and ugly beneath the surface. As fast as the thought crystallized, she pushed it away. Really, there must be something about this place that made her imagination run away with her. Dr. Stamoulis was a respected archaeologist, one of her father's heroes for years.

She stacked the remainder of the dishes on a tray while Eva swept up the broken china, but the simple task didn't slow her thoughts, which grew increasingly uneasy.

Daniel had respected Andreas; he had been honored to be chosen to work with him on this dig. But Sara could not help recalling Daniel's last two letters. He had apparently begun to question several aspects of the dig and had hinted of doubts about Stamoulis's integrity. These concerns had only been part of an otherwise enthusiastic report of their promising progress, but they'd struck a jarring note. She remembered several complaints about Dr. Stamoulis's erratic behavior, his almost paranoid fear that the site would be attacked by art thieves and his insistence that he knew where they should dig regardless of the other archaeologists' suggestions. Andreas appeared an affable man yet the incident of the broken cup, added to her father's letters, showed her another side of him. The man was either unstable or under some kind of strain.

After Eva left with the tray Dr. Stamoulis seemed to recover his former equanimity. In fact, he changed back to the benign host so quickly that Sara shook her head in disbelief. The Mad Hatter's tea party had nothing on this strange breakfast.

"I'm sorry you had to witness that, Sara," Stamoulis said. "Guests shouldn't be subjected to domestic disturbances."

Fighting an inclination to give him a hearty lecture on employee rights, Sara assumed a bland expression. "Accidents will happen," she murmured tritely, gritting her teeth.

Stamoulis regarded her keenly with his glossy eyes giving no hints as to his inner feelings. But he said nothing more as Nick returned. Sara rose with alacrity when

Nick suggested they go down to the stable. She'd had enough domestic disturbances for one day.

By midmorning a fresh breeze was whipping the sea into whitecaps that sparkled in the sun and sent waves surging onto the beach. Nick and Sara, in brief swimsuits that barely observed social proprieties, rode the horses bareback into the foaming surf. The animals loved it, dancing on the hard-packed sand and eagerly plunging back into the water. Sara laughed as a wave broke over her, nearly washing her from the horse's back. Although a less accomplished rider than Nick, she stayed on, her wet thighs molded to the little horse's equally wet hide.

They galloped along the beach, damp sand and seafoam flying from under the horses' hooves. Sara loosened one of her hands, which she'd tangled in her pony's mane, and waved to Nick as he passed her.

"Race you to the end of the beach, slowpoke," he shouted at her, touching his heels to his mount's flanks.

"No fair," she cried. "You've got a head start." She leaned forward, urging the pony on. It leaped ahead as Nick slowed to watch Sara's progress. Smaller and nimbler in the shifting sand, Sara's horse won by a nose.

"You distracted me," Nick complained, pushing back his wet hair.

Sara patted her pony's dripping neck. It responded by tossing its head up and down, sides heaving from exertion. "Strategy," she said, grinning like a kid. She stuck her tongue out at him, wheeling the pony out of his reach as he lunged for her.

"I'll get even for that," he called after her as she sent the pony flying down the beach.

When the sun was overhead they turned the horses loose to graze in the orange grove. The grass was long and lush between the trees, and there was no danger that the animals would run off.

"Enough sun for now, I think," Nick said as he spread a blanket in the shady spot where they'd left their clothes. "We wouldn't want that lovely skin to burn."

Sara tossed back her tangled mane of golden curls as she rummaged in her purse. "I never burn," she told him saucily. "Oh, here it is." Triumphantly she held up the brush, then drew it through her snarled hair.

Nick watched in fascination as her arm curved with the innate grace that was reflected in all of her movements. She let her head fall to one side as she brushed her hair behind her ears. In doing so she bared the nape of her neck, and with a faint groan Nick closed the small distance between them and let his lips touch the tender brown skin.

Sara's arm paused in midair. "No," she said in a whisper. Then, deciding offense was stronger than defense in view of the way her bones began to dissolve, she added with a forced smile, "Nick, I'm hungry. What have you done with the food?"

His mouth was a torment against her neck. "I'm hungry, too," he said in a muffled voice. "Ravenous. And you taste so good."

Sara lightly tapped his bare knee with the hairbrush. "Nick, stop playing around and get the food out."

Nick lifted his head. "Hard-hearted woman. I'm not playing. With you, it's a lot like work. However, there'll be another time when you're in a more cooperative mood." He rolled away from her and began to unload the saddlebags.

"Don't bet on it, Nick," Sara said, placing her brush back in her purse. "I think we should keep this strictly a business relationship, that's all."

Nick turned his head toward her, his expression serious. "So did I when I was walking home last night. But when I'm with you, I forget all my good intentions." He ran his palm lightly down her spine. Sara couldn't stop the tremor that shivered through her. "And I think you feel it, too," he drawled. "Why are you shaking?"

"I'm not."

His breath was warm, brushing softly against her skin. "You are. You can't deny what's between us. From the very first moment on the beach yesterday, it's been there."

"Chemistry," she said in cool dismissal. "Just ignore it. I will."

"Will you?" His tone held amusement but underneath she sensed a hard edge that was almost a threat. But he said no more as he shrugged and began laying out the food.

"Why, it's a feast!" Sara exclaimed. "Are we going to be able to eat all this?"

Nick grinned. "We'll have a good try at it."

And to her surprise, he was right. The riding had given them ravenous appetites. They managed to polish off most of the cold chicken, tomatoes with delicious salty goat cheese and a small loaf of crusty bread still fragrant from the oven. To wash it down, Nick had brought a bottle of a light golden wine that was the perfect accompaniment.

Sara sat back against the tree trunk, her small white teeth sinking into a ripe peach. At a little distance, she could see the horses, their hunger also satisfied, standing side by side, switching flies off each other. Nick's was the larger of the two, but hardly impressive. A nondescript brown gelding, it was the antithesis of the golden steed in her dream. Only its finely molded head showed traces of Arabian ancestry.

The horse she'd ridden was little more than a pony, a motheaten gray whose head hung phlegmatically as it stamped to fend off biting flies. Its hipshot stance did nothing to enhance its appearance.

Sara's light laugh caused Nick to glance at her. "What's so funny?"

"The horses. Somehow I imagined you on a great golden horse along the lines of Pegasus."

Nick roared with laughter. He tapped her temple. "Are you sure you weren't suffering from sunstroke? Wings? Wings were bred out of them long ago. Too hard to catch when they're out to pasture. Besides, horses here don't need glamour. They need to be able to go all day over rough terrain with little food or water."

Sara sighed in mock regret. "Another myth shot down. I grew up dreaming of Pegasus, and Alexander's Bucephalus. And centaurs."

"They were bad-tempered beasts from what I've read," Nick said, reclining at the edge of the blanket, elbow bent, his head propped on his hand. From time to time he took a bite of his own peach. "So you were already interested in history and ancient lore as a child?" he asked lazily.

"With a father who's a history professor, that's not surprising, is it? I grew up on Greek myths. I think when I was small I believed them."

"I guess all only children tend to dream about adventures like the ones in the books they read," Nick said. "I know I did, too."

"You weren't an only child."

"No, but my sister was ten years older than I, and since she brought me up more or less single-handedly, I didn't think of her as someone to play with. And my brother was older yet. So I felt like an only child."

"Did it bother you, Nick?" Sara asked.

The corner of his mouth curved down. "No, not really. I had friends all through school, like Paul."

"The one you mentioned who's at the excavation?"

"Yes, you'll like him. He's serious and perfectly sane, not like me."

Laughter rippled from Sara's mouth. "You're sane enough, Nick, but impulsive."

"So are you, Sara, but you try to stifle that in yourself."

She looked at him in surprise. "I never thought of myself in that way," she said slowly. "But since I've been here I find myself doing things and thinking things I'd never even considered before. It must be the sun."

"The air," Nick said with a superior smile. "No smoke, no pollution. It clears your brain and makes you throw away your inhibitions."

And you, Sara thought. *Your lack of inhibitions makes it easy for me to forget mine.* Their eyes met and that powerful current again arced between them, locking them together in a magical spell. Sara's fingers curled reflexively into her palms until a trickle of juice made her aware she held a peach in one hand. She lifted her hand and sank her teeth into the succulent fruit, her eyes sliding away from the dark magnetism of his.

Some of the juice spilled down her chin, and she wiped at it impatiently with the back of her hand. Nick reached over, moistened a paper napkin from their water bottle and rubbed the stickiness from her chin. Then he slid the wet paper down to clean a trickle that had run into the hollow between her breasts. His fingers brushed the soft skin and Sara could not stop the quiver of response that ran through her.

Nick's pupils dilated as he felt her reaction. He leaned forward and she saw her own image reflected in the violet depths of his eyes. For the first time she realized his eyes weren't black at all but a deep navy blue, like the sea where it meets the horizon. Then his features blurred as he bent lower and placed his mouth, cool and faintly sticky with peach juice, on the spot he had wiped.

"Sara," he murmured, his mouth silky on her skin.

Despite her own reservations Sara found herself unable to move or say anything. She felt as if she were splitting in two, one part of her powerless to control her response to him, the other reminding her that she couldn't afford to get emotionally involved with a man who could never be more than a transient figure in her life.

Nick sensed the turmoil in her, even sensed some of the reasons for it. A moment more and he would stop, he thought, honestly believing he could. He stroked the smooth, sun-warmed skin of her throat where a pulse fluttered at a mad pace. Their open mouths clung hotly, moving back and forth, tasting and biting, sticky and sweet with peach juice and wine.

Sara couldn't help returning the stunning magic of his kisses. She tangled her fingers in his black curls with rapturous intensity, the clamoring of her heart drowning out all the reasons she shouldn't go on with this. But when he raised his head to inhale a long ragged breath, she bobbed briefly to the surface. She forced open her weighted lids and met his gaze, her eyes copper-dark and troubled.

Nick wavered between compassion for her confused feelings and assertive male pride. For a moment pride won. "Sara, don't be so uptight. Let yourself go. The world isn't going to fall apart if you give in to your emotions for once. Let go."

Sara didn't hear the gentleness in his voice as she became aware of the tightening of his arms around her. She was suffocating. She had to get free. Twisting with unexpected strength, she rolled out from under him, sitting up with her hands wrapped around her knees.

Nick made no move to follow her. He lay back on the blanket, one knee raised. Lifting his arm over his eyes, he settled himself with the boneless fluidity of a cat. "Let me sleep a bit. I didn't get much sleep last night."

His other hand came to rest on Sara's thigh, gently wandering up and down just above her knee. Presently his hand was still, and she knew from the rhythmic rise and fall of his chest that he was asleep.

She too closed her eyes, listening to the rustle of the leaves above their heads, the occasional stamping of the horses in the grass and the quiet splash of wavelets on the shore. She needed to think, to analyze this powerful emotion that assailed every fiber of her being whenever she was with Nick. Desire she'd felt before, but never this overwhelming passion that engulfed her senses.

Her presentiment in Stamoulis's library should have warned her. Nick was dangerous; his charm sliced through women like a scythe through wheat. She had been so proud of her immunity, but she was another easy victim falling at his feet.

She should never have consented to this day with him. If she had been able to go to the dig and begin work, he wouldn't have gained this foothold in her emotions. But the holiday feeling and the freedom of living outdoors under the hot sun had weakened her, made her vulnerable. Maybe she was more her mother's daughter than she'd thought. Her frivolous, weak-willed mother had walked out on her and her father when Sara was ten.

A long buried memory exhumed itself, and she was ten again, hearing her parents arguing. Funny, it was the only real fight they'd had that she'd heard. She might have remained ignorant of the real state of their marriage longer, but her school had been dismissed early and her parents hadn't known she was in the house.

She'd been about to enter the living room when the tone of her father's voice stopped her in her tracks. Her father, whom she'd never seen as anything but gentle and quiet, had exploded. "I am sick to death of hearing about Teddie this and Teddie that," he'd shouted. "If you think so highly of Teddie, why don't you go to him?"

There was a short silence as Sara cowered against the partly open door. "You mean you're finally agreeing to a divorce?" her mother asked incredulously. "I thought you'd never let me go until Sara was old enough for boarding school."

"You never wanted her, did you?" The brutal words rang in Sara's shocked ears. "Well, I do. And I never wanted her to go to boarding school. I'll keep her with me."

"Yes," her mother had almost shrieked. "You wanted her, but I'm the one who had to endure nine months of those ugly clothes and that awful nausea."

"You monster," her gentle father snarled again in a tone that made bitter sickness rise in Sara's throat. "What kind of a mother are you, hating your own child?" His voice softened to a terrible weariness. "But I might have known. You were never any kind of a wife, either. Tell me this, Margaret, why *did* you marry me?"

"Because my father had gambled away all our money and I needed a husband to support me or I would be the laughingstock of all my friends. Fortunately Father had that heart attack right after our wedding and no one really knew I was penniless."

This must have stunned Sara's father, for the silence stretched. Then he said quietly, "You could have worked."

"At what?" she said scornfully. "Clerking in a dime store? Of course being married to you and living in this tacky town hasn't been any picnic, but Teddie will take me away from this. I'll never have to shop in discount stores again."

Sara had not waited to hear any more. Crushed with the knowledge that her parents were not what they had seemed and the desolate emptiness of being thought a burden, she crept up to her room and the books over which she dreamed. But even they did not comfort her. *Cinderella* was a fairy tale that didn't come true in real life. Married people didn't live happily ever after, not even her own parents.

In that terrible hour she'd vowed that the same books would be her freedom from that trap. She would never be like her mother, marrying because that was the only road to success in her life. She would have a career. She would support herself. She would never give a man a reason to say what her father had said to her mother.

She had only wavered from this self-imposed life plan once, with Eric. But when she'd consented to marry him, she had nearly completed her education; her goals were accomplished. And she had been sure he wanted her to pursue her career. When she'd found out the truth, that his ego couldn't accommodate her ambitions, their affair had been over quickly and painfully. She had vowed never again to be subjected to a man's whims or desires.

Except now. Nick had seriously undermined her strong foundations of hard work and solitary self-sufficiency. He had tapped the innocence that had been bottled up since she was ten. He'd touched her and made her see the woman she was under the starchy history professor.

Yawning sleepily, she stretched out on the blanket, keeping a prudent distance between her and the man who slept so deeply next to her, whose smile told her his dreams were pleasant ones. Strange, even without touching her he could stir her. Such a delicious feeling...

Her eyelids grew heavier and her brain seemed to be in a holding pattern. Her thoughts began to drift aimlessly. She wasn't ten anymore, she was a woman, in control of her life, and a mere man wasn't going to spoil everything just when her ambitions were being realized. Not Nick. Not any man.

She yawned again. So sleepy. The world was wrapped in somnolent heat; even the cicadas were silent. She cradled her head on her crossed arms and slept.

Chapter Four

She dreamed Nick was touching her and thought it was the previous day, when he'd been only a dream lover. Opening her eyes, she felt as if she was falling into the depths of his, into the blue as dark as moonless midnight. They drew her into a fathomless space that claimed her as if their union had been ordained from the birth of time.

Desire beat heavily and languorously through her veins. "Nick," she whispered.

"Not Apollo this time?" he murmured against her lips. His mouth was sweet and warm, his probing tongue the most delicious taste she'd ever known.

One of his hands lay splayed across her stomach and she felt the fingers flex as she lost her shyness and thrust her own tongue boldly into his mouth. He gasped, then drew back, burying his face in the scented hollow of her throat. "Sara, *chrysi mou*, my golden one."

"Oh, Nick," she breathed. "Love me."

"I will, sweet Sara," he said raggedly, still bemused by her unexpected acquiescence. "But slowly, ever so slowly. And that's going to be the hardest thing I've ever done. You've taken all my control. You're driving me crazy."

Sara gave a shaky laugh. "What do you think you're doing to me? I've never felt like this."

He lifted himself on one elbow, taking some of his weight off her body. "Never?"

She was too aroused, too vulnerable, to prevaricate. "Not with this intensity. I didn't know I could."

He didn't answer as he continued to look down at her. Then he lifted her so that her head lay on his broad chest. "Beautiful hair," he murmured, spreading it in a shining cloak over her shoulders. "Like spun gold."

He sat quietly holding her. Then he said, his voice very gentle and so soft she barely heard him, "Sara, we can't do this, you know."

Bemused, she asked, "Do what?"

His mouth was against her temple and she felt his lips move as he smiled. "You know, make love."

Her stomach did a strange flip-flop. Disappointment? "Why not?"

"Oh, any number of reasons. We've just met, for one. We don't really know each other."

Sara smiled. "That's not what you've been telling me. You said what we feel when we touch was all that mattered."

"Sara, I lied. I didn't want to admit that you were different so I used all the old arguments men use, something I've never really done myself. But you threw me off balance. You're still doing it."

"And what if I say I've changed my mind and I want you now?"

He chuckled, his chest shifting under her. "I'd say you've been out in the sun too long and it's time we went home." He pulled her tightly to him, nuzzling the top of her head. "Sara, I've been thinking. I wasn't asleep all that time. I was watching you sleep and thinking."

He paused so long that finally she asked, "And what did you decide?"

"I decided that this attraction or whatever it is between us needs further exploration. Sex at this stage will only foul things up between us. I've seen it happen too many times. Two people meet, are attracted to each other and go to bed, and then they never get to know each other in any other meaningful way. Physical intimacy too soon can kill a relationship before it really starts."

"And what if I don't want a relationship with you or any man?" Sara asked.

"You'd be cheating yourself and a man who might love you."

"Love, Nick? I haven't seen much of that in my life, except of course my father."

"Then it's time you opened your mind to the possibilities around you. You'll never find love if you're closed up like one of your New England clams."

Sara bit her tongue to smother an indignant retort, but fairness told her he was more than half right about her.

"Nothing to say, Sara?" Nick asked, twisting his head to look into her face. "Then I'll say it. I want to get to know you, to work with you. Then we'll see what develops. I can't promise to keep my hands off you at all times but I'll try to keep within certain bounds. And when I really touch you, you'll know it's not just to satisfy some physical need. It's to make love to you in the deepest sense of the word."

Sara sat up, gazing into his serious face. She was profoundly moved by his insight and his gentle words. He was the first man she'd ever known who had a deep understanding of a woman's psyche. If this was due to his sister's teachings, she must be quite a lady.

Nick gave a faintly sheepish laugh. "Why are we looking at each other like this, as if someone died? Come on, Sara, we're not at a wake." He pushed her to her feet with a familiar hand on her bottom, then tweaked her nose as he hoisted himself to full height. "You know the real reason why we can't make love? Your father has probably been here long enough to absorb some of our customs. Here in the Mani a man comes after his daughter's lover with a shotgun, and if the man won't marry her, he makes sure that he can't marry anyone else, either."

Sara laughed. "I doubt if my father would do that. I've lived on my own too long. I'm not a little girl anymore."

"To a father, a daughter is always a little girl." He eyed her figure in its brief bikini. "No, you're definitely a woman, but you are my responsibility and I'll deliver you safely."

Sara grimaced. "Like a package—" She broke off as Nick interrupted with a hand on her arm.

"What the hell?"

Then she heard it too, the horses, which had moved farther into the trees, were stamping and snorting. "Something's disturbed them. Wait here, Sara. I'll go check. This is private property and if there's anyone here, they're trespassing."

Sara wasn't about to miss out on anything if she could help it. She bent down and picked up her shirt, pulling it over her dry bikini. Stepping into her sandals—she knew her feet weren't as tough as his—she followed.

The horses munched quietly in the long grass. Sara glanced around, puzzled, then saw Nick farther up, climbing a slope leading away from the sea. She scrambled up the rough ground after him.

"Damn it," Nick said as she came up beside him. "What scared them?"

From their vantage point at the top of a little ridge they could see the road on which Sara had reached this beach yesterday. It was deserted, a melting strip of asphalt under the hot sun.

"Maybe another animal," Sara suggested.

"Maybe," Nick said. "But I doubt it. Unless we're talking about the two-legged kind."

He frowned at the road, eyes narrowed against the glare. "I guess there's nothing here," he muttered, turning back. "Wait, Sara. Do you hear that?"

She did, a car engine. And not on the road. That was the grinding of the starter, and a moment later the roar of the engine. A large car, by the sound of it, and not far away.

She came down beside Nick who had crouched so they wouldn't be seen from the road. A moment later a car passed below them, heading for the village, the same red Pontiac that had been parked outside Sara's hotel last night.

"Tourists?" Nick wondered out loud. "Or someone snooping around? I knew I should have looked at the register. We don't get that many strangers in this area."

"What do you mean?" Sara asked in bewilderment. "I drove out here yesterday. They could have been sightseeing."

"Not much to see but orchards," Nick said laconically.

"So maybe they're horticulturists," Sara quipped.

Nick obviously didn't see any humor in her remark. His brows drew together until they met over his nose. "And maybe they're casing Andreas's house. He's got some pretty valuable stuff there and he's well-known. Could be a target for a burglary."

"A New York burglar coming way out here?" Sara asked in disbelief. "You've got to be kidding."

"I'm not," Nick said as he led the way down the slope to where they'd left their things. "Art thieves move all over the world."

The easy mood between them had shattered, and they spoke little as they packed up the picnic dishes and saddled the horses.

Sara shivered at the thought of someone spying on them. They hadn't been doing anything that had to be hidden, but they could easily have been making love. Several times they'd been no more than a breath away from it. Her face was grim as she cinched the saddle with silent efficiency.

She glanced at Nick, busy with the other horse. His face was set, almost angry, and she wondered what he was thinking. Burglars? Or something else, more sinister? This area was isolated, remote from the modern world. In the past, men had killed for family honor in blood feuds spanning generations. Today they might kill for gold, long buried but now brought to light.

"Do you really think the person in that car might have something to do with Dr. Stamoulis and the excavation?" Sara asked as they mounted and set off at a trot toward the house.

Nick shrugged, his expression enigmatic. "I don't know. But it's possible. A good many people know about the dig and if they found something of importance it wouldn't be a secret long. You can't expect the students who work there to keep anything exciting to themselves."

Nick's introspection lasted until they were unsaddling the horses in Dr. Stamoulis's stable. The thick stone walls of the building kept out the heat, and Sara sniffed appreciatively at the smell that pervaded it—the sweet scent of hay and the pleasant, pungent odor of horses. For an instant she was twelve years old again, preparing for a Saturday horse show. Horses had once been a passion with her and her school friends, and she'd been fortunate that her father had possessed the means to indulge it.

"I could sure use a drink and a shower," Nick said as they wiped down the gear before hanging it in the tack room. A smile tugged at the corner of his mouth. It broadened into a grin as he slung his arm around Sara's shoulders. "What are we being so glum about anyway?" he said cheerfully. "It's still a beautiful day, too good to waste on useless speculations."

Sara was conscious of the solid comfort of his arm around her as they walked toward the house. "Are you going to tell Andreas about the car?"

Nick considered. "No, not at the moment," he said slowly. "No use alarming him without good cause. It might have been a lost tourist." His voice was neutral, yet something told her he wasn't so ready to dismiss the incident, any more than she was.

"Do you want to stay for a cold drink, Sara?" Nick asked as they approached the back patio of the house. "Or would you rather go back to your hotel and change for dinner? I'll pick you up at eight."

"Presumptuous, aren't you?" Sara said tartly but with a grin that took the sting out of her words. "Maybe I have another date."

To her surprise he glowered at her. "With whom? You don't know anyone here."

"Maybe I met the man in the Pontiac," she said airily, examining a broken fingernail to avoid looking at him. "Fellow Americans and all that."

A tangible hostility bombarded her and she looked up. The glitter in his eyes dried her throat. "Nick, I didn't mean anything."

"Don't joke, Sara," he said, his voice low and dangerous. "For all we know the man may be a criminal. Even if you do see him, I'd advise you to ignore him, at least until we know who he is."

"You're taking this awfully seriously, aren't you, Nick?"

"It may be serious," he said.

She saw he meant it. "Don't worry, Nick. I can take care of myself."

"Sure you can, but I'm responsible for seeing that you're entertained, fed and happy. And that you get to the excavation site safely."

Sara bristled. "I don't need a keeper, Nick. You're not under any obligation as far as I'm concerned."

Nick heaved a long-suffering sigh. "Will you have dinner with me, Dr. Morgan, and save me from terminal boredom? Please? You'll be doing mankind a valuable service."

Sara choked back a laugh. "Mankind?" she queried. "Or just you?"

He pulled a droll face. "Me, of course. Who cares about the rest of mankind?" His voice dropped to a whisper. "In fact, I'd like nothing better than to lock you away where no one can see you, where I can keep you all to myself."

"Well, I might have something to say about that, Nick," she retorted smartly, not quite sure whether he was teasing or not. "But I'll have dinner with you," she said, giving in to her own wishes.

His grin astounded her with its open expression of delight at her agreement. Had he been that worried she wouldn't accept? She saw a flash in his dark eyes, and the movement of his hands led her to think he was about to enfold her in his arms. But he controlled the urge, merely saying, "Good. I'll pick you up at eight."

When she came down the marble staircase later, Sara found Nick waiting in the tiny lobby, deep in conversation with the desk clerk. His charm seemed to reach out to everyone he encountered.

He heard the click of her heels on the steps and moved away from the desk. His dark eyes glinted approvingly at her crisp linen dress in a pale yellow that emphasized the golden tan of her smooth shoulders. Her hair, caught up at the sides with tortoiseshell combs, hung in loose waves down her back, highlights sparkling in the dim light from the bare bulb over her head.

"Ready?" he asked lightly, with no trace of the disturbing tension of their last conversation in his tone. He'd also changed, into beautifully cut tan trousers and a silk shirt with its short sleeves rolled so they fitted tightly on his biceps. His hair was brushed close to his handsome head, more stringently under control than usual.

"Yes, I'm ready," she replied with a grave smile.

She remembered their resolution to keep their relationship strictly business for a while, but when he took her hand in his big warm one, she couldn't suppress a little thrill of excitement. He was very much a man, masculine and sure of himself. For a moment her determination of noninvolvement wavered. Would it be so bad to have an affair with him? He would be a wonderful lover and the memory of this summer would warm the cold winter nights.

"Sara, get hold of yourself," she murmured under her breath.

"Talking to yourself, Sara?" Nick asked with an amused wiggle of his brows.

"At least I get intelligent answers," Sara threw back at him with a bright grin.

They drove to Areopolis in Nick's car, a battered Citroën of uncertain vintage. Its smooth motion was at odds with its shabby appearance, and Sara relaxed against the worn leather upholstery, inhaling the scent of flowers and sea air that came in through the open windows. The heat of the day had mellowed in this hour before sunset. The fragrant, tranquil air touched a deep place in her, poetry to her soul. Pure magic, she thought, letting her mind drift.

"That red Pontiac wasn't there," Nick said, breaking into Sara's reverie.

"Oh? Then he must have checked out."

"He didn't," said Nick. "That's why I was questioning the desk clerk. The car was driven by a Constantinos Vergis, American passport, occupation and business unknown. But he's been in Greece a while. He entered a year ago and never left. Very accommodating of the desk clerk to be so talkative and of the tourist board to require guests to leave their passports at hotel desks."

"How did you get a look at his passport, Nick? Or are you a member of the secret police?"

"Secret police!" Nick exclaimed. "Greece is a country with very little crime. No, I just used my charm." He paused delicately. "And a thousand-drachma note."

Sara laughed. "You've been watching too much television."

He slanted her an amused look. "It worked, didn't it?" Then he frowned. "I wonder what this Vergis is doing here."

"Maybe he's visiting relatives. Or he's a perfectly innocent tourist."

"Maybe," said Nick skeptically. "But I don't know. I don't trust guys who drive fancy cars and don't have regular jobs."

There was no real reason to suspect the man of anything, Sara mused in the silence that followed. Her feelings of unease with Andreas, however, were much less nebulous. "How long did you say you'd known Dr. Stamoulis, Nick?"

He glanced at her in surprise. "Practically all my life. He knew my father; his family and mine were always close. Why?"

Sara shrugged, unwilling to put Andreas in a bad light by relating the incident of the broken cup. "I just wondered, that's all."

Nick threaded the car expertly through the narrow streets of Areopolis to a small taverna with tables set outside under the trellis of grapevines. Sara sniffed appreciatively as the appetizing aroma of roasting meat drifted to them on the still air. She suddenly realized what a long time it had been since they'd eaten lunch.

"It certainly smells good," she said as they chose a table and sat down.

"You'll find it tastes just as good," Nick commented, waving his hand for a waiter.

A young man who looked about eighteen ran out of the building. With a flick of his wrists he draped a length of clean white paper over the table and snapped a large rubber band into place to hold it. Then he whipped a pad and pencil from his back pocket to take their order.

"We have roasted lamb and chicken, lamb chops and souvlaki and roast pork," he announced in heavily accented English. "You like?" His even white teeth gleamed as he cast a special smile in Sara's direction, which earned him an immediate frown from Nick.

The waiter inclined his head in an almost obeisant gesture. *"Signome, Kyrie, i yineka sas ina poli omorphi."*

Nick made a curt, and to Sara, incomprehensible reply to this, then asked her in English, "Do you drink ouzo?"

Her mouth curved in a smile. "I've never tried it. Isn't it the national drink?"

"You might say that." He addressed the waiter. "Two ouzos, please. And a plate of *mesethes*."

"Very good, sir."

When the boy had gone, Sara asked curiously, "Nick, what did he say before?"

"Time you learned Greek, Sara. He said my wife was very beautiful."

Sara's face suffused with pink color. She'd had to ask. "And did you tell him I wasn't your wife?" she asked with a nervous laugh.

"Of course not. If he thinks you're my wife, at least you'll be spared his stares and lovesick sighs."

His voice held a hardness that caused Sara to look at him in surprise. Why was this bothering him? He was getting as bad as Stamoulis. If he was ashamed that she was thought to be his wife, why hadn't he simply denied it?

An alternative possibility struck her. Amused, she asked, her golden eyes dancing with mischief, "What's wrong, Nick? Surely you're not jealous."

"Jealous? Hell, no," he denied offhandedly, but there was no humor in his face. "I haven't known you long enough, have I? In fact—" his voice dropped while his eyes remained cold "—I haven't really *known* you at all." He picked up his water glass and drank from it, his eyes never leaving Sara's increasingly indignant face. "Or perhaps you like being ogled by every man you meet."

Sara's resentment fled, to be replaced by an irrepressible bubble of laughter. "Ogled? Really, Nick, you can't think I'd be interested in that boy. Where's that arrogant male you were yesterday and this afternoon? Does your ego bruise so easily?"

He had the grace to grin sheepishly. "Sorry, Sara." He took her hand and turned it palm up. It was so small and fragile in his, he marveled at the delicacy of it. Damn it, he *was* jealous, jealous of any man who looked at her. He wanted to be the only one who received her smiles.

The feeling was unfamiliar and disturbing and he didn't like the way it kept sneaking up on him. He'd always been in control of his emotions, but since he'd met Sara that control slipped far too easily, as if the look in her golden eyes had loosened some vital cog in his brain.

His fingers tightened and he felt her pulse quicken. He looked at her face. She was staring back at him, her eyes soft in the lamplight, her lips parted and tender.

"Sara," he whispered. "What am I going to do with you?"

A startled light leaped into Sara's eyes. Before she could form a reply, the waiter appeared with their drinks and a large plate of appetizers. He set the dishes on the table with a flourish, looking for approval. Sara awarded him with a dazzling smile. The boy, flustered and red-faced, nearly collapsed at her feet in the throes of adolescent love. Sara barely noticed the waiter, though, as she directed a defiant look at Nick.

She'd heard Nick's low words, felt the melting heat they ignited inside her. Quickly she brought her dissolving sanity under control. She wasn't going to play games with Nick or let him get under her skin unless it was on her terms. Her smile at the waiter served to notify Nick of her intentions.

Nick had been grateful for the waiter's appearance. He'd been on the point of making a fool of himself in front of Sara once again. The boy had shattered the moment just in time. That look on her face! Nick had wanted to whisk her away to kiss and love her, to make sure she never lost that expression. It hadn't been for him, anyway, he told himself with brutal honesty. On a night like this, soft and romantic, she would have looked like that for anyone.

He dismissed the waiter with a heavy frown and a sharp toss of his head. Picking up his glass of ouzo, he downed half the contents at a single swallow.

Sara, watching him, innocently did the same—and nearly choked as the fiery spirit hit the back of her throat. "What was that?" she sputtered after she had quenched the fire with a drink of water. "You could have warned me."

"Ouzo," Nick said, succinct and unrepentant, absurdly gratified by the small revenge. "One of the weapons in our arsenal of defense."

"No wonder the Turks never entirely conquered the Greeks. One drink of that and the Greeks were bristling with aggression." She sampled her glass again, more carefully this time, finding the licorice flavor refreshing and surprisingly to her taste. Picking up a fork, she tried the tiny meatballs on the platter. They were seasoned with dill, mint and the faintest hint of cinnamon. "Mmm, delicious."

She smiled at Nick, conceding him this round. That smile she'd given the waiter had been a bit overdone.

Nick, still smarting, said the first thing that came into his mind, and wondered as soon as the words left his mouth, what devil had driven him. "How old were you when your mother left?"

Sara blinked. For a moment she felt disoriented at this sudden and irrelevant question. "What do you know about my mother?" she asked defensively.

"Nothing except that she and Daniel were divorced when you were small."

"Why do you want to know?" she asked, taking another careful sip of ouzo.

Good humor restored, Nick grinned suddenly. "I want to know all about you. You intrigue me. You have such a cool exterior, yet I find you lying stretched out in the sun like an uninhibited kitten. I want to know what goes on behind your golden eyes. You must admit you're unusual. Intelligent, well-educated, no obvious vices, all your own teeth. Why isn't there even a suggestion of a man in your life?"

Sara wavered between annoyance at his presumption and laughter at the teasing note in his remark. Laughter won out. She dropped her voice to a whisper, eyes sparkling. "I snore."

"Oh," said Nick, not batting an eye. "And I suppose your excellent teeth came from a dentist. My grandfather always told me to look for good teeth and good health in a woman."

Sara laughed. "Did your grandmother qualify?"

"I'll say. She lived to be ninety-five. Of course Grandfather outlived her, but only by a year. He was ninety-nine."

"Did he have his own teeth?"

"Most of them." Nick grinned, showing off his. "I'm from good stock. So, what's with the men in Boston? Are they all blind?"

"Why should they be?" Sara asked, bristling a little. "Don't you think a woman can make a life on her own? A man isn't really necessary, you know."

His smile turned wickedly gleeful, and she knew she'd laid herself wide open. "I know," he said, deadpan, "but it's so much more fun with one."

Sara laughed in spite of herself. "Are all your interests below the belt?"

He looked smug. "Not all," he drawled, his eyes on the curve of her breasts where the round edge of her dress outlined them. A tingling heat rushed into them, and she was sure he could see the points of her suddenly erect nipples.

"A lot of women aren't getting married these days," Sara said. "Some of them are even having children, their own or adopted. If I want a child, I can have one without getting married."

Nick seemed fascinated but a line was appearing between his brows. "Can you?"

"Of course," she said complacently. "I make enough money to support myself and a child. I have job security. Other women raise children with a lot less going for them."

Nick's frown deepened. "Maybe they do but does that make it right if you have a choice? Besides, you can't make a baby alone."

"You'd be surprised, Nick. Haven't you heard of the latest developments in scientific technology?"

"Sure I have, but it's not natural. People should make children with love, not technology."

A corner of Sara's mouth lifted wryly. "How many children are conceived in love by parents who want them? Even marriage is a risk if you look at the divorce rate. Anyway, I'm sure I could find a man willing to father a child with me. I wouldn't need technology."

"And you'd do that and then forget all about his contribution? Maybe he'd want some say in its upbringing. It would be his child, too."

They were beginning to forget that this was a theoretical discussion as their voices rose and became more heated. "I haven't seen that many men these days who care much about their children," Sara said a little scornfully.

"Men?" Nick retorted hotly. "What about your mother? Didn't she leave you?"

Sara subsided as a peculiar angry pain sliced through her. Even after all these years the hurt remained. Would she never be able to view her past in its proper perspective? She forced a smile to stiff lips. "Touché, Nick. You're right, of course. Children do need two parents, or at least parents with the intention of raising them together."

Nick raked his hand through his hair, tousling its curls. "I'm sorry, Sara. I didn't mean to upset you. But since I have, why don't you tell me about it? You must have been badly hurt for it still to bother you. Don't you see your mother at all?"

Sara gave a brittle little laugh. "I'm twenty-seven, hardly an age to be mourning my childhood. Besides, I wasn't deprived. Father saw to that."

"Tell me about your mother," Nick said, sticking to his original question with the tenacity of a moray eel with a diver in its jaws.

Chapter Five

Sara sighed. "All right, Dr. Freud. You'll let me know your diagnosis, won't you?" She took another fortifying swallow of ouzo, chasing it down with water. The glass was wet with condensation and she toyed with it, her eyes fixed on the series of wet rings she made on the paper tablecloth. "She left when I was ten. She said she'd done her duty with me and now it was my father's turn. Her duty! I was her child but to her I was only a duty." Her voice rose on the last word and she quickly gulped another drink of water.

Nick watched her agitation, his face unreadable. "And you've carried this resentment with you for seventeen years." He leaned over and took her hand, rubbing it between his palms, massaging her fragile fingers. "Sara, you're a grown woman, beautiful, successful and desirable. You can't let what happened with your mother color your whole life. Many marriages work out fine."

"I don't think about her most of the time, and I have no intention of following her example."

"What example?" Nick asked. "Leaving your father?"

Sara stared at their clasped hands, her small one almost lost in the broad warmth of his. "No, her example of chasing men all over the world. She couldn't live without the adulation of men. All they have to do is give her a smile and she's all over them. And since her second husband died and left her extremely wealthy, she keeps falling for the most awful playboys, most of them titled and penniless. She's been married at least five times." She smiled ruefully. "I've lost track of them."

"I take it her marriage to Daniel lasted the longest?" He paused thoughtfully. "Strange, he doesn't seem to fit the pattern."

"He doesn't. She married him because her family was on the verge of disgrace and he was an easy mark." Her voice dropped to a painful whisper. "She never intended having any children. I was an accident."

Nick's heart contracted with sympathy. "Lucky for me," he muttered. In a normal tone he said, "I don't see what you're so worried about, Sara. From what I know of you, you're not in the least like your mother."

Sara's chin lifted and Nick almost laughed at the contrast between her stubborn pride and the picture she painted of her mother's weak-willed gullibility. "But I have her blood. It could come out in me yet, if I'm not careful. If I let myself become dependent on a man I'll never be my own person again. At least I won't have to marry for money. I worked hard and now I've finally succeeded in getting the job I want and the independence."

If she hadn't been so earnest, Nick might have laughed at this convoluted logic. But he saw beneath the woman and perceived the child who had been deeply hurt. "Sara, Sara," he said, shaking his head. "You *are* your own person. You've more than proved it." He stroked the back of her hand, tracing the blue veins and fine tendons, the tensile strength implicit in it. "You can't shut off part of your personality just because you're afraid. You can have a relationship without subjugating your own feelings and needs."

"I tried once. I really tried. But it didn't work out and I don't care to repeat the experiment," Sara said firmly. The set of her mouth told him not to probe in that area. His curiosity was piqued but he let tact prevail, for now.

However, he couldn't resist one more piece of advice. "Let yourself go, Sara. Enjoy life. You'll never be happy denying your true nature."

"And what is that, Dr. Freud?" Sara said, flippancy covering the growing realization that he just might have a valid point.

Nick laughed. "I'll let you discover that for yourself, Sara." He reached for the bottle the waiter had left them and topped up her glass, adding a generous measure of water that changed the clear liquid to a milky cloudiness.

Sara looked skeptically at her glass, then tasted it. "Good," she pronounced with the air of a wine taster.

Nick laughed again. "Watch it, you'll be tipsy before you know it."

Sara made a face. "I never get tipsy. A little dizzy maybe, but I know when to stop."

"Experienced drinker, eh?" Nick said sardonically, helping himself to another meatball. "Ouzo has been known to do in the most experienced. It kind of sneaks up on you." He chewed reflectively for a moment, then leaned back in his chair. "I almost married once."

"Oh?" said Sara with a strange sinking feeling in her stomach. "How did she let you get away?"

Nick threw her a quick grin. "She found a better prospect. At least she thought he was."

"Like my mother," Sara said flatly.

"Kind of, I suppose, but she stayed married." He paused, staring up at the canopy of grapevines, his hands clasped behind his head. "It was four—no, closer to five years ago. She was blond, the pale kind of blond, sort of ethereal, very uncommon in Greece. I was smitten the first time I saw her." He grinned again. "Of course I was a lot younger then."

Sara's straight brows lifted. "A lot?"

"Emotionally younger, I meant." He chuckled. "Boy, was I younger! Anyway, I had bought the land where Andreas's house now stands and I started to build, all the time more or less worshiping her from afar. Oh, we went to the same parties and I talked to her, but she never knew how I felt about her. I wanted to have something to offer her, and I thought the house would be it."

"You designed it for her? I hope she was honored." Sara couldn't keep a faintly ironic note from her tone.

"Yeah, so honored she married some other guy. Actually, I didn't design it for her. I'd planned it for years, in fact it was one of my university projects. Anyway, the day I went back to Athens to ask her to share it with me, I found out she was marrying someone else, older and more sophisticated." His mouth twisted in self-mockery. "Less romantic, too, you might say. They live in New York where she gives elegant dinner parties and appears on the best-dressed list nearly every year."

Sara raised puzzled eyes to his. "You're so calm about it now, Nick. Yet yesterday when you mentioned the house, I could have sworn you were angry."

Nick shifted in his chair, picking up his fork and spearing a slice of tomato. "I was just thinking I shouldn't have sold it. I was angry when I found out that Irene wasn't interested in me. My pride had been hurt. I sold the house to Andreas in a fit of temper, the kind young men have when their romantic dreams fall apart. It was a stupid way to react."

"But a human one," Sara said with understanding and an ever-deepening feeling of warmth toward him.

Later they ate grilled lamb chops and a tomato-cucumber salad washed down with a delicious golden wine that seemed to contain the sun that had ripened the grapes. Sara chattered unself-consciously now that her mother wasn't a subject of discussion. She felt happy and light-headed from the wine she'd consumed on top of the ouzo, not noticing that Nick drank only sparingly. Somehow, his confiding in her about his near marriage had altered her perception of him, or perhaps had shown her another aspect of him. At any rate, he seemed less arrogant in her eyes, more vulnerable. He could be hurt, too.

And she should also forget the past, she realized, and make an effort to embrace the present, living life to its fullest. The years of study and hard work were behind her. Her present work wouldn't always be easy, but there would be less pressure. No more exams to be passed. Now she'd be the one giving the exams.

No, she wasn't her mother; she was Sara Morgan, professor of history, a woman in charge of her own life, dependent on no one and answerable only to herself.

The summer with Nick suddenly seemed full of exciting possibilities and the most tempting of them was not the hope of making the archaeological discovery of the century.

It was late; most of the other diners had long since left. Nick was engrossed in conversation with two men at the next table, fishermen by the look of their battered caps. Sara studied Nick from under lowered lashes, wanting to understand what it was that attracted her. She'd known men as handsome, with even greater savoir faire, but something about Nick set him apart. He had an air of taking command that touched everyone who came into contact with him.

His arm, which rested on the back of an empty chair, was long and muscular. A gold wristwatch was nestled in the fine hairs that sprinkled the back of his tanned hand and continued up his arms. His fingers were lean and strong with clean short nails, and an involuntary shiver passed through her as she remembered their sure touch on her bare skin.

Later, when they returned to her hotel, he might touch her again, might ask to come into her room. And what would she do?

Not yet, said her innate caution. She liked him but it was still too soon. He was right; they couldn't rush headlong into a relationship that would be physical before any real mental or emotional bond was established between them. She'd succumbed to an attraction before that had turned out to be only a shadow of love. She wasn't going to become like so many of her friends, rushing into bed with a new and exciting partner, only to wake in the morning next to an unattractive stranger.

But would it be that way with Nick? Would the handsome prince become a toad in the light of day? She almost laughed out loud at the absurd idea, then forced the rush of mirth down with the uneasy feeling that perhaps she had miscalculated her capacity for alcohol. When she moved her head she felt decidedly tipsy.

Nick shifted in his chair and she watched the easy play of muscles under his thin shirt. He would be a marvelous lover; that confident masculinity almost guaranteed it. He hadn't learned that sensual expertise he used so skillfully in a monastery. Yet she was willing to bet that the women he'd loved and left were still on friendly terms with him, if and when he ran into them after their closer association had ended.

Nick's eyes swiveled to meet hers for an instant and he winked, reaching out his hand and covering hers. "We'll go in a minute," he murmured as he listened to the end of an involved tale the fisherman was relating.

The two men left and Nick signaled the waiter for the bill. He paid it and moved around the table to help Sara with her chair. A wave of dizziness staggered her as she stood up. She grasped the edge of the table, shaking her head to clear it.

"Sara, are you all right?" Nick's voice seemed to come from a great distance.

"Jus' a li'l dizzy," she muttered.

"How much did you drink?" Nick demanded with a frown. He took her arm and began to lead her to the car. "Never mind, let's get you back to your hotel."

Sara found to her dismay that she could hardly walk. She really hadn't had that much to drink. It must have been a combination of hot sun and the day's physical activities that was amplifying the effect of the wine. She'd never felt so disoriented and didn't protest as Nick helped her into the car before moving around it and getting in under the steering wheel.

"You're drunk," he said succinctly as he started the engine. "It doesn't take much in this climate, and you're not used to the heat."

Sara forced a laugh. "Now you tell me." Her head lolled against the back of the seat. "I'm so sleepy." The words slurred and her eyelids drooped as if weighted with lead.

Nick gave a short bark of laughter that was devoid of any sympathy. "You're drunk. You're going to have a colossal headache tomorrow."

"Colossal? That was in Rhodes...." Her voice trailed into oblivion.

"And how the hell can you say you don't need a keeper, Sara?" Nick muttered with a kind of disgusted tenderness, but he doubted if she heard him.

Sara woke in the morning, head heavy, mouth like cotton. Sitting up in bed, she groaned. How much of an ass had she made of herself?

She suddenly realized she was naked except for her bikini panties. Had he undressed her and put her to bed?

She clutched her head. Well, he'd been only partly right about that; it ached but not colossally. She remembered that part. A discreet beep from her watch reminded her they planned an early start. Nothing for it but to get moving.

She was in the bathroom brushing her teeth when she heard the outer door open. "Who's there?"

"Room service," came Nick's amused voice. "I brought you some breakfast."

Breakfast? She grimaced at her reflection in the mirror. But when she mentally examined her body she discovered she was hungry.

She was about to open the bathroom door when she remembered she wore only a tiny lace bikini, a mate of yesterday's. Nick hadn't left. She could hear undefined noises from the bedroom that indicated his presence. For a moment she hesitated, then decided she'd brazen it out. He'd seen this much of her already anyway. What did one more time matter?

Head high and back straight, as if she were modeling the most exquisite couturier gown, she glided across the room to the closet. Outwardly cool but inwardly aware that Nick's dark eyes had surveyed, assessed and recorded every centimeter of her body, she pulled out a dress and put it on. Then she drew a chair to the bedside table where he'd set the tray of food, and sat down.

"How's your head?" Nick asked. His face was serious, but the glint in his eyes gave away his suppressed amusement.

"Fine," she said airily, wishing she could control the blush that crept up her cheeks. She busied her hands with sweet rolls and butter, avoiding his eyes. "Look, Nick, it was rude of me to sleep all the way home last night. I don't know what came over me."

"I seem to bring out a lot of uncharacteristic inclinations in you," Nick said without inflection as he spread honey on a slice of bread. "Or is it only what's buried in you coming out now?"

Annoyed, she frowned. "Do you have to twist everything to suit your own purposes, Nick? Who appointed you my psychiatrist?"

"Nobody. You do it all by yourself if that's the way you think of me. I keep hoping you'll begin to see me in a different light. Why don't you quit vacillating between what you really want and what you think is the right and proper thing to do?"

Sara stared at him, her butter knife poised in her hand, her mind in turmoil. His self-assurance was exasperating. She'd never met a man who could make her run such a gamut of emotions. It was disturbing as well as exhilarating.

"Aren't you ever unsure of yourself, Nick?" she asked.

He looked startled, then smiled. "Frequently, Sara. Especially where you're concerned."

She suddenly found that the food on her plate required her undivided attention. "Well, you certainly don't act it."

There was a short silence and then Nick said, "You don't have to be so prickly, Sara. As I told you yesterday, I'm not pushing you. I won't force you into anything you don't want to do."

Sara raised troubled eyes to his. "That's just the problem. You make me want things I've never wanted before. I don't want to get involved and you disrupt my life."

"Do I, Sara?" Nick asked seriously, his words so simple, yet the tone of them so warm she felt as if his hand had caressed her.

She stumbled doggedly on, ignoring the little curl of desire that awakened inside her. "Yes, you're always crowding me, even after you said you wouldn't. I don't want to be touched all the time. I don't like it."

His laugh was half incredulous, half scornful. "Sara, don't lie. You love it. You love to touch. I've watched you. You're always stroking things. Those pretty cups of Andreas's that you can read a newspaper through, you were caressing yours as if it was my skin. You're a very sensual woman, if you'd let yourself go." His voice dropped to a near whisper. "As you let yourself go in my arms."

She felt as though she was burning up, melting and flaming at the same time. With difficulty she found her voice. "But where will it all end? We have a job to do and we can't let this—this body chemistry interfere with it."

Nick sighed. "Is that all you think it is?" Then he broke eye contact with her and spread butter and honey on a roll. "But you're right. We have work to do." He chewed thoughtfully for a moment. "But when it's all over—"

"When it's all over, at the end of the summer, you'll be back in Athens and I'll go back to Boston, to my new job," Sara said firmly. Only by fixing her mind on the temporary nature of their association could she fight her restlessness and regain control of her disintegrating self-possession. If she allowed her emotions free rein she would find herself his puppet and that would spell her ruin.

Nick leaned forward suddenly. "You've got some honey there."

"Where?"

"Here." He bent his head and, with the tip of his tongue, removed the honey from her lower lip. The contact only lasted a split second, but it was long enough to accelerate her already unsteady pulse.

She glared at him with unconcealed disapproval. "You're very physical, aren't you?" she asked acidly.

Nick shrugged. "No more than you, if you'd be honest with yourself." He drained his coffee cup and began to stack their dishes back on the tray. "How long will it take you to get your things together?"

So it was business again. "Only a few minutes," Sara said coolly.

He eyed her critically. "You might change to something a little less, shall we say, decorative. Shorts or jeans and a covered-up shirt. We'll have to walk a little and you don't want to get sunburned."

For the first time Sara noticed that he'd changed from his clothes of the evening before. He wore a serviceable cotton shirt with the sleeves rolled high in his usual manner, and the inevitable tight, faded jeans. He added, "I hope you've got some sturdy shoes or sandals. It's a rough path."

Sara raised her chin. "I came prepared, don't worry. I knew it wasn't a Sunday School picnic."

"Good." He nodded as he picked up the tray. "I'll wait for you downstairs."

She was down in ten minutes, dressed in shorts with plenty of pockets and a cotton T-shirt that boasted a garish decal of a leaping leopard. Her compact backpack held a change of clothes and other necessities. A single suitcase contained the remainder of her belongings. Since she would be staying at the site she didn't need to keep the hotel room.

Nick lifted his brows in amusement at the sight of her lurid shirt. "Quite the lady professor, aren't you?"

"My students won't see me," Sara replied primly.

"You look young enough to be one of them."

Sara unsuccessfully hid a smile behind a haughty look. "I'll have you know I'm a mature, liberated woman. I'll wear what I please."

Nick threw up his hands. "I'm not objecting. I'm admiring." He picked up her suitcase. "We'll drop this off at Andreas's before we head out."

He carried the luggage to his car while she made arrangements to keep her car parked in the hotel's lot until she found out whether she would need it. If there was sufficient transportation at the site, the hotel could call the rental company to pick it up. She paid for her room, then ran out to join Nick in the shabby Citroën.

"Oh, by the way," he said casually as he turned the ignition key, "you don't snore. Whoever told you that lied."

Sara shot him a murderous look, then asked, "Is Andreas riding with us? Or is he taking his own car?"

Nick took one hand off the steering wheel and struck his forehead. "Didn't I tell you?"

At her blank look, he added, "Andreas went yesterday, while we were out riding. I meant to tell you last night. I guess with one thing and another it slipped my mind."

"What about the supplies?"

"He took them in his Land Rover. There was a lot of stuff to take so he decided we could come along on our own."

The sun was just past its zenith when they stopped for lunch in a village Nick said was the last before the excavation site. They would have another hour's drive over an increasingly narrow, rocky road, then an uphill walk to the site itself.

The village was tiny, sparsely scattered over a mountain slope, the houses half hidden in a pine forest. Spiky aloes and prickly pear adorned with yellow blossoms grew along the cobbled street.

The central square had an air of desolation in spite of the dusty red geraniums growing around the door of the *kafenion*, the village coffee shop. The only sign of twentieth-century technology was the electric meter mounted on the outside wall of the weathered building. Nick's dusty Citroën stood next to the only other modern vehicle, a red Datsun pickup truck. Its gleaming paint indicated its owner's pride, but rock dents in its sides betrayed the reality of stony mountain tracks.

In contrast, and more in keeping with the atmosphere of the place, a moth-eaten, swaybacked mule was tethered to a plane tree next to the village water pump. At intervals a harsh bray erupted from its mouth as it lamented the flies, the heat and the weight of the saddle on its back.

Nick went into the *kafenion* to arrange for a meal. A little group of old men playing a desultory game of cards looked up at the stranger who entered their private domain. There were few visitors to their village these days; even their children who had emigrated seldom came any more.

Sara stood in the doorway, shyly conscious of five pairs of unwinking eyes on her. Only men sat at the little tables in the gloomy room, driven indoors by the relentless heat of the sun, and she guessed that her presence, even at the door, constituted a serious breach of etiquette. There was an atmosphere in this place of time having stood still for a century or more. At any moment Kolokotronis, the hero of the Greek resistance, would come galloping around the corner to partake of refreshment before resuming his badgering of the Turkish interlopers.

Her fantasy was spoiled by the appearance of a small boy wearing a T-shirt that proclaimed itself a souvenir of Disney World. He looked with envy at the leopard on her chest, and she gave him a slow smile. He stared for a moment longer out of wide, almost apprehensive eyes the color of ripe olives. Then, at a word from one of the old men, he ducked around her and fled across the square.

Sara backed out of the doorway and stood in the narrow strip of shade outside the building. Lifting her hand, she pushed the heavy hair off her neck. It was hotter than the hinges of hell and she wished she'd worn her hair up.

"They're not used to serving meals here," said Nick behind her. "But he's going to cook us some eggs. With bread and a salad that should keep us until we get to the dig."

Sara nodded. "That sounds fine. It's so hot. Can we get something to drink?"

"Lemonade all right?" Nick asked.

"Great," Sara said, licking her parched lips. In spite of the sunscreen lip gloss she'd applied they were uncomfortably rough. The dry heat sucked the moisture out of everything exposed to it. "Do we eat outside or in? I think outside is better. From the funny looks I've been getting, I think the men feel awkward having a woman in the coffee shop."

Nick laughed. "Yes, you're probably the first female to venture in that door for a hundred years."

He moved a table into the shadow of the plane tree, under the disapproving stare of the mule. Sara brought two chairs, sitting on one of them as Nick went to fetch the lemonade. It was tart and deliciously cold, and Sara found herself grateful for refrigerators, an item she'd always taken for granted.

Condensation misted the bottles, forming a puddle on the metal table. "Nectar of the gods," Nick said, taking a long swallow and wiping his hand casually across his mouth as he put the bottle down.

"How do they live here?" Sara asked a little later when the man had brought their omelets and salads. "No industry, completely isolated from the rest of the world, no decent road. How do they stand it?"

"Not everyone has a craving for shopping malls," Nick said dryly.

Sara bristled slightly. "I know that. But it just seems so poor, so hopeless."

"They manage," Nick said. "A few sheep or goats, a garden, some olive trees. It doesn't take much to live here."

"Are they happy?" Sara asked.

Nick shrugged. "Probably no less than people anywhere. They could move farther down the mountain. Others have. But you have to realize these people have their roots here. You can't dig up a mature tree and expect it to prosper out of its native soil." He gestured at her half-eaten omelet. "Come on, Sara, eat up."

Chapter Six

Sara felt as if every bone in her body ached as the Citroën toiled up the last steep incline and came to a halt on a flat area ringed with boulders and thorny shrubs. She stretched stiff muscles as she got out of the car, letting a tiny breeze from the mountain peaks around them stir her loose hair. The sun was copper in a sky from which all the blue had been bleached by its intensity. Even the faint breeze gave no relief from the unrelenting heat.

"What the hell?" said Nick explosively, his face darkening in a frown.

"What's the matter?" Sara asked, wiping perspiration from her face with her forearm.

"There should be more vehicles," Nick said. A Land Rover, presumably Dr. Stamoulis's, an open jeep and a dusty Fiat occupied most of the limited space. Heat waves shimmered over the hot metal roofs. "The students who are working on the dig for the summer must not be here.''

"Maybe they took a long weekend," Sara suggested.

"Maybe," Nick said, still frowning. "But usually they don't leave on weekends because of the difficulties of driving that road."

Rocks and debris made the path hazardous and Sara was glad of her sturdy shoes. Nick moved ahead of her, marking the path that seemed nonexistent at times. They were following a gully and the heat was oppressive, trapped between stone walls. Sara's shirt was wet with sweat, uncomfortably sticky. In fact, she thought, blinking against the glare of the sun, even her eyeballs seemed to be sweating.

She kept her eyes on Nick's back as he set a steady pace. His arms, tanned and strong, swung with the easy rhythm of his stride.

He moved like an athlete, with superb muscular co-ordination. She wondered what sports he played. He must do something besides sit in an office to maintain that edge of fitness and condition. Perhaps he ran, or played tennis. He had the well-developed arms and shoulders of a tennis player, and the long legs.

"Did you ever play tennis?" she asked without really intending to. She was surprised that she'd voiced the question.

Nick turned his head, never pausing in his stride. His eyes as they touched her were quizzical. "Some, at college," he replied. "Why?"

Sara shrugged. "Nothing. It just struck me that you look like you could have been a tennis player."

"Not for many years, sweet Sara."

Sweet Sara. A hot awareness ran through her and she almost stumbled. That seductive note in his voice. Did he do it on purpose or was that just his particular trait in dealing with women? The ease with which he did it seemed to indicate it was as natural to him as breathing, this playing on her senses. But how sincere was he? Could she trust him when her emotions were tumbling with breakneck speed toward a giving that was much more than physical?

She turned her mind from this fruitless speculation, staring again at his broad back, forcing herself to forget the heat and the aching tiredness in her legs.

How well he wore his clothes, the jeans molding his narrow hips snugly, his long thigh muscles flexing with supple grace under the faded cotton. Perspiration stained his shirt under his backpack and she knew he must be feeling the intense heat as much as she was.

They reached a comparatively level area, sparsely shaded by pines twisted and stunted from harsh mountain weather. Nick handed Sara his water bottle and she drank deeply before handing it back. Without wiping the top he too drank, smiling at her with his eyes. Her lashes drooped as she felt that sexual pull that was never far from the surface with them.

"Tired, Sara?" Nick asked quietly as if he was unaware of the crackling currents in the thick heat.

She smiled, brushing back clinging tendrils of hair from her temples. "Just hot. You don't have to worry about me."

Nick grinned. "I know. You don't need a keeper."

Sara gave a soft, husky laugh. "That's right, Nick. I can take care of myself."

Nick's expression grew thoughtful. "Sure you can, but isn't it nice sometimes to have someone else look after you? It's the nature of any species for the female to turn to the male for protection and security."

"Oh, come on, Nick. This is the twentieth century. We're not living in caves anymore."

Nick screwed the top firmly back on the water bottle and tucked it into the outside pocket of his pack. "I know, and women don't need protection." He got to his feet, then took her hand and brought her up beside him. For a moment she was aware of the warmth of his fingers so different from the harsh heat of the day, and of his fresh masculine scent. "Wouldn't you want the man in your life to cherish you, Sara?" Nick asked softly.

Without waiting for a response he turned and strode up the poorly marked trail. Sara shifted the weight of her pack a little higher and followed, her thoughts chewing over his last remark.

Cherish? Her first impulse was to laugh at what seemed an archaic notion. But was it so out of date? Did women still not only want men to treat them as equals but to complement and complete them as well? Perhaps modern couples had lost track of this, become too concerned with what each could get, rather than what each could give to a relationship.

Her mouth curved in a smile. Cherish. What a beautiful word, almost as beautiful as love, and so much a part of love.

Nick might consider a woman as an equal in many respects, but he never lost sight of the essential difference between the sexes. He was a man, secure in his maleness. He didn't need to prove it to anyone. This inner security gave him a strength that also had gentleness, a quality many men seemed to suppress. He could be tender without being ashamed to show it, and it wasn't a weakness in him—only another facet of the complex male he was.

What would it be like to be loved by him, really loved, in every sense of the word?

Before this unbidden and faintly shocking thought could take root, Nick called back to her, "We've made it."

And there it was. The ruin of a small stone shed such as shepherds use was the only evidence that others had camped there in the past. Beside the broken walls stood a hastily erected metal hut with a formidable padlock on the door. Nearby, on a level grassy spot, several tents were pitched, their flaps moving lazily in the light wind that breezed over the exposed plateau. "But where's the dig?" Sara asked.

Nick gestured with his arm. "Up there. It's a cave in the side of the mountain."

His fingers fumbled with the strap at her waist, finally releasing the buckle. He pulled the pack from her shoulders and hoisted it in his hand as if it weighed nothing. "We'll leave these things here," he said, "then go and see what the others are doing."

He moved to the middle tent, a large one that Sara saw was used as an office. A makeshift desk at one side held several books she recognized as her father's and a photo of herself taken at a friend's wedding some years before.

Nick dropped the packs beside the open flap and entered the dim interior. Picking up the framed photo, he stared at it for a moment, then looked across at her. "The same, yet different," he muttered obscurely. His shoulders lifted, then fell in a shrug as he set the picture carefully in its place. "Let's go, Sara."

The trail up the gorge was well defined, although so narrow at times that thorny shrubs crowded them, catching at their clothes. It was difficult keeping an accurate sense of direction on the shrouded trail, but Sara could tell by the pull on her calves that their progress was steadily and steeply uphill. She was breathing in labored gusts by the time they emerged from the shrubbery and stood on a wide ledge that clung to the face of the mountain.

Directly above them gaped the dark opening of a cave. Nick handed Sara one of the powerful flashlights he'd picked up in the office tent. "We won't need both as long as we're together, but it pays to be prepared for emergencies."

"Emergencies?" Sara asked. "How big is the cave? It looks small."

"The entrance is. Inside it's pretty big. We don't know how far it extends so don't go wandering off on your own."

The mouth of the cave was larger than it appeared from below. Scrambling over a tumble of boulders Sara went through the opening ahead of Nick, then paused to look around. The flashlight wasn't necessary; the white glow of a gas lantern chased the shadows deep into the corners of an enormous cavern.

"Good, they've left a light," Nick said with satisfaction. "We can take that with us instead of using the flashlight batteries." He unhooked the lantern from the wall and moved toward the back of the cavern.

Sara shivered as the dank air raised goose bumps on her arms, wishing she'd worn a sweater or jacket. The floor was level near the entrance but sloped upward toward the rear, slippery with condensed moisture. From somewhere in the darkness she heard the monotonous dripping of water.

As Nick advanced with the lantern, Sara saw the back of the cave narrowing to a hole perhaps five yards across. She shivered again, this time more from a sudden feeling of apprehension than from cold. The cave resembled nothing so much as the gaping mouth of an exotic beast, the narrowing at the rear its throat. They had to walk down the throat.

Nick paused in front of her. "Listen. Do you hear that?"

She strained her ears but at first could hear only the irregular pounding of her heart. Then other sounds filtered in. The hiss of the lantern, the more marked drip of water, then the sound of voices rapidly becoming more distinct.

"I think they're coming out," Nick said. "We'll wait outside." He hung the lantern back on its hook and helped Sara clamber over the rocks that littered the entrance.

She stood with her head lifted toward the glassy sky, breathing in air that seemed clean and free after the stale atmosphere in the cavern. Nick looked at her closely, frowning as he saw the color come back into her face. "You were scared in there, weren't you, Sara?" he asked almost harshly. "Why didn't you say something?"

She swung her head around to meet his gaze, her hair falling back over her shoulders. "I'll get used to it. It was just the sudden cold after the heat out here."

Nick shook his head. "I don't know. Some people get claustrophobia in caves. Maybe you're one of them."

Sara shook her head firmly, a little glint of anger coming into her golden eyes. "I'm not. I can't be. Otherwise how will I work in there? Don't worry, Nick. I'll get used to it. I'll have to. I want to do this."

She turned quickly toward the dark mouth of the cave. Out here in bright sunlight it lost most of its sinister air. She was about to go back in and conquer what she perceived as an irrational and inconvenient fear when three men emerged from the darkness.

"Father," she cried, running to him and kissing his cheek.

His arms folded around her. "Sara, I see you made it." His voice was calm, so dearly familiar that tears stung her eyes. "Hello, Nick," he added. "Thanks for bringing her."

Nick's smile was offhand and his eyes remained on Sara as he said, "My pleasure."

Daniel Morgan was a tall, spare man whose scholarly demeanor hid a sharp mind and a curiosity about the world that was undiminished by the years he'd lived and the places he'd visited. Sara had the same quality, Nick realized, although physically she hardly resembled him at all.

Andreas Stamoulis greeted them with perfunctory terseness, then lurched off down the path with that awkward gait of his that covered ground with deceptive rapidity. The man who had come into the sunlight after him stood quietly, letting the others complete their greetings. Now he stepped forward and shook Sara's hand. "I'm Paul Heras," he said in a rumbling voice.

His handshake was firm and cool and left a smudge of gray clay on Sara's fingers. He saw it and apologized, his swarthy face reddening under its tan. "I'm sorry. I should have realized my hands were dirty."

Sara smiled warmly. "It's all right. I'm sure I won't be clean for long when I'm digging in there. Have you found anything?"

He hesitated. When he spoke at last, his tone was guarded. "We're not sure. We're digging through a fall of rock that looks as if it didn't happen from natural causes. Another day or so and we'll be through to whatever is on the other side."

Excitement coursed through Sara. So she might be in on a major find. "Are you going back in today?"

"Perhaps," he said. "It depends on Andreas." He extended his arm in a courtly manner. "Shall we go down with the others?"

Sara saw that Nick and her father, deep in conversation, had preceded them toward the camp. She tucked her hand into the crook of Paul's elbow, already feeling an affinity with this quiet man who was Nick's childhood friend. He was about her height, not tall for a man, but broad and muscular without an ounce of fat. He had none of the vital electricity that seemed to fly around Nick like a science-fiction force field. A man who could be depended on, Sara decided, but who would never generate the excitement and reaction that was so much a part of Nick.

The absence of the students working at the dig was explained during the evening meal, which Nick and Paul had efficiently cooked. Apparently the work was divided evenly with no discrimination, Sara saw with satisfaction. She would have been very unhappy if she had been relegated to kitchen duty every day. Cooking was not her strong point. To judge by the savory taste of the lamb stew, it was Nick's. Was there nothing the man couldn't do, and do well?

"I gave them a few days off," Dr. Stamoulis said, referring to the students. "I think we're on the verge of a major discovery and the fewer people who know about it the better."

"Do you think someone might come up here to steal artifacts?" Sara asked skeptically. "How would they ever find this place?"

"It's widely known that we're digging here," Andreas said with a stern look at her. "If we found something significant we'd have the press, other archaeologists, tourists, and other undesirable characters scrambling all over here. We can't take the chance."

"I'm no longer convinced that there's anything here," Nick said.

"Then why did you put up money for the dig?" Sara asked.

"My company did," Nick corrected her. "It looked promising, but the digging has been going on for two months and very little has been found."

"We found a small gold cup at the entrance of the shaft in which we're digging now," Paul said. "And of course you've seen the rings, earrings and other small items. Those bits of carved stone may be fragments of statuary. We haven't had a chance to check them out."

"The earrings aren't modern," Andreas interjected. "We had a pair of them tested and the gold is the same type used to fabricate the finds of Mycenae."

"But there's no sign of a settlement," Nick said. "Will any of the discoveries further our knowledge of the early inhabitants of the region? That's supposed to be the point of all this. I'm beginning to think that what you've found is the loot of grave robbers, stuff they dropped when they recovered their cache." He paused, his eyes going from one dejected face to the other. "Still, you're the experts. If you all agree, we'll keep going."

Daniel set his empty plate to one side and took out his pipe and began to fill it from a worn leather pouch. "Is that why you've come, Nick? To stop the dig?"

"Not exactly," Nick said. "If you find something behind that rock fall, I'd like to be in on it. But the present grant runs out at the end of the month, which is less than a week away, and I have to justify putting further funds into what looks like a dry hole."

"A damp one, don't you mean, Nick?" Paul said drolly. "Some places it feels like an underground riverbed."

Nick smiled faintly at Paul's comment, grateful for Paul's dry humor and the friendship they'd shared since childhood. He didn't want to shut off the supply of money that was the major financing of this work; it would be a shame to disappoint his friend. Daniel didn't need the publicity; he was internationally known and respected. But Paul could use a boost in his career in a difficult field. And Andreas, well-known as he was in academic circles, deserved this chance for fame.

If there was anything...

Well, he would judge for himself tomorrow.

The cavern where they were digging was small, barely head high, and only wide enough for two men to stand abreast. Nick's head brushed the ceiling and Daniel, taller still, bent in a perpetual stoop.

Daniel was polishing his steel-rimmed glasses on his shirt. "The humidity," he grumbled. "It keeps fogging my glasses."

Strangely, it was less cold here than near the entrance, and a trickle of water running down the stone wall near Sara's hand was tepid. Hot springs? She knew they existed in many parts of Greece. The country was a geological hodgepodge, the result of aeons of earthquakes and other upheavals in the earth's crust.

Since only two men could dig at one time, she and Nick left Paul and her father to dig while they explored several adjoining tunnels. Andreas had remained outside to catalog the small items that had been discovered while he was at his house. Sara had been impressed by the number of items found, but the scholarly significance of them was less certain.

The mountain was riddled with tunnels, some cavernous, others the size of rat holes. Nick cautioned Sara to take spare batteries and bulbs for the flashlight, since they'd be leaving the lantern behind. He also reminded her to always check the ground before moving forward. Although the prevailing rock strata ran horizontally, cave-ins over underground streams created vertical shafts that could be bottomless. "And don't go far," he warned her. "If the tunnel is straight without any other adjoining, okay, but if there are several tunnels make sure you mark the ones you enter and remember how far you've come." He frowned at the battery lanterns they carried. "Mining lights would have been more practical. They leave the hands free."

Sara found she was becoming accustomed to the dense blackness outside the circle of light. She was no longer frightened and even experienced a thrill of excitement at the possibility of discovering something the others had missed in their explorations.

"Okay," Nick said. "You take that tunnel there, and I'll take this one. We go for fifteen minutes, or less if you run into complications or a dead end, then meet back here."

"Fifteen minutes," Sara repeated, eyes sparkling as she waited in a flurry of impatience to start on her first solo excursion into the unknown dark.

Nick, seeing her excitement, smiled slightly. "Just don't get carried away. Remember what I've told you and be careful." The last was said slowly and with implicit warning.

"I will, Nick."

He looked at her for a moment longer, then dropped a quick, hard kiss on her mouth before striding off down his assigned tunnel. Sara touched her lips, then ran her tongue across them, licking off the indefinable sweet taste of him. She hadn't kissed him back.

Her first tunnel led to a dead end and she spent ten minutes in barely controlled irritation waiting for Nick to rejoin her. When he did get back, Sara learned that his tunnel had run into a limestone-encrusted cavern with no apparent exit. Nick quickly guided her to the cave.

They moved back to what seemed to be the main tunnel and decided to explore another set of passageways. This time Sara's went on and on, the damp green moss on the floor squelching under her sneakers. The silence was eerie and complete except for the ever-present trickle of water.

She came to a fork, one tunnel leading left, one right. She decided to try the right; it was larger. If it led to nothing, she could try the left. The tunnel sloped downward at a steadily increasing angle. She ran her free hand along the damp rock wall beside her, grimacing in distaste at the slimy feel. The floor was equally smooth and slippery.

She stopped and checked her watch. Ten minutes had passed. She would have to go back. As it was, she would be late.

A fine strand of her hair drifted across her face and she brushed at it impatiently. It was then that she noticed the air smelled different, no longer dank and stale but fresher, as if she were nearing trees and water.

She turned out the light. Nothing. The darkness was a cloak that enveloped all her senses. For a second panic rose in her. What if the light wouldn't go on again? Then logic returned. She pushed the plastic button and a reassuring glow lit the tunnel.

She sniffed again. Definitely fresher. She decided to go a little farther before turning back.

The tunnel leveled off, making walking easier, then took an abrupt turn to the right. A stir in the air ruffled Sara's hair. She switched off the light. This time she could see a glow in the far distance.

Excitement filled her, making her want to shout the discovery to someone. Another entrance to the labyrinth of caverns! She quelled her exuberance. Even if it was, the find might not amount to anything.

She looked at her watch. Eighteen minutes. Nick would be frantic by the time she reached him. Turning, she hurried up the slope, which seemed steeper now. Her knees ached and once she stumbled, quickly recovering. She leaned for a moment on the wet wall beside her, struggling for breath. How far had she come? Downhill distances were deceptive.

She moved forward again. Odd, the ground was softer here, dry and resilient. She hadn't noticed that earlier. She swung the lantern to illuminate the entire tunnel. It was higher than she'd realized. Her limited area of light had given her the illusion of a roof immediately over her head.

All hell broke loose. A wild squeaking and a flurry of a million wings filled the air and her head. She fell again, groaning with pain as her knee struck an outcrop of limestone. The flashlight fell from her hand and went bouncing down the tunnel.

"Damn, damn," she muttered, rubbing the circulation back into her numb knee. "Bats can't hurt you. They don't even fly into your hair." In the total darkness they would be much more adept at avoiding her than she would be at avoiding them.

What good were spare batteries and bulbs if you dropped the flashlight, she asked herself in disgust as she picked herself up. She flexed the injured knee. A little stiff but okay.

The bats had settled down again, or up, she thought with a near-hysterical laugh. She couldn't get lost. Even without a light, she could find her way back to Nick. Besides, he would be looking for her by now.

No use wasting time on self-recriminations. Her chin set in determination she started to walk up the slick grade. The tunnel was silent except for the faint sound of her rubber soles on the stone floor. She kept her hand on the wall as a guide, shutting her mind to the tons of rock over her, under her, and all around her. What if she didn't find Nick? What if she wandered here forever, through a dark eternity of damp and cold?

Her knee throbbed painfully and her throat ached with the laboring of her breath, as she trudged up the sloping tunnel. Nick, she screamed silently. Nick. Surely he'd missed her by now. But what if he'd gone down the left tunnel at the fork?

"Sara!"

She stopped, listening. Had she heard the faint calling of her name, or was it only her imagination, the vivid imagination she kept firmly in check for the sake of her sanity in the darkness?

"Sara?" Closer this time, and her heart leaped.

"Nick," she cried. "I'm coming."

The tunnel had leveled and as she rounded a bend she saw the uneven play of light moving toward her. She broke into a run and in a moment had covered the distance between them. Blessed light and blessed Nick. With an incoherent cry she threw herself into his arms, nearly knocking him off his feet.

He felt warm under her hands, but she knew by the tension in his body that his anxiety was being rapidly replaced by anger. "Sara," he said harshly, holding her away with one hand. "Where were you so long? And where is your light?"

"I lost it," she said, gulping in air and forcing herself to stand free of him when her every instinct cried out for his touch. "I was in a cavern full of bats and when I disturbed them I stumbled and lost the light."

He tightened his arm, pulling her close again. "Sara," he said into her hair, his voice tense. "You could have been lost. I tried the other tunnel and it ended in a sheer drop-off. I thought you'd fallen."

She closed her eyes. If she had gone down that shaft, she might well have fallen. She might now be lying hurt or dead at the bottom of a rock cliff. She felt the movement of Nick's face against her hair, and she savored his warmth and the fact that she was alive. "I told you fifteen minutes only, Sara," Nick said in a muffled voice. "What took you so long?" He felt the shivering of her body and disengaged his arms from around her waist. "Come, Sara, let's get out of here into light and sun."

"I think I found another entrance," Sara said as they walked quickly toward the main cavern. "Of course it may be of no use but there was an opening. That's why I didn't come back."

"It could have waited," Nick said. "You could have come for me."

Sara's fear had diminished. "I didn't want you to have to come all the way there if it turned out to be nothing," she said firmly. "But now I still don't know for sure."

"And you nearly gave me heart failure when I realized you weren't back," Nick muttered. They had reached the point at which the tunnel branched off to the one where the others were digging. "Do you want to see how Paul and your father are doing, or do you want to go out into daylight?"

"Let's see how the dig is going," Sara said promptly, causing Nick to smile. She had been scared, as evidenced by the uninhibited way she'd thrown herself into his arms, but he had to admire her quick recovery. His own recovery might take a while longer, he realized as he felt little residual surges of adrenaline in his blood. He clenched his fists, fighting an urge to shake her for frightening him so much.

Daniel and Paul had put down their shovels and were talking excitedly as Nick and Sara approached the rock fall. "I'm convinced there's a room behind these stones,"

Daniel said exuberantly. "Maybe even a burial chamber."

"And we're almost through," Paul said, shaken out of his normal calm. "I can put my arm into an empty space."

The air was stale and heavy with the scent of the lamp fuel. The lanterns gave off little smoke, but in the confined space even that small amount made breathing uncomfortable.

"I'll dig for a while," Nick suggested. He decided to make no mention of Sara's experience. With luck the flashlight could be retrieved when he explored the tunnel later. "Daniel, why don't you take Sara to the camp? She's a little cold."

She was nothing of the kind. She was about to protest, but the thought of clean light and air beckoned temptingly. She looked at her father, and the exhausted lines of his face and stooped shoulders made her decide against arguing. "I'll make lunch," she said. "Give me an hour."

Nick and Paul barely acknowledged their departure as they picked up shovels and began to dig with renewed vigor. The rhythmic sound of metal striking stone followed them as Sara and Daniel slowly made their way down the narrow tunnel to the surface.

Outside the air was as breathlessly hot as the day before. The sun was an amber ball in a colorless sky. In the distance, from the cloud-enshrouded slopes of Taygetos, thunder rumbled into the mountain valleys.

"Will it rain?" Sara wondered aloud as they trudged down the airless gorge to the camp.

Daniel regarded the cloudless sky above, then the thunderheads over the peaks. "It's been like this for days. If it rains, it doesn't get as far as here."

They had nearly reached the camp when Sara said casually, "I may have discovered another entrance to the caves."

Her father paused in the act of lighting his pipe, holding the match until it was cold, then dropped it carefully in a pebbled area on the ground and began to walk again. "Would you be able to find it if you went back into the caves?"

"I think so," Sara said. "Didn't you explore most of the caverns?"

"We did but we might have missed something. If the area we're digging comes to nothing and Nick's firm approves more money, we might explore farther and try another spot. By the way, I drew a map of the tunnels we checked out. Maybe you could show me where you found this place."

In the office tent he rummaged through the scattered papers on the desk, giving a grunt of triumph as he pulled out a rough map drawn on a sheet of lined paper. "It may not be very clear," he said doubtfully. "Can you make anything of it?"

Sara looked at the seemingly haphazard lines on the diagram, then closed her eyes, mentally picturing the route she and Nick had taken. Opening them, she traced her finger down one line. "There. That's where the fork was. Nick says the left one had a sheer drop-off." She moved her finger up to the end of the line. "About there, I'd say." A red slash bisected the blue ink line.

Daniel bent closer, the smoke of his pipe fragrant in the stuffy heat of the tent. "Yes, we found that too. If it's not too deep, we plan to climb down. So your tunnel went off here. Oh, yes, there's the cavern with the bats."

"Yes," said Sara, suppressing a shiver. "I found them. It's just a little farther that I saw the light coming in. And felt fresh air."

Daniel puffed on his pipe thoughtfully. "You know, if I recall it was nearly night when we were in this area. We decided to leave it for another day since it was a long tunnel. Then we discovered the closed-in tunnel and started digging. We never went back."

He stepped to one side and pulled another paper from an overflowing file. "This is a topographic map of the area. You see, the entrance, if it really is one, must be about here. That's closer to the camp than the one we're using now. That might prove useful. It's certainly worth looking into."

Sara straightened away from the desk, surreptitiously rubbing her sore knee. "But not now," she said. "I'll go start lunch."

Lunch—sandwiches, coffee and fruit salad—was a lighthearted affair. Paul, showing none of his usual calm dignity, could barely force himself to eat. He fairly bubbled with excitement and even managed to penetrate Nick's conservative pessimism. "I told you there was something to be found," he kept saying, punching Nick playfully in the arm.

Nick punched him back, grinning good-naturedly. "We haven't got it yet."

"An hour's digging and we'll be able to crawl through," Paul said, refusing to let his enthusiasm be dampened. He looked speculatively at Sara. "Actually Sara could probably—"

Nick interrupted sharply. "Don't even think about it."

"I'll go first," Andreas put in. "I'm as small as Sara."

She knew she should have resented their attitude, especially Nick's, but her experience of the morning cautioned her against rushing into a situation that might well prove dangerous. What if the rock slide they'd dug through decided to collapse and imprison whoever was in the chamber beyond? Coward, she told herself. "You can't leave me out," she said, perversely opposing the instinct she saw as weakness in herself. "I'm in this too."

Nick reached over to pour himself another coffee. "Sure you are, Sara, but there's a difference between being brave and risking your neck. We'll keep on digging until the opening is big enough for any of us." He lifted his cup toward her. "Good coffee, Sara. Who said you couldn't cook?"

Chapter Seven

It is a chamber!" Paul exclaimed as he stood beside Dr. Stamoulis in a vault seemingly carved out of solid rock. Andreas had been the first through the opening; the senior archaeologist on the project deserved that honor, the others had mutually conceded. Sara was amazed at how well the men cooperated with one another. Her father had told her stories of bitter rivalry on digs, and given Andreas's peculiar temperament, Sara had expected to see some of it here. But it hadn't materialized. Paul's good nature precluded arguments, and Nick's firm leadership bound them into a cohesive unit.

"Is there anything there?" Nick asked with a trace of his earlier skepticism.

"Bring more light over here." Andreas's voice sounded hollow and thin from the far end of the chamber.

Daniel hurried over with a lamp, and a moment later he whistled low between his teeth. The others rushed forward.

"Will you look at that," Paul breathed. "See, Nick, you were wrong."

"Only partly wrong," Nick said. "Wooden crates? They would never have survived for four thousand years."

"No," said Dr. Stamoulis. "But let's see what's inside."

Someone handed him a crowbar that had been used to pry rocks away from the opening. The wood of the crate was dried and pulled readily away from the nails holding it. In this enclosed chamber the limited ventilation had slowed decay.

Still, Sara's heart sank. The condition of the crates and the manner of their construction showed them to be no older than a century or two, young by archaeological standards. The best they could hope for was a cache of gold hidden from the Turks during the Greek wars of independence in 1821, or the loot of church or grave robbers. The three crates suddenly seemed symbols of shattered dreams.

Sara was about to turn away to seek the fresher air of the outer tunnel when Daniel gave another whistle. "What is it?" she asked, leaning over Nick's shoulder.

Paul swung a lantern closer, and in its light she saw a canvas bag, green with age. Daniel lifted it out of the remains of the crate. It clinked with a dull, metallic sound.

"You do the honors, Andreas," he said, handing the little man one of the pouches, which were the size of currency bags used by modern banks. Disappointment clung to Sara's spirits. What if this turned out to be the loot of some simple robbery perpetrated during modern times? What a letdown for all of them. She slanted a look at Nick's face, but it was set and expressionless, telling her nothing, neither disappointment nor anticipation.

Andreas set the bag on the ground and fumbled with the cord that held it closed. It was rotted and came away in his hand, allowing the bag to spill on its side.

Gold! Gold, hundreds of coins that gleamed in the white light from the gas lantern. Nick picked one up and turned it between his fingers. "Early nineteenth century, just as we might have guessed," he said flatly.

"At least you'll have something to show the company for its investment," Sara said in an effort to lighten the gloom that was descending on all of them.

"Not likely," Nick said. "The government will confiscate it, and there won't even be the artistic satisfaction to sweeten the disappointment."

Andreas was sitting back on his haunches, his fingers sifting through the rain of gold coins. Sara glanced at him, and in that moment he raised his eyes. The gleam in them sent a chill through her and she looked quickly away, wishing she hadn't seen the unmistakable light of greed. Still, she might have expected it after the incident of the broken cup. How galling it must be for Andreas. He wouldn't have the fame of an artistic discovery nor the gold of this mundane find.

Stamoulis got to his feet. "We'll take these crates out and lock them up. Since you're the sponsor of this dig in a manner of speaking, Nick, will you go down to the village and notify Athens?"

"Of course, Andreas. When we get it out, we'll have another look at it and then I'll go."

The crate they'd opened was the largest of the three, and two men were required to carry it out after they haphazardly nailed it back together. Nick and Paul went back for the smaller boxes, leaving Daniel and Andreas to make room in the metal storage shed for them.

Once inside the oven-hot shed, Sara had her first chance to examine the earlier finds. She had to agree that they looked promising. Thin gold earrings, a bracelet in an intricate design, a gold cup and other assorted pieces of jewelry could all have been used by ancient civilizations. Most significant of all was a fragment of stone covered with strange symbols that might date back to Minoan times. Its authenticity hadn't been confirmed, but officials had verified that a similar fragment discovered years earlier by a shepherd had been of that period. How the new fragment had come to be in the cave remained a mystery. And the discovery today had done nothing to solve the puzzle.

"What made you realize that wasn't just a rock slide in the cave?" Sara asked her father to beat off the crushing disappointment within her. Nick had been less than enthusiastic about this dig before today; now he would see that it was shut down unless they found something else to justify further explorations. She had barely arrived here and now she might not even have her chance to work. As for a confirmation of her theories that the Mycenaeans and the Minoans had close connections, that had really fizzled out.

"The first layer of rock was very regular and at the top we found traces of mortar. We felt that the tunnel had been closed on purpose but because of the jewelry found in other parts of the cave where the ground was softer, we expected a burial site." He sighed. "It's all very disappointing."

"What if we go on and dig further in the soft area?" Sara asked, her hopes reviving.

"It may be too wet. It looks like an underground river may have been seeping in there. Of course if we had a pump—" He broke off. "But that takes more money and we don't have it."

"Nick?"

"Yes, Nick, but you saw how he feels."

"Do you want to come down to the village with me, Sara?" Nick asked her after he and Paul had placed the two small boxes in the shed. They had pried them open and glanced at the bags inside, virtually identical to those in the larger crate. It was late afternoon and the sun was lowering in a fiery ball toward the jagged horizon.

"We'll have to stay overnight," Nick added. "And we'd better get started so we don't get caught in the dark on that trail." He smiled at her. "You'll have a chance for a bath."

Uncannily he managed the one argument that would do the most to sway her. The lack of water at the site was the only hardship as far as Sara was concerned, and the thought of a real bath was irresistible. "Okay," she agreed. She turned to her father. "You won't need me to help with your notes, will you, Father?"

He smiled ruefully. "There won't be many notes. No, go on, Sara. We'll see you in the morning." Bending, he kissed her cheek, letting his palms rest against its smooth curve for a moment. "Take it easy on the hike down."

The packs were considerably lighter than on the hike up, and they made good time going down to the parking area. The vehicles shimmered in the slanting sunlight, so hot Sara had to use the tail of her shirt to protect her hand as she opened the door. Nick slung both packs into the trunk.

"Leave the doors open for some of the heat to escape," he said. "If we get in like that, we'll cook."

He led her into the sparse shade cast by a clump of stunted pines. With one hand he smoothed the curling tendrils of her hair that clung damply to her temples. The tawny gold was streaked with sun-bleached white that contrasted with the smooth brown of her tan. "Sweet Sara," he murmured, holding her close to the lean, hard length of his body.

Sara felt the heat of his body and her heartbeat stirred at his touch. When his warmth and masculinity enticed her so, how could she resist the dangerous emotions that were sure to cause her heartache? And now that the project appeared to be fizzling out, they had so little time to explore those emotions.

"Nick," she whispered as he tilted her face up to his. Then all thought of speech was lost in the devastating hunger with which he covered her mouth with his.

"Sara, Sara," he said, his breath mingling with hers. "I hardly slept all night thinking of you in that tent so close by. Did you know, with a lamp on inside, those nylon walls don't hide anything?"

Sara's face suffused with hot color as she recalled that she had undressed with the lantern on last night. But it had been late; she'd read most of her father's notes on the dig before preparing for bed. She drew back a fraction, very much on her dignity. "And did you know that all decent people would have been in bed by that time?"

Nick's mouth quirked endearingly. "Who said I was decent?" The smile faded. "But you certainly contributed to my insomnia. I couldn't clear my mind of your graceful movements silhouetted by the light. I wanted you to be undressing for me."

An insidious little voice inside her reminded her that at times she'd yearned for the same thing. To stop its clamoring, she said smartly, "Forget it, Nick. It's time you got back to Athens. This country air is addling your brain."

"It's not the country air, Sara. It's you. And it's not my brain that's suffering." To reinforce his statement he slid his hands down to her firm buttocks and pressed her against the part of him that was suffering.

Sara closed her eyes as a wave of heat rushed through her. Then with a quick twist of her supple body she freed herself. She couldn't let the seductive feel of his body subvert her will and destroy her self-control. "The car should be cooler now," she said in as normal a tone as she could manage with her heart crowding her dry throat.

"Well, I'm not," Nick said acerbically as he got in on the driver's side.

Sara sat beside him, gritting her teeth against the jarring of the wheels on the stony track. His profile was impassive. No, he looked thoughtful, and she had a strange feeling his thoughts were not on his driving. She concentrated on the shrubby landscape baking in the setting sun. Soon the withered leaves and grass would have respite from its scorching rays as soft night descended. Over the mountain range the sky lit up at intervals, as heat lightning played over the brooding clouds.

The darkness was nearly complete when the pitifully sparse lights of the village came into view. With a sudden sinking in her stomach Sara remembered they were to stay overnight.

But where? There were no hotels, no sign of any kind of inn. But Nick had promised she would have a bath.

"Did you mean it about a bath, Nick?" she asked.

His face was serious as he glanced at her, but in the dim light she could have sworn she saw a twinkle in his eyes. "Would I lie, Sara?"

"Yes, you would, if it suited your purpose," she retorted.

He turned his eyes back to the winding street. "You'll have your bath."

"What about a bed?"

"Unless you'd like to share mine, you'll have that, too. This place has several houses that have rooms 'to let' as the tourist signs say. Students come and hike in these mountains every summer. And the landlady will see to it that your virtue remains intact. The rooms are dormitories. Boys and girls strictly segregated. Does that suit you?''

His sarcasm was light but unmistakable. Sara felt reduced to the status of a difficult child. Her mind rebelled. What would he say if she followed a momentary wild urge to tear off her shirt and shatter his infuriating arrogance? She squelched the thought, tempting though it was. Why should she give him the satisfaction of knowing how he disturbed her?

''Are you going to be able to get more money to keep the dig open?'' Sara asked Nick as they lingered over the late supper of succulent lamb chops that their temporary landlady had cooked for them.

Nick shrugged. ''If there is any reason to justify it, I'll see what I can do. It's up to Andreas to convince the company that there is a good chance of finding something significant.''

''Father thinks we should dig farther in the soft area where they found the jewelry.''

Nick shook his head. ''Not only is a pump needed, but the whole cavern would have to be shored up with timber, all of it brought in from somewhere else. Can you see transport trucks coming up that excuse for a road?''

''So it's hopeless.''

Nick didn't reply other than to make a very Greek gesture with his hands that indicated it was in the lap of the gods. Sara wondered how much influence Nick had with this mysterious company for which he worked, but it was not her nature to nag. If she kept on, he might well accuse her of just that.

She finished the last of her wine and pushed back her chair. ''Since we have to get an early start in the morning, I'll go in. You did get through to Athens, didn't you?"

"Yes, while you were splashing in the shower. I had a hard time concentrating on the call." The phone had been in the hall of the little house where they were staying. The walls, added to the main structure, were very thin.

"And what did they have to say?" Sara persisted.

"They'll send someone down from the department of antiquities and history to formally identify the gold. In the meantime we'll dig some more, if we find a likely spot that looks productive."

"Until the money runs out," Sara said glumly. "Good night, Nick."

She expected him to detain her, but to her mingled relief and disappointment he leaned back in his chair with his coffee cup in his hands. "Good night, Sara. Pleasant dreams." His voice could not have been more offhand.

"Isn't that the car we saw that day we rode on the beach?" Sara asked as they were driving across the village square the next morning.

Nick stood on the brake, making her grateful for her seat belt. She turned angrily to him, but her anger faded when she saw the grim look on his face. "Constantinos Vergis," he muttered.

The red Pontiac, as out of place here as a dinosaur at a tea party, was parked in an alley, its glossy paint lackluster under a film of dust. Nick called out to a young boy who was passing. The boy replied briefly, then hurried away.

"He says Vergis is visiting relatives here." He set the Citroën in motion once more. "Trouble is, I don't recall any family named Vergis here at all. There are only about twenty families in this village, and very few of them have relatives in the States."

"Maybe he likes hiking," Sara suggested.

"Maybe." But he didn't sound convinced.

The cave mouth lay like a scar on the pale hillside, more forbidding than ever. Inside Nick and Sara found Daniel and Paul digging at the edges of the chamber where they'd found the gold. "Anything?" Nick asked.

Paul straightened, resting against the handle of his shovel. "Solid rock," he said, wiping his forehead with a large handkerchief. "We're about to knock off for the day."

"Where's Andreas?" Nick asked.

Paul's mouth twisted. "Where he usually is, in the storage shed, gloating over those pitiful pieces of jewelry." He sounded disgruntled.

Sara had an uneasy feeling that Andreas might well be gloating over the more mundane but infinitely more lucrative gold coins. Either as collector's items or melted down, the intrinsic value of the find must be astronomical. She was sure she hadn't mistaken that feverish light in Andreas's eyes yesterday. None of the others, though, seemed affected by the worth of the gold.

"Strange," Nick mused. "The shed was closed and locked when we passed it. I wonder where Andreas is. I'd assumed he was in here too."

"Maybe he took a nap," Daniel suggested. "He was complaining of a headache earlier."

Andreas was in the office tent, scribbling in a journal. He looked up as Nick and Sara entered. "Are you back already?" he asked in lieu of greeting. Sara thought his voice sounded abrupt and strained. Perhaps his headache was worse.

"We've been back a while," Nick said, moving around the makeshift desk.

Andreas glanced at his watch, his manner abstracted. Sweat beaded his upper lip, and he pulled out a handkerchief and mopped his face. The heat was a tangible entity in the close confines of the tent, but Sara hadn't noticed it bother him to this extent on the previous day.

"Didn't you want to check on their progress?" Andreas asked in a querulous voice.

"We've been," Nick said briefly, picking up a list of the finds and running his eyes down it. "They're coming out soon." He broke off, his head lifting. His nostrils flared like those of an animal sensing danger.

Sara heard it too, a low rumble that suddenly began to shake the earth under her feet. Thunder? The thunderheads had been quiet this morning.

Before she could speak, Nick charged out of the tent, overturning a chair in his way. She cast a quick glance at Andreas. He was sitting in his chair, eyes staring, body motionless. A trickle of sweat ran down his temple and into a crease in his cheek. Sara registered this in less than a second, then as the rumble became a roar, she ran out after Nick.

She met her father halfway down the ravine. His face was colorless under its tan, and he was breathing in ragged gusts. "Rock slide," he gasped between breaths.

"In the cave?" Sara asked.

"Outside. It's a miracle we weren't caught inside the cave. As it is, Paul is half-buried. You go on and help Nick dig. I'll get Andreas and some more shovels."

"Is he all right?" Sara put a hand to her throat to stop the frantic racing of her heart.

"Don't know," Daniel tossed over his shoulder as he loped down the trail.

The entire mountainside had vanished under a blanket of rock and earth. The mouth of the cave was buried. At the near edge of the slide Nick was digging with a shovel, his movements tense and jerky. Even as Sara approached, she saw him throw down the shovel and pull out a rock with his bare hands.

Then she saw Paul. He lay half-buried, his eyes closed. The only color in his dead-white face came from the dark fan of his lashes and the bright red blood seeping from a wound in his forehead. Sara's stomach heaved, but she managed to control its convulsions by swallowing hard.

Nick saw her and with a quick grateful look handed her a shovel. "If you can move some of the soft dirt from under his hips, I think we can get him out. There's a tree under there holding most of the weight off his legs."

She set to work, not daring to dwell on the thought that Paul might even now be dead. As if he'd read her mind, Nick said, "He'll be okay if we get him out. That head wound is superficial."

She gave a choking laugh. Superficial with so much blood? She wondered what he considered serious.

Andreas and Daniel came running up with a pick and two more shovels, and Nick directed them where to dig. Fortunately there were no large rocks in this area of the slide, and the digging, though tedious and heavy, progressed steadily.

Paul moaned and Nick put down his shovel and bent over him. "Hang in there. We'll have you out in a few minutes." He noted that the wound had stopped bleeding and he quickly felt for a pulse at Paul's throat. Steady and strong. Apparently no internal injuries.

He glanced at Sara as he began to dig again next to her. She was a worker, putting in just as much effort as the men. In the heat her face was scarlet and little sun-bleached curls of her hair stuck to her temples. A trickle of perspiration crept down her cheek making a clear track in the dust that covered her skin. She bent to move a large rock and her teeth bit into her lower lip as she grunted with the effort. Nick dropped his shovel to give her a hand and together they sent the rock rolling down the slope.

Andreas and Daniel had managed to clear the area around Paul's legs. The tree, a twisted little pine, had protected him from the worst of the rock fall. Working carefully, Nick and Daniel were able to pull him out and move him to a patch of soft, sun-dried grass where there was a little shade. "Sara, will you go down and fetch the first-aid kit and some water?" Nick asked. "And, Andreas, get down to the village and phone for a helicopter. It should be able to land in the parking area. I think his leg is broken and he has a concussion. We can't waste any time, especially in this heat."

Sara scrubbed her hand across her hot face as she trudged beside a silent Andreas. A half hour for him to walk down to the cars, then perhaps an hour to the village in the Land Rover. How serious were Paul's injuries? Broken bones and concussion? None of them had medical training, unless Nick had talents he hadn't revealed.

Andreas stepped into the office tent to pick up a bunch of keys. Sara found the first-aid kit at once. She caught Andreas's arm as he prepared to leave. "Please," she said, her eyes wide with anxiety. "Please hurry."

Andreas nodded jerkily, his glance sliding over her face but avoiding her eyes. "I'll try. They'll have to pick him up before dark." He turned and hurried down the mountain.

Nick was cutting away Paul's pant legs with a pocket knife when she returned to the site. One leg, though bruised, seemed intact. The other showed a livid bulge on the shin, and when Nick ran his fingers over it, Paul groaned even in his deep unconsciousness. Nick felt the jagged ends of the shattered bone under the skin and swore viciously.

"Is it bad?" Sara asked, crouching next to him. "Can you set it temporarily?"

Nick shook his head, sending droplets spraying out from his perspiration-wet hair. He glanced up at the white merciless sky where a large bird hung motionless near the zenith. This heat wasn't going to help, and it would be several hours at best before the helicopter arrived. In the meantime they had to get Paul down to the parking area.

"Daniel, would you bring up one of the cots to use as a stretcher?"

"Of course," said Daniel, his face lined with concern. "But it's going to be rough."

Nick let out a pent-up breath. "Don't I know it. And the only thing we can do is fill him with painkillers. And take a chance that we don't damage anything permanently." He turned to Sara. "Is there some brandy in that kit?"

Sara came up with a small flat bottle. "Here. But do you think it's a good idea for Paul—"

"Not for him. For me," Nick cut in, unscrewing the flask and taking a long swallow. "I need a little fortification to launch my medical career."

"Oh," Sara said, clenching her teeth on a laugh she feared would become hysterical.

"Can we splint the leg?" she asked, checking through the other contents of the kit. She, too, was suffering in the heat, her thin cotton shirt sticking to her back, its front also damp, delineating the tender curve of her breasts.

"That would probably be best," Nick said. "If we can find some wood that's straight enough."

"The handle of one of the shovels," Sara suggested. "We can chop it into strips with the hatchet."

"Good idea." Nick grunted. He reached into the first-aid kit and handed Sara a packet of large gauze pads. "Will you wash that head wound with some of this disinfectant? It'll have to be diluted. Damn, we've got nothing to pour the water into."

"I'll moisten a pad and then pour a little disinfectant over it. That should do."

Nick got to his feet and picked up the hatchet he'd used to chop up the tree that had saved Paul from more serious injury. Its wood was gnarled and knotty and of no use as splints. As he reached for one of the shovels, his eye fell on Sara's bare legs. "While you're mopping, you might clean that scratch on your leg, Sara," he said quietly.

She looked down and gasped. On her thigh was a long angry abrasion. In her adrenaline-fueled anxiety over Paul she hadn't noticed the pain. It began to throb. "Compared to Paul, it's nothing," she said, wetting a new square of gauze and adding antiseptic.

"Nevertheless, make sure you clean it. In this heat it's easy to get infected."

She threw him a quick grin that belied her fatigue. "Yes, Doctor."

Paul's head wound turned out to be a shallow cut, not nearly as dangerous as the amount of bleeding had led Sara to fear. She placed a clean gauze pad on it and taped it securely. He was still unconscious, his face pale. In spite of the heat he felt cool, and she wondered whether he was in shock. Perhaps his injuries were more serious than they'd looked. "Damn," she muttered. "Why didn't I take a first-aid course?"

"You're doing okay, Sara," Nick said as he came back with the shovel handle neatly splintered into long strips.

"Good thing there are yards of bandages in here. We'll get this leg wrapped and get him down to the parking area."

"Where will the helicopter have to come from?"

"I'm not sure. Probably Sparta. Or Kalamata. They're about the same distance from here so either way it won't make much difference."

Paul's eyelids fluttered and he moaned once as they wrapped the gauze bandages around the makeshift splints that held his leg motionless. As an added precaution against the dust, Nick covered the white gauze with the pant leg he'd cut off.

Sara leaned against the twisted pine that shaded them, closing her eyes for a moment, feeling tired in every pore. She opened her eyes and looked at Nick as he straightened after checking Paul's heartbeat. He had taken off his shirt to dig, and his naked bronze torso gleamed in the harsh sunlight. Sweat had plastered his chest hair to his skin and his jeans hung low on his narrow hips. In spite of her fatigue and worry Sara found herself suppressing an urge to trace the damp line of black hair that bisected his concave stomach and disappeared under the waistband of his jeans.

"Sara?" Nick waved his hand in front of her bemused eyes and she started to attention.

"What did you say?"

"I asked if you wanted a drink but you were off in some never-never land."

Never-never was right. But she said nothing as she took the canteen from his hand. The mouth of the container was warm from his lips and as she drank her eyes met his. The now-familiar warmth awakened deep inside her, a visceral reaction to his unconscious sex appeal. Nick touched her dusty cheek, then withdrew his hand when

Daniel joined them with the light folding cot that would be used as a stretcher.

The walk down the ravine and the steep mountain path was harrowing for the wounded man. Nick and Daniel carried him on the cot, but frequent stops were necessary as Paul groaned with pain every time they stumbled on the rough trail. Nick checked his pulse regularly and cursed each time. Noting the increasing anxiety on his face, Sara scanned the sky praying that the helicopter would arrive quickly.

Chapter Eight

They waited another hour after they reached the parking area, and Nick began to debate the merits of loading the cot on Paul's jeep and risking the difficult track down. Before he came to a decision, the welcome chop-chop of spinning blades cut through the afternoon quiet.

They'd all sprawled in the narrow shade of the shrubs surrounding the flat area, but at the first sign of the approaching helicopter they jumped up and began waving frantically. Like a prehistoric butterfly the machine landed, a rescuer in olive camouflage paint. Dust flew around them in a cloud until the blades slowed and stopped.

The pilot and a man carrying a black doctor's bag stepped out of the glass cockpit. Both wore uniforms of the Greek air force. "You got him down," said the doctor. "Dr. Stamoulis wasn't sure you'd be able to make it." He knelt in the dust beside the wounded man. "What have you given him?"

"Nothing," Nick said. "He's been unconscious and I didn't want anything to aggravate possible concussion."

"Good." The man nodded, peeling open one of Paul's eyelids and peering at the pupil. He checked the other, then muttering to himself, withdrew a hypodermic needle and a vial of liquid from his bag. Quickly and efficiently he administered the shot, then gestured that they could load the improvised stretcher.

Nick and Daniel had a quick discussion on what would have to be done to close the camp. Since Andreas might not return for an hour or more, Daniel was responsible for security. "I'll stay," he said. "You go on with Paul and take Sara with you. You might need her. I'll get everything secured and wait for Andreas. He can check it over and decide what to do about the government men who're coming. We might have to stay so the gold isn't left unguarded."

Nick frowned. "There shouldn't be any problem as long as no one knows about it."

A peculiar expression crossed Daniel's face. "I don't know. Andreas was acting strangely all morning, ever since those hikers came by."

Nick's eyes sharpened. "Hikers?"

"Yes, a middle-aged man and a younger man. They had coffee with us at breakfast. Asked quite a lot of questions about the dig. We didn't tell them anything, of course, but you never know if they might return and start snooping around." He scratched his head, a familiar gesture to Sara. Her father always did it when he was puzzled. "Funny, they didn't look like hikers. The older man was too out of condition, and the younger man looked like he'd never left the city." He shrugged. "It's probably nothing. I'm just getting infected with Andreas's paranoia about art thieves. Besides, there's no art up there of any consequence."

"But the gold would be worth stealing," Nick said thoughtfully. "Do you want me to send someone up to guard it?"

"No, I don't think so. They wouldn't get here until morning. Andreas and I should be able to handle it. And the government men will be here tomorrow."

"We'll try to be back tomorrow as well," Nick said, his frown deepening.

The pilot started the engines and the rotors began to circle in lazy arcs over their heads, stirring the fine dust. Sara squinted against the flying grit and touched Nick's arm. "We'd better get going."

"Yes. Goodbye, Daniel. Be careful."

"Goodbye, Nick. Take care of Sara." The two men shook hands and Daniel kissed Sara, giving her a quick hug. "Bye, Sara." He touched his fingers to his temple and set off up the trail.

By nightfall Paul was conscious and comfortably installed in a white bed in the hospital in Sparta. His leg had been set in a thick plaster cast and hung from a complicated system of pulleys above the bed. Only a small white bandage marked the cut on his forehead. All in all he'd gotten off lightly although he admitted he ached all over.

"Just goes to show you can't get rid of me that easily," he joked as Sara and Nick stood beside the bed. Then he grimaced in pain. "Oh, my head." He smiled as the pain subsided. "Anyway, it only hurts when I laugh."

Nick grinned. "It's certainly affected your originality."

"Give me some time here," said Paul. "And I'll work on my lines. Did you manage to get hold of Sophie?"

"Yes," Nick said. "She and Dino will be down tomorrow."

Sara hadn't realized Paul was married or that he had a child until this afternoon when Nick had mentioned it. "She must be worried about you," she said quietly.

"I've had accidents before," Paul said. "We used to go motorcycle riding before we married. We took a spill a week before the wedding and almost didn't make it to the ceremony. I can tell you it wasn't much fun honeymooning on crutches with a sprained ankle."

Nick laughed. "Never mind. You would have spent your honeymoon in bed, anyway. The ankle only gave you an excuse."

Paul lifted his hand feigning a swing at Nick, then changed his mind. "I'll have you know I didn't need an excuse. Just wait until you're on your honeymoon."

"I'll have to find a wife first, won't I?" Nick said, his voice suddenly serious.

Paul's eyes swung to Sara. "Isn't it about time you did, Nick? Don't overlook what's under your nose."

Nick looked at Sara, his black eyes taking in the tired lines of her face, the uncombed tumble of her hair. "I haven't."

But your thoughts aren't on marriage, I'll bet, Sara thought as she saw the light in his eyes. Only lust at first sight. Yet was it as simple as that? On several occasions when he could have taken advantage of her urgent attraction to him, he'd resisted. He'd kept his word to wait until they knew each other better. Was it because of respect for her father, or was his interest in her more than physical? She pushed the tantalizing thought aside. The dig was closed, useless. She would be going back home soon, and she would never see him again.

Forcing a smile on her face to counteract the sudden desolation that filled her, she bent to kiss Paul's cheek.

His eyes were heavy with fatigue and pain. "Rest, Paul," she said gently. "You'll want to be fresh when Sophie comes."

"Yes," Nick said. "And in the meantime watch out for that pretty nurse."

Paul's eyes popped open. "Pretty? She's old enough to be my mother and built like a female wrestler."

"Must be my eyes," Nick said, turning as the nurse walked in. "Yes, we're just leaving."

She said something in Greek, then shooed them out the door. "In the morning, come back," she added in broken English for Sara's benefit.

"Aren't we going back to the site in the morning?" Sara asked as they stepped into the luminous glow of a starlit night. "And if we are, how do we get there? I don't suppose the Greek air force would be so accommodating as to take us?"

Nick laughed. "No, they wouldn't. I'm sure they stretched some regulations in rescuing Paul. Yes, we'll go back to the site and as for how we'll get there, simple. We take the bus, dear heart. There is a bus, you know. With excellent service. Even one to that village where we stayed last night."

Last night? Had it been only last night? It seemed a lifetime had passed, compressed into a single day. "What about tonight?"

"Sparta has a number of excellent hotels," Nick said, amusement lacing his deep voice. His dark eyes searched her face. "But first dinner, I think."

"This is a very busy place, isn't it?" Sara commented as they found a table outside one of the numerous restaurants that did business out of a cramped kitchen. Modern Sparta bore no resemblance to the ancient city where austerity had been a way of life. The streets were broad and straight, shaded with decorative orange trees and offering pedestrians water coolers on nearly every corner. The buildings were attractive and clean-lined, many of an Italianate design that was appropriate to the dry air and spare landscape.

Nick frowned. "Unusually so, I'd say." As if to prove his words, a squadron of bicycles ridden by lean young men in skintight shorts and singlets poured by, led by a Mercedes sports car that honked to clear a path in the traffic. Nick waved to the waiter, who walked smartly to their table and stood with his pencil poised over his pad.

Nick gave the order for their food and Sara made no objection. She was so tired she was glad to let him take charge. Under lowered lashes she studied him. His shirt was wrinkled and dusty, but otherwise he looked none the worse for having spent half the day either digging or acting as a field doctor.

The waiter left them and Nick turned to Sara, his expression faintly amused. His amusement must be at her expense, she thought immediately. She'd seen that look before. "We may have a problem getting a room," he said. "That bicycle race has filled the town with spectators and the hotels are booked solid."

"What about a guest house like last night? Or a park bench? It's certainly warm enough." It didn't matter as long as she could lie down and pass out. Fatigue was making her light-headed and after the harrowing day she'd been through, she wasn't overly concerned about the quality of her bed for the night, as long as there was one. Even a cot in a garden would do.

"Sleeping in parks is frowned on," Nick said. "Here comes our waiter. He said he'd check into a place for us to sleep."

They exchanged a few words in Greek, then Nick turned again to Sara. "He's found a room." He paused and she waited, knowing the rest of the statement. "One room."

Sara closed her eyes, too exhausted to care if it was a cell in the city jail. "As long as it has a bed," she said with studied indifference. "I could sleep a week."

Nick's smile was tender as he cupped her cheek in his palm. "Poor baby. It's been a long day, hasn't it?"

She jerked her head away. "I'm not your baby," she snapped, then regretted her tone as she saw the hurt expression on his face.

"No, you're not," he said slowly, reflectively. "You're very much an adult."

He was silent and thoughtful, almost moody, during the meal. Sara ate doggedly, fighting to keep her eyes open, and refused to allow her thoughts to dwell on the upcoming night. Nick was unlikely to be a gentleman who would let her have the room and take himself elsewhere, and she couldn't ask it of him. He must be just as tired as she was.

The room was similar to that in which she had slept the previous night, except that it contained two neatly made-up twin beds and had its own adjoining bathroom. It was a wing added to a private house, and their hostess was a comfortably plump, motherly woman who spoke a few words of English and promised breakfast in the morning. As she went out, she winked at Sara. "Your husband, very beautiful."

"And she hasn't even seen him clean and dressed up," Sara muttered sourly beneath her breath.

"Talking to yourself again, Sara?" Nick asked.

"Husband, huh?" Sara retorted. "Suddenly I'm married. And of course you did nothing to enlighten her."

Nick pretended to look shocked. "Would you rather she thought we were living in sin? Besides, wouldn't I make a suitable husband?"

"Maybe for some people, but not for me," Sara said firmly without giving herself time to think. "You're too arrogant. "Too—" she groped for a suitable word to describe him. "—too untamed."

"So tame me."

"I couldn't be bothered. I could just see you at a faculty tea."

"I've attended a few of those in my life," he interrupted. "Universities aren't much different here."

She made a disbelieving sound. "I suppose you sat there nibbling on finger sandwiches, holding out your pinky."

"I didn't nibble on the dean's wife's ear, if that's what you're thinking."

"Didn't you? What remarkable restraint."

Nick closed his eyes, his expression exasperated. "Sara, shut up. D'you want the bathroom first?"

"Don't be a gentleman on my account," Sara said, sweetly astringent.

Nick sent the ceiling a long-suffering stare. He pulled a coin from his pocket and deftly flipped it, slapping it down on his wrist. "Okay, call it."

Sara won the toss. She undressed and ran water in the sink to wash out her underwear, grimacing at the thought of wearing the same clothes again the next day. She bit her lip in indecision, then tossed in her shirt and shorts. The material was thin and would dry overnight.

The shower flowed over her in a tepid fall that seemed like sybaritic luxury to her overworked muscles. She could have stayed there for an hour but the sound of Nick's fist on the bathroom door reminded her that it had no lock and there was nothing to stop him from joining her.

"Sara, have you drowned? Hurry it up, will you?"

Hurry up what? Her drowning? She made a face, then stuck her tongue out at the closed door. Chivalry was certainly dead. And buried.

She scrubbed herself dry with a large towel, silently thanking the landlady for an ample supply of the largest towels she'd seen in Europe. She used a dry one to tie around her body, sarong fashion, then rinsed out her clothes, hanging them on a little clothesline thoughtfully strung under the window. She had no toothbrush but made do with water and a vigorous forefinger.

"All yours," she said breezily, sailing past Nick, wearing her towel like a glamorous gown.

"Thank you," he said with cutting sarcasm, slamming the door behind him. In shock, she found herself staring at the white-painted panel of the bathroom door. He'd been dressed in the scantiest underwear she'd ever seen.

She was trembling and disgusted with herself as she slid beneath the sheets on one of the beds. His swimming suit had been one of those nylon things that were virtually transparent when wet so why did she get so hot and bothered over seeing him in his underwear?

Because it was underwear and emphasized the intimacy of their situation. "Get hold of yourself, Morgan," she muttered. "He's only a man, like every other man."

But he wasn't. Not to her. She heard the shower running and wild heat flared inside her. She quelled it firmly, shutting out the image of Nick's naked body, streaming with water, and her own hands washing him, touching him.... Making a sound of self-derision and frustration, she turned her face to the wall.

She knew when he came out, knew it with every pore in her tense body. His bare feet were silent as he crossed the floor, and she waited for the rustle of the sheets that would indicate he'd gone to bed. It didn't come. Instead the side of her bed dipped as he sat on the edge of it. She forced her breathing to remain steady, but the gasp she'd uttered when he sat down had betrayed her.

She didn't know what she expected from him but certainly not that he would gently begin combing her hair. "You're not asleep, are you, Sara?" he asked, his voice low and, to her overcharged nerves, seductive.

"No," she mumbled. "Where did you get a comb?"

His hand brushed her scalp as he lifted a section of hair to work out the tangles in it. "Oh, I always carry one. Sit up, will you, Sara?"

She struggled up, her joints protesting, and tucked the sheet firmly around her chest, well above the curve of her breasts. Resolutely she kept her back to him, telling herself she was giving him greater access to her hair.

Oh, it felt good to have him comb it, to feel it floating free on her shoulders. She had washed it as best she could with the bar of soap and rinsed out most of the snarls under the shower but Nick was completing its restoration to well-groomed order.

She turned slightly to glance at his face. He was absorbed in his task, his expression brooding and enigmatic. Only his eyes were alive, with a glitter in their depths that his heavy lashes did nothing to hide. A half-delicious, altogether disturbing throb started in her lower body and she pulled her eyes away lest her transparent face reveal her thoughts.

"You have beautiful hair, Sara," Nick said huskily. "Very unusual, especially in Greece. I assume it's real."

"Of course it's real," she said unsteadily. "It's not a wig."

"I meant the color, sweetheart. But of course it is. The rest of you matches." He groaned and dropped the comb, at the same time pulling her down so that she lay across his lap. His voice sank to a heat-charged whisper. "How could I forget how you looked lying in the sun?"

The languorous heaviness invading her limbs and weakening her defences owed nothing to the physical exhaustion of her body. "Nick, don't," she said but even to her own ears the words lacked conviction.

"I only want to kiss you good-night, Sara," he murmured, his mouth a breath away from hers.

His arms enfolded her in an embrace so warm and secure she wanted it to go on and on. She didn't want to think; she wanted the warm magic of darkness and his touch to chase all thought and leave only sensation.

But it wasn't dark. The overhead light was still on, with moths and other insects that had come in through the open window hurling themselves suicidally against the globe. With a shiver she came back to reality. She struggled against his strength, which now seemed threatening. "Nick, let me go."

Her sharp tone penetrated and with a look that combined chagrin and an amused mockery he loosened his hold.

"Just one kiss, Sara," he said with good-natured lightness. "Then I'll let you sleep."

His kiss was light, the embodiment of tenderness, barely fleeting over her lips. She wanted to deepen it but her head was suddenly too heavy for her neck. Nick kissed her once more, letting her feel the hot tip of his tongue against hers, then he drew away, one hand trailing gently from her temple to the curve of her jaw. "Good night, Sara. Sleep well."

She was too far gone into sleep to answer.

It seemed to Sara she barely closed her eyes when it was morning and Nick was calling her. "You've got ten minutes to get to the table for breakfast if we're to catch the bus."

She groaned as she struggled up from the soft blanket. Every muscle ached, crying out its protest against the workout she'd given her body yesterday. "Aren't we going to see Paul?"

"I saw him this morning, lazybones. It's late." He pulled on her arm as she showed signs of snuggling down under the pillow. "This is the only bus that will give us a connection to the village, so get moving."

A warm shower did much to restore her muscle tone and the substantial breakfast their landlady served them filled all the empty spaces in her stomach. By the time they were on the bus moving ponderously south she felt almost human again.

Nick teased her. "How did you enjoy the shortest marriage in history?"

"Marriage?" Sara snorted inelegantly. "You don't look like the marrying kind."

Nick rolled his eyes. "That's what everyone thinks until they fall."

"But you won't fall, will you, Nick?" she asked sweetly, taking a perverse pleasure in needling him.

He gave her a long look, his face serious. "I doubt if one has much say in the matter when it happens."

Sara returned his look, a dozen sensations grappling for supremacy inside her. Then she turned away to stare out of the window at the sere tan hills the road looped through. No, one didn't have any control over falling in love. She had, so easily. It had crept up on her and taken her by surprise.

But what was she going to do about it? What could she do with a man like Nick?

In the village they were lucky to find a Land Rover parked in the square, and two linen-suited men Sara took to be the representatives of the government drinking lemonade outside the little *kafenion*. Nick, who apparently knew one of them, walked up and they shook hands, greeting Sara politely in accented English.

"We can get a lift with them," Nick told her. "I was afraid we'd have to go up by mule."

As they drove out of the village a short time later, Sara looked over her shoulder at the alley where the Pontiac had been parked the other day. Nothing today, only a dense shadow from the buildings crowding the street.

"It's gone," Andreas gasped, staring at the empty space in the shed as if he couldn't believe his eyes. "Everything's gone."

Even the little trays that had held earrings, bracelets and the small gold cup had disappeared. Vanished. The two small boxes from the cave and the canvas bags from the larger crate, all missing. Only the shell of the larger crate remained in the corner.

"But how?" Sara asked. "The door was padlocked." A dull glitter on the earthen floor caught her eye and she bent, picking up a thin gold ring, twisted out of shape as if the thief had stepped on it.

Andreas snatched it from her hand. His mouth worked and he looked as if he would cry. "The key was hanging in the office tent, along with the Jeep and the Land Rover keys. Anyone could have taken the gold."

"Turkish gold, was it?" said one of the government men.

"Yes," Daniel said calmly. He seemed the least disturbed by the theft. "And some quite desirable artifacts."

"I knew we should have kept a guard posted," Andreas wailed.

"Too late now," Daniel said. "Besides the key wasn't here when we were all away from the site yesterday. I had it in my pocket. Later when we were both here, I put it back in the tent with the others. So when could the gold have been stolen?"

"Any time in the night," Andreas said. "Or when we went up to the dig to check how much rock covered over the cave entrance."

"We would have heard something," Daniel said positively.

Andreas seemed not to hear him. "Or you could have taken it." He suddenly rushed to Daniel and waved his fist in front of the taller man. "You moved it. You did, before I got back."

"Andreas!" Nick said sharply, taking him by the shoulder and pulling him away from Daniel. "Don't make rash accusations. Why would Daniel want to take it? It wouldn't be easy to smuggle out of the country."

"Why wouldn't he?" Andreas retorted heatedly. "It wasn't just gold coins," he added, stunning them all. "There was a mask in one of the smaller boxes. I would have told you, but the accident happened and in the excitement I never had a chance to mention it."

So that would explain Andreas's peculiar behavior, Sara thought. A death mask like those found at Mycenae? That would be a find. Her questions were lost as the men all began talking at once, reverting to staccato Greek in their excitement. Only Daniel said nothing as he puffed on his pipe, his face impassive.

The rest of the day was spent rolling up the tents and packing the office materials and tools for transport down the mountainside to the vehicles. Around three o'clock a man from the village came up with a string of mules to move the equipment. The heat continued unabated, punctuated at intervals by the rumble of thunder, and the dry air seemed to draw all the moisture from their bodies.

It was late afternoon by the time the mules left, followed soon by the government men, who insisted that Andreas and Daniel accompany them in order to file a complete report on the landslide and the theft. Sara's eyes were sympathetic as she watched them trudge down the mountainside. Bureaucracy at its worst.

"What do you think, Sara?" Nick asked as he came up behind her.

She shook her head, rubbing perspiration from her face. "I don't know. Maybe those hikers did come back when we were waiting for the helicopter. But it would have taken more than two men to carry it all unless they made several trips. We would have seen them. Besides, Father had the key in his pocket."

So he'd said, Nick thought silently. He didn't want to put any stock in Andreas's wild accusations, but logic forced him to consider every angle. "Yes," he said to Sara. "Maybe the police will find something but they won't get here until tomorrow." He took hold of her arm. "Let's have another look in the storage shed in case we missed something. Then we'll get out of here. I don't like the looks of that sky."

A livid thunderhead lay almost overhead. Even as Sara looked up lightning slashed a path to earth. High against the blue and white cloud an eagle soared on motionless wings. She shivered in spite of the heat. What an awesomely lonely place now that everyone had gone.

A search of the shed turned up only a handful of gold coins among the ruins of the crate. The puzzle remained: How had the gold been spirited away so thoroughly in the short time the camp had been deserted after the accident?

When they stepped out of the shed a short time later Sara wondered if they had miscalculated the time of sunset. The sky was dark with an ominous heaviness that triggered a strange primeval fear in her. That suffocating feeling she'd had the first day in the cave came back, shortening her breath. This was no ordinary storm; this was the buildup of weeks of drought and extraordinary heat. When it broke it would be a cataclysm to rival Noah's.

They had reached the edge of the flat area that had housed the camp, walking amid a fireworks display of lightning, when the clouds dropped their burden. The sheet of water they could see descending from the peaks into the valleys suddenly surrounded them, a pounding, enveloping shroud that soaked them to the skin in seconds.

Sara jumped as lightning took the top off a tree a hundred yards from them. Nick pulled her against him, covering her ears as thunder reverberated around the peaks.

In the instant of eerie silence that followed, he raised his head, listening. The roar he'd heard faintly before the lightning strike grew louder, then louder still until the ground shook and the sound filled the rapidly cooling air.

"A freight train?" Sara asked, her heart racing under his hand.

He gave a humorless laugh. "Unless they built a track in the past couple of hours, it's unlikely. What we're hearing and what we'll be seeing in about five minutes is a flash flood."

She drew back her head from where it rested on his chest. "A flash flood? You mean like in the movies, swallowing whole herds of cattle?"

"Something like that. Only this one's going to block our path to the car."

The roar built up to a crescendo, then it was upon them, a torrent of water crashing down the ravine they'd followed so many times in their hikes to and from the cars. Nick cursed fluently and imaginatively as the newly formed river boiled past their feet and the buckets of water from the heavens poured down on their heads.

"Nothing we can do except stay at the camp," he finally said as his extensive vocabulary exhausted itself.

"But the equipment—"

Nick gestured at the pack he carried. "We'll have to make do with what I've got here." Even Sara's pack had gone down on the mules.

They turned and fought their way back to the shed, against the slashing rain and a rising wind that drove through their wet clothes and clawed at their bodies. Lightning strobed around them, illuminating the little plateau with an eerie blue brilliance that hurt the eyes.

Sara was shivering in earnest, her teeth chattering despite the tight clenching of her jaw. Nick could feel the tremors that racked her body as they made the final dash to the shed.

Fortunately the door was on the sheltered side of the shed so they were able to build a fire near it, leaving the entrance open to let out the smoke.

"At least these pieces from the crate are dry," Nick commented as he fed small bits of wood into the fire. When it flared brightly, it gave off a steady heat that was more than welcome, and lit the gathering gloom in the little building. Sara shook her head at the perversity of nature. In the afternoon she had thought she'd roast; now she was shivering in wet clothes.

"What about more wood?" she asked. "That won't last long." She looked at Nick and realized how she must appear to him, clothes soaked, hair plastered to her head in rat tails.

Something sparked between them in the same instant and they burst into gales of laughter. "If you could see yourself, Sara," Nick gasped. "You look like a drowned cat."

"And so do you, Nick," she said, rumpling his dripping hair.

"So who's going out to look for more wood?" Nick asked. "Do we draw straws or are you going to volunteer?"

Sara cast her eyes, alight with mischief, around the room. "In the caveman days, the man provided the wood."

"Is that so? Well, as you pointed out once before, this isn't the caveman days. This is now. What happened to those equal rights you women always talk about?"

Sara wasn't about to let a mere man get the better of her. She squelched to the door in her wet sandals. Thunder and lightning had subsided but the rain poured down. She was about to step into it when Nick grabbed her arm. "I was only kidding, Sara. I'll get the wood. You take off those wet clothes before you catch pneumonia."

The glow from the fire revealed the way their wet clothes clung to them, Nick's faithfully outlining the muscles of his chest and shoulders. His thin faded jeans, wet through, emphasized rather than concealed the heavy masculinity of him. Sara tore her eyes away from his body, only to find his on her.

She looked down and saw how her nipples, erect with cold, strained against her T-shirt. A light flared in his eyes for an instant, then as quickly cooled.

Sara swallowed to moisten her dry throat. "How can I take everything off? What will I wear? I can't just stand around naked." She bit her tongue at the unfortunate choice of words, red washing up her cheeks.

Nick looked at her with an impudent grin. "Fine by me." He bent and rummaged in the pack. Tossing her a shirt, he added, "Put that on. It'll be too large but it'll warm you. Take your time. I'll be a while getting the wood."

Chapter Nine

By the time Nick returned with an armful of wood salvaged from the ruins of the nearby shepherds' hut, Sara was dressed in his shirt. It reached to the tops of her thighs, an adequate if not exactly elegant covering.

He dumped the wood on the sandy floor next to the fire. Sara was arranging wet clothes over the shelves that had held the artifacts found in the early stages of the excavation. Keeping her back turned, she pretended to straighten the few items until Nick had changed into the dry jeans he carried in his pack. His chest was bare and she realized he had only one spare shirt, the one she was wearing.

"Damn, why did I let my stuff go on the mules?" she muttered.

"We didn't plan this, Sara." He handed her his jeans, shirt and undershorts, and she hung them next to her clothes. There was a curious intimacy in seeing her lacy underwear hanging next to the utilitarian dark cotton of his.

He must have been thinking the same thing for his eyes were black and intense on her, making her conscious of the length of leg the shirt left uncovered. A shimmering thread of tension stretched between them, tighter and tighter, until she looked away from him, snapping it. She heard the hoarse intake of his breath and nervously licked her lip.

"Sara." It was a groan, and Sara felt his longing as if it were her own. Excitement burgeoned in her but she grasped the last dangling safety line.

"Do you have anything to eat in that pack?" The words were mundane but tension made them stick in her throat.

Nick gave a sigh as he forced himself to relax. "I'm afraid not. But there should be a couple of cans of lemonade."

"I guess we'd better drink that and imagine the rest of the meal," Sara said, aware that she was chattering but unable to stop herself. She felt as though she stood on the edge of a precipice and she wasn't sure she wanted to step back from it. Wasn't it time she honestly faced the attraction between them and decided what she felt? Attraction? Love had crept up on her as silently as cat's feet.

Nick centered his attention on finding the cans of lemonade in his pack, his thoughts skittering around his brain like demented mice.

Every time he looked at her he wanted her, with a passion that turned his insides into a blazing inferno. But it was so much more than physical, this emotion that had crept stealthily around the outskirts of his consciousness. Now it revealed itself, like one of the bolts of lightning lashing the earth around the little hut.

He loved her. With surprise he realized he probably had from that first moment on the beach when he had seen her, a golden mermaid in the sun. Perhaps it had been passion then, but now that he had begun to know her his passion had altered, tempered with a desire to cherish her as well as to ravish her.

He loved her, all of her, her unquenchable spirit and the proud strength she'd revealed yesterday when she'd worked to free Paul. And he loved the joyful light in her golden eyes when she was happy and the way her wet hair snarled like a bird's nest when it dried. And her independence.

Her independence? Yes, even that, he realized in astonishment. Though it was the most difficult problem between them, he could never take it away from her. There had to be a way to have her and yet leave her in possession of that essential quality that shaped so much of the person she was. For he knew that her body would never be enough for him, although he wanted that, too. But he wanted to be her friend as well as her lover, her companion. She was his other half, without whom he would be forever lonely.

But did she love him? Could she let herself go enough to feel the deep emotion that made him want to spend eternity in her arms? He ducked his head as a sly, contemplative smile crept over his face. He would make love to her, slowly and delectably, find out what pleased her and use all the skills he possessed until she couldn't move or think without his image coming into her mind. He would teach her to love him, and then they would sort out all the other problems.

His hands were shaking as he pulled out the two cans; he couldn't control them. Not here, in this dilapidated place. He wanted the first time he made love to her to be in a proper bed, preferably one they needn't leave for a week. His love was too important to be consummated in these sordid surroundings.

Yet how could he wait when he burned just watching her struggling to unsnarl her drying hair with his comb? She gave his shirt an allure it certainly never had on him. He closed his eyes, sure he was going mad. He even envied the shirt, so close to the skin he ached to touch. He shook his head to erase the picture of how she would look in nothing but that golden skin.

Shifting his legs to ease his aching body, he popped the top of one can. "Sara, come and get your drink." Sara, come and let me love you, bury myself in you, in your silken softness, love you, love you....

He kept his eyes downcast as she took the can from his hand. His own lemonade was tepid. That it was wet was about all that could be said in its favor.

Holding her lemonade can in her hand Sara went to stand by the open door. The rain continued to fall, pattering on the metal roof, and she breathed deeply of the scent of parched earth and grass refreshed by the moisture. The thunder had receded to an irritable mutter in the distance.

Nick came up beside her, resting his arm lightly across her shoulders. She wasn't oblivious to his mood. She'd seen how he looked at her as she moved in the firelight. Hunger radiated from him and it wasn't for food. She understood, for the same hunger gnawed at her.

Should she let him know she knew? That she would welcome anything he wanted to do? Questions filled her mind but she could only wait for him to take her on a journey that would show her the answers.

"Sara," Nick said softly, his warm breath caressing the tendrils of her hair where they curled against her temple.

She looked up, anticipation drying her mouth, sure he was about to kiss her and take the decision out of her hands. Electricity arced between them and she felt her heartbeat jump into high gear.

"Nick," she whispered, waiting, yearning. She wanted to press her suddenly painful breasts against him, to feel his soothing touch on them and revel in the hardening of his body in response to her nearness. But she couldn't move, caught in the spell of his eyes.

Nick almost gave in, then he remembered his resolve to wait until they were out of here. Without changing his physical position he managed to pull back into himself.

Sara shivered as she sensed his withdrawal, and looked out into the back night. Nick's voice sounded faint and strained. "Sara, if you want to go out for a moment, the rain has almost stopped." He forced a laugh. "Sorry this hotel doesn't have a bathroom. A hot tub would have been nice."

Sara suddenly remembered the others who had gone ahead. "Father must be worried."

"He'll assume we've holed up somewhere to get out of the storm. I'm sure we're not the first to be stranded in these mountains."

"We'll be home tomorrow." Sara went out, slipping on the muddy ground that this afternoon had been powdery dust. When she came back she saw that Nick had spread a blanket over a thin groundsheet on the sandy floor. The realization hit her that they would have to share it. She would sleep close to him all night, touching him.

"There's only one blanket. We'll have to keep each other warm." His voice was low, husky with the emotion he kept in check.

How could he sound so cool and unaffected? Sara's heart pounded erratically as she nodded and lay down under the blanket. He stretched out beside her, tucking it around her. Cool air blew in the open door, bringing with it a scent of woodsmoke and more rain.

"Won't you be cold, Nick?" Sara asked. "You don't even have a shirt."

"You'll warm me," he said. And how! He was burning up. He gave her a little pat and turned his back. If he faced her, he would explode.

Tired as she was, Sara found she couldn't sleep. She was deliciously warm, curled against Nick's back, but the tension in his body communicated itself to her until she was as keyed-up as he was. And she was sure he had turned his back because he was being noble.

If only he knew—it was totally unnecessary.

Slowly, carefully, she edged her arm over him until her hand rested in the soft curls on his chest. He didn't move but his body grew more rigid. Laying her cheek against his smooth back, she allowed her hand to creep stealthily over his chest until she found one flat nipple nearly hidden in whorls of hair.

Nick's reaction was explosive. He flipped over so that he faced her, the blanket sliding off her. "Sara, what are you doing?" His voice was hoarse and he couldn't control the way it shook. "Why don't you sleep?"

"Why don't you?" she asked, a provocative smile in her voice, an equally provocative fingertip tracing along his collarbone.

For a moment he said nothing, his harsh breathing seeming to fill the space between them. Then he crushed her against him. "How can I?" he groaned in an anguished whisper. "How can I sleep when you feel so good, so close to me? I can't stop myself from touching you. I can't!"

"Then touch me, Nick. Why, are you scared?" She nuzzled the hollow of his throat, the salty-sweet taste of his skin an absorbing wonder.

Nick shifted restlessly. "Yes, scared as hell. I want it to be perfect and for the first time in my life—"

"It will be perfect," she cut in, stopping his words with a finger on his lips. "Kiss me, Nick. Oh, kiss me."

He kissed her, his lips covering hers in fierce hunger, a hunger that was not satisfied but intensified with every taste of her delectable mouth.

"Sara, sweet Sara," he groaned. "I want you so much. I want to touch you, to touch all of you. I want to feel you under me, to make love to you...."

Heat flashed through her and she felt as if she would melt. "Yes," she said. "Yes."

The shirt she wore had ridden up to her waist, and she could feel the rough fabric of his jeans against her tender skin, sensitizing every nerve ending. The desire to remove all barriers between them burned within her.

In him, too, she soon realized. Their hands went at the same time to the buttons of her shirt and tangled as they struggled to undo them. They finally gave way and Nick raised her slightly to slide the shirt from her shoulders. When she was free of it, he did nothing for the longest time. Only his eyes moved, taking in every crevice and hollow of her slender nakedness, every curve and mound as it was highlighted by the flickering fire. He was a beggar at a feast who couldn't decide which delicacy to sample first. He wanted it all.

Almost in slow motion he began to touch her, running a gentle palm over the small creamy breasts with their exquisite pink nipples. With a low sound of longing he took one of the nipples into his mouth, caressing and tasting with his tongue and gentle teeth. Shock waves shafted through her until every nerve reverberated with sensation.

She gave a little whimper as his mouth left her breast and returned to her lips. Grasping one of his hands she brought it up to cover her aching nipple, moaning her satisfaction as he massaged it. She opened her mouth, welcoming the entrance of his tongue, the firm thrust of it as it sank deeply to explore every crevice. His hands slid over her skin, caressing and stroking as if they loved the silk and velvet texture of her. Sara had never felt so beautiful or so thoroughly loved.

When he lifted his head to drag air into his starved lungs she placed her hand behind it and drew him back to her. With the tip of her tongue she investigated the corners of his mouth, dimly aware of the rough silk crispness of his hair around her fingers. He waited, scarcely breathing, to see what she would do next.

Slowly, like a cat tasting cream, she licked the inside of his lower lip, relishing the slick texture, then continued to his teeth. They were smooth, set in a faintly uneven line. She probed deeper, and he parted them, then closed them over the end of her tongue with gentle ferocity. Tension wound tighter between them until Nick made a peculiar sound and pressed Sara down onto the blanket. His mouth skated over her face, returned to her mouth and drank from it as if he were dying.

Sara writhed against him, wanting him. She felt his arousal and she pressed herself to him, her legs parting in invitation. Nick pulled away slightly, resting his weight on his elbow. "Sara, sweet Sara, are you sure? Because if you're not, I'm not sure I'll be able to stop beyond this point."

Clinging to his neck, her hands tangled in his hair. The musky man-fragrance of him filled her nostrils and she moaned. "I want you. I want you." Her hands moved from his head, frantic, restless little animals greedily scrambling over him, tugging at his neck, sliding up and down his back and chest but always returning to his waist where the one barrier still separated them. "Please, Nick. Please."

He gently removed her hands and stood up. Facing her in the firelight, he stripped off his jeans. His skin was bronzed in the flickering light, his rampant arousal undisguised and triumphant. For a moment Sara wavered. Could her uncertain love and inexperience guide her to satisfy him, to pleasure him? And would he satisfy her? Or would he now concern himself with only his own need and forget about hers, as Eric had so often done?

No, not Nick. He did nothing without fixing his whole mind on it. He would make love with the same concentration, no halfhearted gropings that left her in a limbo of frustration.

She held out her arms with a radiant smile and he came down to her, trembling with an urgency he could barely control.

Still he did not hurry, but took his time, stroking her breasts with his hands and his mouth. He trailed his fingers with agonizing slowness down her body. When they brushed the golden curls at the base of her abdomen she whimpered. When they delved deeper, she had to bite her lip to keep from screaming. *Nick, Nick, get on with it, touch me, don't play—love me. Oh, love me!*

She was spinning toward the end of the universe. *No, not yet, not without you.* Boldly she ran her hand lower on his body, drawing back at the first contact with the rigid, satin heat of him. But hearing his moan of pleasure, she touched him again, delicately stroking her fingers over him.

"Yes," Nick gasped and entered her so quickly her hand was trapped between them.

A swift pain shot through her, but she controlled the cry that rose to her lips. She was immediately swamped in a hot gush of pleasure that made her forget all pain, all previous conceptions of love.

Wrapping her legs around him she held him as he thrust deeper and deeper into her. *I love you, I love you,* she cried silently as she matched her rhythm to his. This was what she had been born for. Past and future vanished, leaving only this all-consuming present. The shabby hut, the cold, the discomfort were nothing; only this pleasure mattered.

But even that had to reach a conclusion. She felt the tingling start and went rigid in wonder as it burned up to where Nick was so alive, deep inside her. As the explosion rocked her, she dug her nails into his back, the last solid object in her world. She was falling, falling, and then, miraculously, he was with her, pouring a liquid heat into her that restored them to reality.

For a long time they lay, unable to speak or move. Sara caressed Nick's head as he lay heavily on her breast, gulping air into his lungs. "Sara, Sara," he murmured, his hand lightly stroking her. He was still joined with her. He didn't want to move, but he finally did when her breathing became shallow.

"I'm heavy," he said, reluctantly pulling free of her damp, silky thighs.

"Nice heavy," she murmured drowsily. "Nice everything."

"Speaking of nice everything," Nick said, "you haven't done this kind of thing much, have you?" In spite of her readiness and his painful urgency, he hadn't been unaware of the slight resistance of her body to the tender invasion of his.

Sara was silent. Why did he have to talk? Couldn't they sleep and discuss it in the morning?

"Have you?" Nick persisted. "Or maybe you haven't done it at all?"

Recognizing the implacable insistence of his tone, she took refuge in flippancy. "Done what? Had sex?"

Nick groaned. "Had sex? Is that what you call this wonderful happening between us?" He framed her flushed face with his two palms and gently ran his lips over her cheeks, then nuzzled her chin before softly kissing her mouth. "Sara, we made love. We didn't 'have sex.'"

She sighed, ashamed. "I know, Nick. It was wonderful."

"But you haven't answered my question, Sara. Was I the first?"

He didn't sound too pleased by the idea, Sara thought, forcing her eyes open and her mind out of the encroaching cotton of sleep. "No, you weren't, Nick. You weren't the first."

He sighed and the tension went out of him. "Then why did you practically freeze up every time things got a little hot and heavy between us, especially at first?"

Sleep was gone for good. "I told you, Nick. I don't have casual affairs. You were just playing around."

"And now?" His hands were almost painfully tight around her, as if her answer was more important to him than anything in his life.

Sara closed her eyes, afraid of what he would see in their transparent depths. *Now I love you. I love you.* Aloud she said, "You know why. We both wanted it."

"We wanted it before. Oh, I know I also suggested we cool it for a while. But now you've changed. Why now and not then?"

"I didn't know you well enough then." Sara knew she had to be careful with her answers. He was more intuitive than most men. There were depths of perception in him that made most of the men she knew seem as deep as a puddle on hot concrete.

Nick was not happy. After the euphoria of their love-making, which had far surpassed his more fevered imaginings, he was conscious of a letdown. Under her cool answers he sensed she was being evasive. He had hoped—counted on—his lovemaking to open complete communication between them. Her soul would be as trusting and receptive as her body. Now he saw that it hadn't happened. If anything, she was more elusive than before, and that withdrawal, that little distance she kept between them, enraged him. He had to know the real Sara beneath the surface sophistication.

His future happiness depended on it.

Sara waited for him to speak again. In the protracted silence her drowsiness returned but altered almost to depression. Maybe they shouldn't have done this. Maybe she should have waited until a more auspicious time and more glamorous circumstances. Maybe she shouldn't have pushed him.

No, whatever the circumstances, their lovemaking had been right. She shivered at the thought of never knowing that soaring ecstasy again, and without conscious thought she snuggled her body close to his, seeking his warmth.

Nick, feeling the trembling in her limbs, reached over and covered her with the blanket. He stood up and tossed another chunk of wood on the fire. It flared up, outlining his nakedness. Then he turned away and pulled on his jeans.

"How many men have there been, Sara?" he blurted suddenly as he yanked up the zipper.

"Men?" Sara echoed, sitting up and wrapping the blanket more firmly around her body. "Why do you want to know? I haven't asked you how many women you've had."

"No, but I'd tell you if you did." His smile was fleeting. "How many, Sara?"

"One," she admitted reluctantly.

"I thought so." He didn't like the sinking feeling in his gut, but plowed on. "And that was a long time ago, wasn't it?"

Sara picked at the edge of the blanket, worrying at a thread that had separated from the fabric. Should she tell him? As far as she was concerned, it was buried in the past, but she knew Nick would persist until he'd wormed it out of her. "Yes, when I was doing postgraduate work. I was one of the youngest in my classes and Eric took a liking to me. He was young, one of my profs, actually. I was flattered by his interest. I guess I had a belated crush on him. I was so busy during high school and my first years of college that I never had time for dating. We started to go out together, sort of on the sly. He was new there, and part of the attraction on his side was that he thought it was a game to be unconventional and daring. Having an affair with a student was his way of thumbing his nose at the structured establishment."

Nick made a derisive sound.

Sara looked at him and snapped. "If you don't want to hear about it, I won't say any more."

He gestured impatiently, pacing back and forth in the confined space. "Go on, Sara. What happened? When did you become lovers?" Instinct told him even if she were infatuated she wouldn't go into her first affair without weighing all the consequences.

Sara sighed, sadness washing through her as she remembered the painful events surrounding and affecting her relationship with Eric. "I didn't want to rush into anything with him," she said quietly. "But he was becoming impatient, calling me a tease."

"He would," Nick said with a snort. "I can imagine just the kind of line he'd use."

"Stop interrupting, Nick." She paused for a second to collect her thoughts. "Then my mother married again, her third husband. She didn't invite me to the wedding, her own daughter, even though it was only fifty miles away. I had to read about it in the newspapers. It was like a slap in the face. That night I let Eric make love to me for the first time. I guess I did it to prove to myself that someone could still want me."

"Did you enjoy it?" Nick asked with a morbid fascination.

"Not the first time," Sara said honestly. "He was in such a hurry. I don't know if it was because he'd had to wait so long for me or if he was just plain nervous. He hurt me, then he gave a grunt and it was all over. He said it would get better, that it was always bad the first time."

Nick's heart wept for her rude initiation into what could be the most profound form of communication between two people. "And was it better later?"

Sara shrugged. "Sometimes it was, sometimes it wasn't. I thought it was me, that all the stories I'd read were exaggerated. Eric didn't seem to know the difference. He asked me to marry him and I agreed." She laughed shortly. "For six weeks I wore a large diamond, then it was all over."

"What happened?" Nick asked in a monotone, still pacing.

"Ambition was what happened. Eric became conventional. I got into an argument at a dean's party with some rich muckamuck, and the dean let Eric know that I wouldn't fit in as a faculty wife if I offended someone who could endow the university with a substantial donation. So Eric asked for his ring back."

"And you threw it in his face," Nick guessed, leaning against the wall and folding his arms over his chest.

"Something like that." There was a silence broken only by the soft crackle of the fire, then Sara added reflectively, "Funny thing, a couple of years later they offered me a position in their history department."

Nick grinned. "Oh? I would have thought you'd be blacklisted."

"I guess not. Eric didn't teach there anymore, and some of my other profs must have recommended me. The dean had probably forgotten my name, if he ever knew it. Anyway, the man I had the argument with—pompous ass—made twice his usual donation. Seems he liked arguing obscure points of history, so I was vindicated even before Eric and I broke up."

"Were you badly hurt?" Nick asked softly.

"At first, yes," Sara said, wondering now how she'd let a shallow man like Eric capture her heart, however briefly. Compared to Nick, he faded into insignificance. If she hadn't gotten over him long ago, she would have now, since knowing Nick. "I worked hard, cut six months off the time I figured I'd need to get my master's. In the meantime Mother divorced number three and began actively hunting for number four with all the accompanying publicity in the papers, while her proper Boston family pretended to be scandalized. I was even more determined not to be like her and chase everything in trousers."

Nick uttered a sharp, humorless laugh. "Don't be a fool, Sara. You couldn't be like that in a million years. You've got too much self-esteem. You wouldn't let anyone use you."

"Playing psychiatrist again, Nick?" Sara asked lightly to hide a sudden rush of emotion. At least he wasn't using her. He understood her so well it was like finding the other half of her soul.

"You don't need one." His voice dropped to a lower register as he came nearer. "But maybe you need me."

Yes, she needed him. And wanted him. If they only had this one night together, so be it. She had to make the most of it, to store away the memory of him, in case memories became all she had left. "Nick, I'm cold," she said while fire licked at her veins. "Come and keep me warm."

Nick's mouth curved in a slow, honey-sweet smile as he sat down next to her. "Are you sure I can do that, Sara?"

Her answering smile was seductive, as if she knew all the secrets of the universe. "I'm sure, Nick. Shall we prove it?" She leaned forward and whispered in his ear. "Take off your clothes and I'll take off mine."

"They're already off," he reminded her with a grin. "Under that very fetching blanket." He gave her shoulder a little pat. "Lie down. I'll just fix the fire so it'll burn till morning."

He arranged the last chunks of wood on the fire so they would burn slowly, then walked to the door to look out at the night. It was clear, a vast sky filled with points of light. He inhaled the pungent smell of wet earth and grass, its evocative after-rain fragrance. In the distance a jackal called and was answered from a ridge at the other side of the valley. The lonely howling sent a shiver up his back and the hair rose on his nape.

"Nick, come and sleep."

Chapter Ten

He turned at the sound of Sara's low voice. She was standing up, the blanket a rumpled heap around her feet. Her body, bathed in golden firelight, had a primitive beauty that called out to everything masculine in him. As if in a trance, he came to her.

"Let me help you, Nick," she whispered, and he couldn't suppress the groan that escaped his lips.

She released the button at his waist and slid the zipper down, ever so slowly, a tooth at a time. Her eyes, shining gold in the dim light, held his and in their transparent depths he saw everything he'd ever wanted in a woman. Pleasure enveloped him as she freed him from the suddenly painful restriction of his clothes. She pushed the jeans off his hips and he stepped out of them, at the same time crushing her to him, bringing both of them down on the blanket.

"Sweet, sweet Sara, you're driving me crazy. Or is it this place? I think we're both bewitched."

"Shut up, Nick," Sara said with a laugh. "Shut up and kiss me. We can talk later."

He kissed her with almost bruising force and she opened her mouth to the invasion of his tongue, meeting and matching his passion with her own. She'd never tasted such sweetness, such delicious rapture that went to her head and sent her spinning endlessly through space. She clutched his shoulders in a panic. She was falling into an enormous void that would swallow her. Falling...

"Sara, *kardhia mout,*" Nick murmured, bringing her back from the edge of the abyss. "Touch me."

Shyness overwhelmed her, totally unexpected after her earlier boldness. "I don't know how. Nick, show me what to do. Teach me."

"Do what pleases you. What feels good to you. That's what will please me."

"But I want to know all those things they tell you in books."

"Forget that. We're making love, not performing. All those sex manuals talk about is technique. There's no substitute for emotion."

Sara's heart seemed about to burst. He couldn't say anything like that if he didn't mean it, could he? Was it really possible that this meant as much to him as it did to her?

She let him guide her hand over his body, forgetting her shyness in the pleasure of caressing the smooth skin with complete freedom. Such an array of textures, soft curls on his chest, satin-smooth skin on his shoulders, the play of sinuous muscles under that skin, the fascinating hollow of his navel in the center of his flat belly, the crisp, tight curls farther down. She hesitated, then made a detour to his muscle-corded thighs.

Nick chuckled and reached down for her hand. "Don't be shy, Sara. You touched me before."

Her face burned. Her whole body burned. "But that was in the heat of the moment." Heat of the moment? How could she be any hotter than she was now, with molten lava flowing through her body?

Nick echoed her thought. "I'm burning. Touch me, Sara. Make me better." He guided her hand and she touched him, jerking back as he groaned. Firmly he put her hand back, wrapping his fingers around hers and holding her there. "Yes, like that. Oh, yes."

He tangled his hand in her hair and brought her mouth down to his, burying his tongue so deep she felt she was drowning in his sweetness. Her remaining reticence fled and she caressed him ever more boldly, savoring the hot vibrancy of him. What a marvel a man's body was, so resilient, so responsive.

Nick felt the all-consuming pleasure of her touch. What sweet hands she had. Never had he been so aroused, transported beyond the rapture of the body into the realm of the soul. Nothing had ever prepared him for this. She gave so utterly that everything faded into insignificance except the feel and the presence of her. With sudden clarity he knew what had been missing in his previous relationships with women: love, the magic ingredient poets extolled. He had always considered love an unattainable fantasy.

Until now. Until Sara.

Did the same feeling touch her heart? Did she feel the same sense of completion he did?

She had to. He couldn't bear it if she didn't love him, at least a little.

The need to make himself one with her was becoming excruciatingly urgent. He grasped her tenderly exploring hand. "Sara, Sara, no more." He brought the hand up to his mouth and kissed her palm, "I want to love you, too."

Sara felt his hand on her breast, the faintly callused palm rubbing over the sensitive nipple until it stood erect and waiting for the touch of his tongue. A deep pleasure shafted through her as he took it into the warmth of his mouth, suckling and pulling at it. She whimpered her loss when he let go, then pressed his head to her as he engulfed the other one.

He stroked his hand down her body, over her hips, then around the creamy brown thighs, until he reached the center of her. She strained to meet him. Why did he keep drawing back? "More, Nick," she moaned. "More."

Nick slid his mouth down to caress her navel, then back up to her mouth. His breath mingled with hers as he murmured, "Already? So quick?" His fingers were exploring, skimming over her velvet softness, then venturing deeper. "So warm, darling."

He placed one hand beneath her to protect her from the rough ground. She willingly opened her thighs to receive him, giving a long sigh of pleasure as he entered her, gently, with infinite care, a fraction at a time. She strained her hips toward him, but he would not be rushed. "Slowly, Sara. Slowly," he whispered, his breath hot and uneven against her throat.

He seemed to know her body better than she did herself. Every time she almost reached the top, he would gentle her down enough to delay the moment. Sweat dripped from his forehead with the strain of holding back his own fulfillment.

Sara twisted beneath him, trembling as though with cold, but her skin burned with fever, a fever he stoked hotter and hotter. His almost leisurely thrusts stroked her inside while his hands caressed her moist and burning skin. She couldn't wait. "Now, now," she cried, locking her legs about him and clutching his back. Nick, at the breaking point, teetered on the edge, then gave up his control in a shuddering convulsion, searing pleasure hammering into his brain.

"Oh!" cried Sara. Then again. "Oh!" in such astonishment that Nick knew the ultimate triumph. She was soaring, floating, higher than eagles, unafraid now. Nick would catch her as she came down, bringing her safely back to earth.

"Is it always like this?" Sara asked in wonderment as the cataclysmic tremors subsided.

"No, not always, my Sara," Nick said fervently, not sure he had come back to reality. "In fact, I think very few people ever have this."

His body languorous and content, he stroked her hair. Tangled, filled with dust, it still seemed to contain golden flame. A wave of tenderness brought tears to his eyes. He tried to tell himself it was smoke from the fire but he knew he lied. He'd never in his life felt like this.

"Sara, I love you."

As soon as the words were out of his mouth he knew he hadn't meant to say them yet, not so soon. But in the next instant he was glad he had, and his arms tightened protectively around her.

Sara's breath was trapped in her throat. Had she heard him say he loved her? Was that what she felt, too? Could she say it, even though she wasn't sure? "If this is love," she said carefully, "then I love you too." She sighed, the practicality of a lifetime coming to the surface. "But what are we going to do about it?"

She shivered as the cool night air sighed over her heated skin. Nick pulled the blanket around them. "We're going to get out of here in the morning, go back to Andreas's house and find out what's going on, where the gold disappeared to. Then we'll see." Gently he folded her close to him, her back cradled against the curve of his chest and belly. He dropped a kiss on her back and tucked his hand under the pleasant weight of her breast. "Sleep, Sara."

Even the turmoil of her thoughts couldn't keep Sara awake. They slept until the sun invaded the dark corners of the shabby room, shedding its light and warmth on their closely entwined bodies.

Nick woke first and as he shifted his weight, Sara opened her eyes. Her cheeks dusty, her hair snarled like a Medusa's, she had never looked more beautiful and alive.

She slid her fingers delicately over Nick's unshaved face, finding a tactile pleasure in the rasping of the hard stubble against her skin. "Did it really happen?" she asked, mirroring some of the astonished wonder of the night.

Nick smiled, a smile that held so much sweetness and warmth that her heart lurched, then went on at a quicker pace. "Yes, my darling Sara, it really happened."

"It seems like a dream." She nuzzled his wrist as his hand cupped her throat, gently pushing back her hair.

"It was a dream," Nick said. "Only it was real."

They looked at each other wordlessly, their eyes locked, suspended in a rainbow bubble of pure unadulterated happiness. Outside a wild canary celebrated the new day with an ecstatic warbling that seemed to perfectly symbolize the way Sara felt, joyous and carefree.

Nick lowered his head and kissed her with tender sweetness. She even tasted good in the morning. Sara clung to him, knowing they had to move but reluctant to get up. This might be the only true union between them. In a few days they would go to Athens, Nick to his work and Sara on a plane headed for home. There was no future so she had to hold on to the present.

Nick gently disengaged her arms, wanting her but holding his hunger under rigid control. If he gave in to it now they would never get out of here. He smiled, the thought tempting, but the realization that other people might be worrying about them forced him to his feet.

Their clothes were dry, and after pulling on his underwear and jeans, Nick tossed Sara her shirt and shorts. He left her to put them on as he walked to the door to survey the weather and the state of the ground. He hoped the flash flood had subsided enough to allow them to follow the ravine to the car, and that the rough track to the village was navigable.

Sara pulled on her wrinkled clothes, aware of an unfamiliar but pleasurable ache in her lower body. Had she really been so wild and wanton? She couldn't believe that her practical self had so easily let go of all its built-in cautions. And seeing him there, so tall and straight and dear, she wanted him again.

Nick whistled cheerfully as his eyes roamed over the newly green shrubs and the rapidly drying puddles on the path. A sense of well-being pervaded him. He loved her. She loved him. A frown etched itself between his brows. Did she? Or had she merely said the words because she sensed he expected it? Had that been uncertainty in her tone, or had he only imagined it out of his fear that she might not return the momentous feeling that burned in him?

Sara came up beside him, driving away his dark thoughts. He watched her face brighten with pleasure at the freshness of the morning. The air was crisp, like laundry dried in the sun, heat haze dissipated by the rain, all the leaves sparkling with rainbow drops of moisture.

Hidden birds sang their unrestrained joy in just being alive on such a morning.

The ravine was muddy but easily passable. Nick's Citroën still waiting in the flat parking area.

As they drove down the mountain Sara was silent and thoughtful. The warm glow of Nick's love and their mutual passion lingered in her mind, but reality was beginning to intrude.

Her eyes slanted to his profile as he concentrated on negotiating the rough road. Had it meant anything to him, really, at a gut level? He'd said he loved her. Had he meant it or had it only been the right thing to say in the aftermath of a night of love? Had the urgent passion already dissolved like so much morning mist?

Her love was firm, stronger now that they had shared the mystical union of man and woman, mind and soul. She felt less confused and hesitant—about the present. The future was less clear. Their lives and careers were worlds apart—hers was in America and his was in Greece. What possible chance did they have to unite them?

Hunger pangs brought her mind back to more practical needs. Love might be nourishing to the spirit but her stomach demanded something a little more substantial.

They stopped for breakfast at the village. Their bedraggled appearance elicited odd looks from the old men who sat outside the *kafenion*, but Sara was too hungry to be self-conscious.

"We look like refugees," she said with a chuckle. Nick's shirt was wrinkled and had a tear on one shoulder where he'd caught it on a thorn bush. She shuddered to think what she looked like. At least her hair was under some control again thanks to Nick's comb and a bit of string she'd found in his pack.

Nick took her hand and rubbed his thumb along the palm, sending a tingling sensation all over her body. "It wasn't so bad, was it, Sara? Being stranded with me?"

Her hand was small and fragile in his and a fierce protectiveness swept through him. He kissed her palm, nuzzling the soft skin. Salty and sweet at the same time. "I do love you, Sara," he said, seeing the amusement fade from her eyes.

Confusion began to cloud them. "Why, Sara," he said incredulously, "you didn't believe me. Did you think it was only physical, that wonderful happening between us?"

As if mesmerized she shook her head. "I hoped it wasn't. I hoped you meant it."

"And did you mean it, too?"

She hesitated, searching for words, the right words to convey her uncertainty, her happiness, her fears that it couldn't last. She knew Nick needed her to say she loved him, but she was afraid, afraid of the inevitable parting. If they could ignore their emotional attachment, pretending it was all physical, a mere joining of two bodies in the lovely night, they wouldn't hurt each other in the end.

"Sara." His voice was urgent, his hands squeezing hers. "Did you?"

Before she could speak, the man arrived with their breakfast. Nick cursed under his breath at the waiter's timing; but Sara felt relief at the interruption. She didn't want to put her feelings into words, only to experience them, to hug this precious time to her heart, for as long as it lasted.

Dr. Stamoulis's house was wrapped in siesta quiet by the time they arrived. No one greeted them as they tiptoed down the hall to the guest wing. Nick opened a door and glanced inside. "Good, your things are in here."

Sara would have entered the room, but he took her wrist and pulled her into a room across the hall. "Let me go, Nick," she protested, laughing. "What will everyone think if I stay in your room?"

He nipped at her earlobe, his arm firm around her waist. "Who's to know? Don't be so straitlaced, Sara. Everyone's sleeping and that's what we're going to do, too."

"Sleep?" She arched a mischievous brow.

He dropped one eyelid in an exaggerated wink. "Maybe a few other things first."

She made another attempt to free herself but Nick pulled her closer. "Sara, don't you think it's a little late for coyness?"

"I wasn't being coy," she whispered back, although she knew they were unlikely to be heard through the thick walls. "But I want to change."

He gave her a humorous leer. "You won't need clothes for what I have in mind."

He pushed her farther into the room, closing the door and locking it behind him. Sara glanced around. This room was decorated less formally than the main part of the house, she noted. The furniture was pine, the decor brown and tan, masculine yet warm and inviting.

"It's your room, not a guest room, isn't it?"

He came up behind her and put his hands on her shoulders. "Yes, Andreas doesn't live here all the time and I still have land nearby so I have my own room for whenever I'm here." She turned to face him and his arms enfolded her. Gently he nudged her backward until she felt the edge of the bed against her legs. Pushing her down, he lay beside her, his leg over her thighs.

"Nick, don't." She made a laughing protest that had no sting in it. She loved the feel of him on her, the way his body was already stirring against her thigh. "I need a bath."

"You do," he agreed, grinning. "We both do, but later." He held her hands above her head, kissing her leisurely, until she was trembling and his desire was so obvious that she yearned to strip off the clothes that lay between them. "Mmm, delicious," he murmured, his tongue making a warm circuit of her ear. "Just as you were on the beach that first day."

Sara went all hot inside. "But I didn't know it was you and you didn't know it was me. How would you have found me again?"

He wrinkled his nose at her. "I would have. It was meant to be." His tongue delicately traced her lips, teasing them, advancing and withdrawing. "Didn't you want to meet me again, sweet Sara? Tell me what you thought when you saw a man standing over you. Were you afraid?"

She shook her head, her hair fanning over the pillow. "I thought I was dreaming."

"And what else? What did you think when I kissed you and you weren't dreaming?"

She squirmed beneath him, evoking an interesting reaction from him. She lowered her hand between their bodies to investigate further but he held it, bringing it over her head again. "Not so fast, Sara. You won't distract me like that. Tell me what you thought."

She set her lips stubbornly, holding back laughter. "I won't, Nick. You can't make me."

"Now that's an interesting proposition, Sara." His hand came down to her side and he suddenly whisked his fingers across her ribs. "Tell me, or I'll tickle you to death."

Gasping, she cried, "Nick, don't. Stop."

Her distress was real and he moved his hand at once, fitting it over one of her breasts. "In that case we'll try another method." Pushing aside her shirt he wedged his finger under the lacy edge of her bra. With no effort at all he unclipped the front clasp.

His mouth closed on one rosy nipple, softly at first, then his teeth nipped gently, inflicting a pleasure that ran through her like hot honey. She went limp and pliant under him.

"Nick, please."

"Tell me what you thought that day." His hand was making exploratory forays at her waist, caressing her flat stomach, and she strained toward him.

"I thought you were beautiful, like Apollo," she whispered, sinking under the sensuous spell of his touch.

"And what else?" His voice was thick with desire, his body hard against hers.

Avoiding his eyes she admitted, "And I wondered what it would be like if you touched me, if you kissed me."

Nick didn't laugh as she'd expected. Instead he drew in his breath with a sharp hiss and said, "How was it?" He cupped her chin in one hand, forcing her to look up at him.

Sara closed her eyes, shutting out the passion in his. "I liked it," she said haltingly.

"Liked it?" he yelled, startling her so much that she jumped.

"Nick, someone will hear you," she hissed, glancing at the door as if she expected it to burst open.

He lowered his voice. "You only *liked* it?" His eyes were black and intense.

She freed her hands and touched his face in a placatory gesture. "Nick, I more than liked it."

He studied her with burning intensity. "And last night, did you more than like that, too?" he asked, his face dark, his breath harsh in the silence.

Wordlessly she nodded, framing his face with soft palms. "Yes, Nick, you know I did."

Nick closed his eyes against the clear gaze of hers. What had driven him to torment her? His behavior had bordered on cruelty and he wasn't sure why he'd done it. Was it his own uncertainty with her elusiveness that made him show his physical superiority because he was unsure of anything else? When he asked her to declare her love she did so but without the depth he wanted, as if she were a child repeating a lesson to gain praise from the teacher. She kept him off balance and he didn't know how to handle it.

He forced his mood to lighten. "Sara," he whispered tenderly against her mouth. "Would you like to do it again?"

For answer she put her arms around his neck, pulling his face down to hers, uncaring that they hadn't bathed and that Nick's skin was rough and unshaved. "Yes, Nick," she breathed into his mouth. "Oh, yes."

Dr. Stamoulis was out on the terrace when Nick and Sara joined him later that afternoon. A glass-topped table set with a proper English tea had Sara surreptitiously raising her brows. Crumpets out here, in the Peloponnesus? Baklava would have been more appropriate. But Andreas was inclined to be pretentious, as she'd already found out.

"And where have you two been?" Andreas greeted them in a disgruntled tone.

"To heaven and back," Nick muttered near Sara's ear. Aloud, he said, "There was a flash flood and we were stranded in the camp."

"Where's Father?" Sara asked.

"He's gone to Athens. If you'd been here this morning, he would have told you himself. They wanted to question him further," Andreas finished hastily.

"He's not under arrest, is he?"

"Easy, Sara," Nick murmured, his hands on her shoulders.

"No," said Andreas. "He finished talking with the police. Some of the museum officials had questions. He went to see them. Naturally they're very concerned."

"Surely you don't still think Father stole the gold," Sara retorted.

Andreas shrugged. "Does it matter what I think?"

Nick poured Sara some tea. "Don't get upset, Sara. There's absolutely no evidence."

Sara swallowed the angry words she wanted to address to Andreas. Instead she asked. "How is Paul?"

Andreas's eyes were dull and listless as he answered her. "He's been released from hospital and flown to Athens. There've been no serious aftereffects other than the cast on his leg."

"That's good to hear," said Nick. "I guess we'll be going there in a day or so as well. We'll go see him."

"Are you going tomorrow?" Andreas asked.

"Not tomorrow," Nick said. "I thought Sara and I would take another look at the excavation site." He ignored her questioning look as he stirred sugar into his tea. "I've been thinking about that possible second entrance Sara saw from inside the cavern. I want to see if we can find it."

Andreas bristled. "Why didn't you look while you were up there last night?" He sounded disapproving, almost hostile, and his face became animated for the first time.

"Because of the storm," Nick said patiently. "And we weren't exactly prepared for camping overnight. We had no food or a change of clothes."

"I don't see what good it will do," Andreas insisted. "They've revoked our permits to dig, so even if we find another entrance we can't do anything with it."

"Maybe not." Nick shrugged. "But I want to look. Do you have any objections?"

Andreas fixed his eyes on his plate. "No, but you're wasting your time." He wiped his mouth with a napkin before carefully folding it and placing it next to his plate. With a mutter about work in his study, he left the table.

Later, Sara was quietly thoughtful as she and Nick walked on the beach in the soft amber twilight. Some part of her savored the warm strength of his fingers entwined with hers, but another part mourned the brevity of their time together. Unless the authorities held Daniel as a witness in the gold theft, he and Sara would be flying home in a few days.

"Sara, we have to talk," Nick said, pulling her to a seat against a boulder at the rocky end of the beach. The sun was down, the sea quiet. In the darkening sky a sliver of moon cast a gentle light.

He gathered her close to his side, sighing with the delicious feel of her slender softness. "Sara, have you thought that these two days could have lasting consequences?"

Something in his tone told her his mind wasn't on the missing gold. *Of course it will have consequences,* she thought dismally. *I've fallen in love with you and I don't see how we can ever make a life together. The consequence of our impulsive lovemaking is pain.* But she said nothing, waiting for him to go on, to supply some kind of miraculous solution to their dilemma.

"You could be pregnant, you know," he said starkly, the words hanging in the quiet. "I don't suppose you're on the pill or anything, are you?"

His matter-of-fact words rocked her. Pregnant? It was a possibility she hadn't thought of, and she should have. "No, I didn't think there would be any need."

"And I didn't think at all," Nick groaned.

"But I don't imagine there's much possibility that I've become pregnant," Sara added quickly. The idea boggled her so that she couldn't think of anything else. A child. Nick's child. What if there was to be a child? She could raise one. Maternity leaves were generous, and with careful management she could take a year off to nurse it, perhaps even keep on working. Her new position gave her a good salary and flexible hours. It was feasible. However, it wasn't likely.

"I suppose you know best," said Nick doubtfully, unwillingly remembering an earlier, supposedly purely philosophical discussion they'd had. His voice grew intense as he added, "But I want you to promise me that you'll tell me if you are. I don't want you to have my child on your own. I'll take care of you, no matter what. We'll get married."

"Married?" Sara echoed incredulously. "It's not possible. You know that."

A trickle of perspiration ran down his side. The storm had broken the heat and the evening was pleasantly cool, no reason to sweat except from the tension that assailed him.

He hadn't intended mentioning marriage so soon. He'd wanted to wait until all the other problems in their lives were wrapped up. But nervousness and her lack of an immediate response had caused him to blurt it out.

"What do I know, Sara? Why is it impossible? We love each other. We've both said so." If only it were that simple. Though he knew his love was real, he was uncertain about her feelings. Her declaration might have been only an impulse of emotion. Often people justified their sexual encounters by imagining they were in love. By her own admission she'd been celibate for years. Saying she loved him might be her way of rationalizing going to bed with him.

"I know," Sara said slowly, her mind in turmoil. "But you can see why it can't happen. Love doesn't just remove all obstacles. You have your life here and I have mine in New England. A long-distance affair just wouldn't work."

"Couldn't you move here?" Nick asked with little hope. He'd always enjoyed the company of women who were involved in a career, who were confident of their abilities and independent. Now he realized his acceptance of a woman's career had been largely cerebral, and he found himself wishing for simpler days when women dropped their own ambitions and followed their men. He wasn't proud of his sudden chauvinism, but he couldn't help it.

"Nick, you know that's out of the question. I've worked all my life to get where I am now. All I've done up to now is study and work. This teaching position at the university is the culmination of all my dreams. I can't give it up."

Not even for love, Nick thought bleakly, wondering if her love was worth fighting for in that case. "And if you are pregnant?" he repeated his original argument, sensing its futility. "What then?"

Sara heard the anxiety in his voice and closed her eyes as an indefinable response shot through her. "I'll tell you. But I don't think it's happened. It's not the right time."

He wasn't sure whether he felt relieved or disappointed. He accepted her statement; she knew her own body. But frustration lay like cold lead in him. He had nothing further to offer as a bargaining agent to keep her with him. He had offered himself and she had refused him.

"You have to understand, Nick," Sara added when the silence became oppressive. "I can't give up everything I've worked for. I wouldn't be happy without my work."

Anger flared in him and he hated himself for letting it show. "A fancy degree won't keep you warm in winter," he said in a clipped voice. "Neither will your work, even if it is in the most prestigious university in New England, or the whole United States for that matter."

"Then why don't you come with me? You haven't even suggested that." Her temper rose, and her voice with it. "Does it always have to be the woman who makes the sacrifices?"

Nick sighed again, his anger running out of him. "My business is here," he said quietly. "People depend on it. I can't leave."

So there they were, Sara thought, at an impasse in a struggle without a solution.

They walked in silence beside the whispering sea back to the house, and parted for the night without touching. Standing against her closed door, Sara felt scalding tears sliding down her cheeks but she dashed them angrily away.

She wouldn't cry. She wouldn't. Time enough for that when she left Greece.

But late in the night when she lay sleepless, she fought to keep from going to him.

Chapter Eleven

I found it," Nick shouted. "Sara, over here."

And there it was—another entrance to the caves, hidden behind a shrub near the spot Daniel had estimated it to be.

Nick shrugged off his small backpack and took out two flashlights, handing one of them to Sara. "It's better to have both lights even though we're not going that far. And we're going to stay together. I don't want you to get lost."

Sara's expression was somber. "After all that's happened, you don't have to worry. I'll stick like glue." She'd been concerned that the atmosphere between her and Nick would be strained after their argument last night, but Nick acted as if nothing had happened. The only change she'd noticed, and it hadn't struck her immediately, was that he seemed to avoid touching her. After the natural and easy physical contact that she'd grown accustomed to and found immensely pleasing, this was disturbing.

The opening was small, a narrow cleft between two enormous boulders, and they had to crawl on their knees to enter. Once they were inside, the shaft was as evenly proportioned as if carved by machinery.

Sara had worried that she would be frightened in this part of the cave where she'd lost her light, but no fear materialized. Even when they entered the bats' cavern she was only a little uneasy upon hearing the rustling of the creatures' wings.

Nick was careful not to shine the light on the ceiling as he swept it around the chamber. "Nothing here," he said, not really sure what he'd hoped to find. "Let's go back and check that other tunnel we passed."

Veering off the main tunnel near the hidden entrance, this passageway was almost too narrow to admit them. It was short, ending in a small chamber. Nick's lantern cast its beam around the rock-lined room and suddenly he whistled. "Will you look at that? They've been here all the time, under our noses."

There they were, the two small crates and the moldy bags of gold coins. "I knew they couldn't have been moved far in the time we were all away from the camp. And I'm willing to bet they're coming back to pick them up when the dust settles." Excitement animated his voice. "Come on, Sara. Let's get out of here."

"Aren't we taking the gold?" Sara asked as he propelled her toward the entrance.

"No, we'll leave it here and see who comes for it."

Sunlight blinded them for an instant as they stepped outside. "What the hell?" Nick exclaimed as the sound of voices traveled up to them.

His tensed muscles relaxed as the small group of uniformed policemen came into view. "That must be the police summoned to investigate this whole thing. Let's go down and have a talk with them."

After Nick and Sara finished with the police, they drove back to the house to find that Dr. Stamoulis had gone to Sparta. He was expected back that night, Eva informed them as she handed Nick a sheaf of accumulated mail that had been forwarded to him from Athens.

"So real life catches up," he grumbled. He turned to Sara. "Go on and have a shower. We'll eat as soon as you're back. Eva's left some dinner for us in the oven."

"Fine," Sara said, her tone preoccupied. Who had moved the gold? The police were going to keep a round-the-clock watch on the cave. Someone was bound to come and pick up the loot. She had to admit that their discovery didn't clear Daniel of suspicion. He'd had opportunity, if not motive. But then so had Andreas. And for that matter, so had the hikers who'd been in the camp that morning. Sara had to admit, though, that the hikers were less likely suspects since they couldn't have known about the second entrance to the caverns.

A crazy maze of possibilities chased around her head as she showered and changed. But no solutions.

Nick shifted through his letters. Nothing that couldn't wait, he decided as he took them into the library. He checked the desk for telephone messages. There were several but only one caught his attention. An urgent request to phone Professor Psaras at the university in Athens.

He pulled the telephone closer and began to dial, a frown drawing his brows together.

"What was that?" Nick asked incredulously a few minutes later. "You mean he didn't show up?"

"And he's not at his hotel and his car hasn't been returned to the agency." Professor Psara's voice crackled over the long-distance telephone lines.

"Have the police been notified?"

"Yes, but they're not too excited by the one-day absence of a grown man," the older man replied.

Nick raked his hand wearily through his hair. "I suppose you've checked the hospitals and emergency clinics."

"Of course, but nothing turned up."

"Okay," Nick said. "I'll get someone on it here, to check the route he took. We're probably panicking for nothing but in view of the theft and everything, I don't like the look of this." He went on to explain about the second entrance to the cave and what they had discovered there.

After he had hung up the receiver he sank into a chair. What could have happened to Daniel? One of his characteristics was his punctuality. If he had been delayed he would have contacted Professor Psaras and canceled his appointment. He would never have just forgotten or purposely missed it.

Unless—

He stifled the thought before it could take hold. Daniel couldn't be the thief, any more than Andreas or Paul or, for that matter, he or Sara.

Sara. How to tell her. No, he wouldn't tell her yet. No use worrying her for nothing, for something that might turn out to be only a lapse in communications. Time enough tomorrow after he'd talked to Andreas. Daniel might have contacted him and Andreas might have forgotten to relay the message. Andreas was often forgetful and erratic, especially lately. Yes, that was it. He'd wait until tomorrow.

He had to have tonight with Sara, without more problems distracting them. He knew she was puzzled by his attitude today but he'd been thinking about their discussion last night. She thought loving him would interfere with her career, did she? His jaw hardened. Well, he could still try to show her that she could have both—that his love was worth taking a risk. She could start a new career here if she married him. He wouldn't stand in her way, as long as they could be together.

When Sara came into the dining room, she found Nick there ahead of her, immaculate in cream-colored pants and a white cotton shirt. His hair was tamed by a vigorous brushing and still damp from his shower.

Her own dress was white, a frothy confection in eyelet, perfect for the warm evening. "Any messages?" she asked with a bright smile, determined to lighten the dark mood that had been hanging over them for most of the day.

Nick looked startled for an instant, then he smiled and she wondered if she'd imagined his surprise at her question. "No, no messages," he said quietly. "Were you expecting any?"

"Not really. I thought Father might have called to say how his meeting went, whether he was coming back here."

"But we're going to Athens tomorrow, aren't we?" Nick said. "You'll see him then."

"Of course," Sara said, her smile slipping as she observed Nick's peculiar agitation. "But since he didn't know exactly what day we were coming I thought he might have phoned."

The tension seemed to leave Nick's body as he pulled out her chair. "Perhaps he did, but Andreas didn't leave any notes. You can ask him when he returns."

Andreas hadn't returned by the time they were seated in the living room after the meal. Nick offered Sara a drink and she consented to a brandy. His mood was strange; he seemed nervous, jumping at every sound, most unlike him. His fidgeting was beginning to affect her, and she scanned the shadows in the far corners of the room, the play of light that came from the moon on the restless sea.

It was a beautiful room, furnished with lovingly polished antiques set on a muted pastel Aubusson rug, but tonight it seemed fraught with unrest. She cradled the snifter between her palms, inhaling the fragrance of the brandy. Dutch courage.

She wanted to be with Nick tonight. She didn't want another night like last night, when she'd lain sleepless in her bed, longing for him. But his abstracted manner didn't encourage her to make the first move. And after their argument last night she didn't blame him if he thought he should keep his distance.

She patted the sofa cushion next to her as he hesitated, deciding on a seat. "Sit down, Nick."

He sat, but she had the impression he was poised on the edge of the seat, ready to leap up at the slightest excuse.

Nick, for the first time in his life, was at a loss. He wanted her but he didn't want her to think her body was all he wanted. Seduction scenes had always been easy for him when it had been only a game. Now, when it meant his life, he didn't know what to do. He couldn't just grab her and start kissing her. She'd probably throw the brandy in his face. Why, when they loved each other, had they erected this wall between them? If they could communicate, he was sure they could overcome their differences. No problem was insurmountable when there was love.

He had to say something. She was sitting there, her face maddeningly composed while her pulse beat wildly in her throat. He could see the tiny flutter under her skin where a gold heart on a thin chain nestled. He wanted her in his bedroom where the pounding of the sea would be an accompaniment to their love.

The way he felt, he was reluctant to start anything here. Once he touched her he was afraid he would lose all control, and Andreas could walk in any minute.

They had to go to his room, not only for privacy but because there he had the protection he would use to prevent Sara from becoming pregnant—if she wasn't already. A baby might make it easier for him to persuade her to marry him, but he didn't want her that way. He wanted her only if she came to him out of her own free will, without coercion of any kind. With this in mind he had nipped into a pharmacy this afternoon during a brief stop in Areopolis.

Sara shifted her legs, crossing them. The front opening of her dress parted, revealing her knees and the beginning of her thighs. She was about to pull the dress back into place when she noticed that Nick's eyes had followed the movement of her legs. He no longer looked indifferent.

She parted her lips, moistening them with the tip of her tongue. "Nick," she whispered, and was rewarded by the sharp inhalation of his breath.

His heart leaped. "Yes, Sara?"

"Do you think Andreas may have heard something new about the gold?" It wasn't what she'd intended to say, but at the last minute her courage failed her. *Nick, I love you. I want to love you, and you to love me, in every way possible.*

"He didn't leave any message," he said. Was that all she was thinking? No, her pulse was fluttering even more quickly in the hollow of her throat. "Of course he doesn't know that the gold was in the cave all the time." His voice sounded strained and unnatural, and Sara turned to gaze at him.

"Sara," he groaned suddenly. "Don't do this to us. Let me have you tonight, in my room, in my bed." *In my heart.*

He broke off, appalled that he'd voiced his longing aloud. Bracing himself for her scorn or anger, he waited, his eyes fixed on her face.

Sara drained her glass and set it carefully on the table next to them. Delicately she took his from his hand and set it beside hers. "Nick, kiss me."

Wonder and love filled him as he tangled his hands in the abundance of her hair. "Sara, my darling, my love."

His mouth covered hers with a sweetness that flowed through her with tingling rapture. She gave a faint inarticulate moan of longing and pulled him closer. As she touched him and opened her mouth to receive the thrust of his tongue, raw hunger exploded between them.

Nick broke off the kiss, looked into her eyes. "Will you come to my room, Sara?"

She saw the soft glow of love in his eyes and in that moment everything—love, trust, maybe even a future—seemed possible. "Yes, Nick. Yes."

He picked her up as if she was the most precious thing in his life. Sara was aware only of the clean scent of his skin, the power of his arms and the burning of excitement in her body.

In his room, he set her on her feet before going to close and lock the door. He came back to her and slowly released the belt of her dress. The wrapped front fell open, revealing that she wore nothing underneath.

"Sara," Nick breathed, his hands brushing down her body, their touch almost reverent.

Sara forced her heavy eyelids up. "I want you, Nick. I want it to be perfect for you."

He was having trouble breathing. "Sara, it's a good thing I didn't discover that in the living room. We might not have got here."

He began to unbutton his shirt but Sara laid her fingers on his. "Let me, Nick."

He pushed his hands into her glossy hair and gave her a deep, searching kiss. Her knees went weak and her fingers trembled as she opened his shirt, one button at a time, caressing and stroking every inch of his chest as it was uncovered.

Pulling the tails out of his trousers, she worked her hands around his back, feathering teasing fingertips up the tiny indentations of his spine. Nick groaned, his hands painfully tugging at her hair. He let her go and ripped off the shirt, tossing it to the floor. He would have done the same with his pants, but Sara took his hands away, putting them on her bare breasts, soothing her tingling nipples.

Desire raged in her but she held it rigidly under control. She wanted him to remember this, her love. He would look back to this summer, and every subsequent encounter would pale in comparison with what he'd experienced with Sara. Instinct guided her, giving her skills a courtesan would have envied.

She peeled off his trousers and he kicked them aside. Then she hooked her fingers in the elastic of his low-slung briefs, slowly sliding them down his legs. Kneeling, she grasped his ankle and made him lift first one bare foot, then the other, to remove this last garment.

He had been forced to release her breasts when she knelt. Again his fingers threaded through her hair, weaving passion into its silky strands.

Sara put her mouth against the skin of his calf, the sprinkling of hair tickling her face. She moved slowly upward, her hand caressing just ahead of her lips.

His thighs were corded tendons under her palms, braced to hold his weakening legs. The hair on them was rough against the softness of her lips, brushing over her face. He shivered as she stroked his hipbones where the skin was smooth and hairless. Her mouth followed and the shiver became a shudder.

"Sara," he breathed. Her mouth became bolder, hot and sweet and wet on him. "Sara!" His hands clenched in her hair, the only solid object in a world gone crazy. Waves of heat swept up through him and suddenly he could take no more.

He collapsed backward on the bed, taking her with him. One sinuous twist of his body and he had her positioned under him, his mouth devouring hers.

"Sara, Sara, I thought I would die."

Sara was sure she had, as he touched her in the most intimate way possible, stroking and caressing until she was wild with the need to join herself to him. She moaned as he held himself away from her for a moment, then sighed rapturously as he came back. He lifted himself slightly, parting her thighs, and entered her, stroking her so softly the fire overwhelmed her without warning. The sensations took her breath away, as fire poured into her and over her, the fire of life itself. And as the ripples of completion faded, Nick gave a final convulsive shudder and lay still beside her.

"Sweet," he murmured as he fought to draw air into his lungs.

Yes, Sara thought drowsily, too spent to speak, sweet as liquid sugar. And, like sugar, the consumption of it only stimulated a craving for more.

"I only slept with you one night and I'm already addicted," Nick muttered. "I want you beside me every night."

Sara placed one finger over his lips. "Ssh. We have tonight." His legs shifted, sleekly moving against hers. With a sigh of contentment that refused to contemplate tomorrow, she burrowed against his body, letting sleep take her away on a billow of softness.

The light of dawn was in the room when she awoke. She was alone. She moved to Nick's side of the bed but it was cold. Where was he? Sitting up, she looked about. The dresser and chest of drawers were darker shadows in the faint light. Had he gone into the bathroom? No, the door was ajar, the room empty.

She got up, finding a silk bathrobe on the chair near the bed. It was much too large and she giggled as she rolled up the sleeves. She could have wrapped it around her waist twice. Tying the belt she padded into the bathroom. She turned on the tap and rinsed her face, drinking a little from a cupped hand.

Her thigh muscles ached slightly, pleasurably. Nick, she thought with a gentle smile. How loving he was. How beautiful he'd made it for her. She would have this to take home with her, this summer of love.

Back in the bedroom, she was about to slip off the robe when a sound arrested her attention. Straining her ears, she listened. Inside the house? No, it seemed closer. In any case the nearest rooms were unused.

A balcony ran past a wide sliding window. She pushed the sheer curtain aside and found the window partly open. This room was on a lower level of ground than the living room, only a short flight of steps above the beach. She stepped out onto the balcony.

Voices. She heard them again. Leaning over the rail she searched the lemon grove that grew beside the house. No one was in sight, but she could hear the tone of Nick's voice.

Footsteps sounded on the path leading to the beach. She held her breath. What had been important enough to draw Nick out of her arms and into the cool morning?

Nick and his companion were almost under the balcony.

"Have you told her yet?" Dr. Stamoulis. Her mind leaped. Her? Some instinct warned her they must be discussing her, Sara. Told her what?

Nick's voice too was clear. "No, I didn't want her to worry for nothing. We don't even know how long he's been missing."

Missing? Who was missing? Her fingers clenched on the rail. It could only be her father. Hadn't he reached Athens?

They were directly beneath her now and Sara could see the top of Nick's head as he emerged from under the balcony. She moved back, making sure she was in the shadows.

Dr. Stamoulis started to speak but Nick interrupted, "Not here. Sara might wake and hear us. Wait until we're in the house."

Their feet crunched on the graveled path as they went past. Sara stumbled back into the bedroom and sank down on the bed. The rumpled sheets seemed almost obscene in the light of day. So that was why he had made love to her. To keep her here so she wouldn't find out whatever it was he and Dr. Stamoulis were hiding from her, to ensure her blind trust.

And she had so willingly fallen into his trap, in fact had encouraged him, seduced him. Humiliation gnawed at her stomach. Damn, how could she have been so stupid? The gold theft, he was probably in on that.

Wait, maybe she was jumping to conclusions. Maybe she was all wrong. She looked around the room. If this was Nick's permanent quarters he must have an office and perhaps a telephone of his own. There were two doors, other than the closet and bathroom, in Nick's bedroom and she'd never had a chance to investigate where either door led. She got up and opened one of them. It was a storage cupboard filled with filing cabinets and assorted sports and camping gear.

She tried the door next to it and made a sound of satisfaction. A small office lined with bookshelves. On the desk by the window was a telephone.

She picked up the receiver, then bit her lip. What was the number of the hotel where her father was staying? She pulled open a drawer. Good, an Athens directory. Quickly she ruffled through the pages. Yes, here it was.

Five minutes later she knew. Her father hadn't checked into the hotel, and worse, hadn't notified them to cancel the room. Totally out of character. Her father was nothing if not methodical in his habits.

Something had happened to him, and Nick and Dr. Stamoulis knew about it and had deliberately kept it from her. She could understand Andreas doing something this underhanded—she'd never really trusted him—but Nick, she had been sure of his integrity.

She went back into the bedroom and began pacing. A sucker born every minute! She'd been a gullible idiot. She'd trusted Nick, allowed herself to be beguiled by his magic touch and his lying mouth, and all the time he and Dr. Stamoulis had been plotting against her and her father.

Her anger began to cool, and reason reasserted itself. Very few people knew the gold existed at the time it was taken from the shed. If Nick and Andreas had plotted to steal it, they had to keep her and Daniel out of the way until they disposed of it. Of course the gold was under police guard, but she had no doubt that Nick's cleverness would find a way around that.

But what had they done with her father? Were they holding him some place? Perhaps they'd even killed him. And what about the rock slide? Had that been an accident or a deliberate attempt to remove one of the witnesses?

The question remained: How were they going to keep her from going to the police? Did Nick really think that she was so blindly in love with him that she would keep quiet?

Nick with his deceitful mouth and treacherous hands. He'd even had the gall to say he loved her, all the while entangling her with lies. A memory from the night they'd just shared came to her, momentarily slowing her headlong tramping of the floor. He had whispered just before she fell asleep the last time, "No matter what happens, sweet Sara, I love you. Remember that, I love you."

"Love!" She spit the word into the empty room with its sweet love-scent and tangled sheets. "Cheat. Liar!"

The door opened, and Nick walked in and found his gentle lover transformed into a raging vixen. The face she turned up to his was murderous. "You heard," he said without inflection, all hope sinking to his toes. Nausea twisted his stomach. Nothing he could say would repair this.

"And what haven't you told me?" Fury made her voice shrill. She wasn't far from tears but she held them back by sheer determination. "My father's disappeared, hasn't he?"

His brows lifted. "You know?"

"After I heard you, I phoned his hotel in Athens. He hasn't been there. Nick, where is he? What have you done with him?"

"Done with him? You don't think I had anything to do with this?"

"Don't I?" she snarled, fists clenching at her sides. "Then why didn't you tell me he was missing?"

"I would have, this morning, but there's been another development."

"What?"

"They found his car," he said tonelessly.

Anxiety replaced some of her anger. "And Father?"

Nick shook his head. "They haven't found him."

"Of course not," Sara said scornfully, fanning her anger to overcome the sinking fear that threatened her equilibrium. "If he's been kidnapped or killed."

"Kidnapped or killed?" He looked so shocked that for a moment Sara wavered. "Who would do that? And why?"

"You and Andreas would, to gain time to get the gold out of the country."

He gave a harsh, humorless laugh. "Sara, you're crazy. If I'd wanted to steal the gold, why did I take you to it yesterday? That'd be pretty stupid of me, wouldn't it?"

This gave her pause. "Then where is Father? And why didn't you tell me he was missing last night?"

"Because I wanted to talk to Andreas first. I thought he might know something and hadn't left a message. He's pretty forgetful sometimes. And he did know something. That's why he was in Sparta. They have the car there. It was just lucky some shepherds found it. It went off the road between Kalamata and Sparta, into a deep gorge. It could have stayed there for years without being discovered in the heavy brush."

Sara's face was white, her eyes wide and fightened. "But they didn't find...a body?"

"No, and there's no way to tell whether he was in the car at the time of the accident."

Sara began to pace agitatedly around the room. "You had no right to keep it from me."

Nick sat on the edge of the bed, his face buried in his hands. "I know, Sara, I know. But I wanted last night with you. I had to be with you. I didn't want to upset you in case it turned out to be only a foul-up in communication."

"Upset me?" Sara's anger came back in a hot flood. "I'm not a child that needs to be cosseted. I had a right to know." A sudden thought struck her and she calmed. "At least this clears Father's name."

Nick lifted his head. "Not necessarily. He could have staged the accident."

"He wouldn't have," Sara declared. "He would have known how I'd worry. But you could have staged it."

His nostrils flared and his eyes glinted with a dangerously angry light. "I didn't, Sara. I couldn't have, as you'll realize if you stop and think. You've been with me all the time."

A tiny hope that she might have been wrong about Nick ignited inside her. "Well, Father didn't steal the gold, or stage an accident. I know him. He just wouldn't do anything dishonest. But what about Andreas? He had the same opportunity when we were away from the camp. Maybe you should check him out. This is a very luxurious house. How can he afford it on a professor's salary?"

"His family has money," Nick said sullenly. He'd expected her anger and once it cooled, he'd hoped she would look at matters objectively. Obviously blood was thicker than water, and their relationship hadn't progressed. He'd deluded himself. She didn't trust him.

He tried again to reach her. "Sara, I was only looking out for you, trying to prevent you from being hurt until we had something concrete to go on. I thought you would trust me."

"How can I trust you? You've done nothing to warrant my trust. You keep defending Andreas when you should be just as suspicious of him as of my father. Father was puzzled by his behavior at the site but he didn't accuse him of anything without proof."

"I'll look into it, Sara, but I'm sure you're wrong about Andreas."

"Just check it out."

"It may take a few days." Nick sighed. "I hate to go behind his back. Good thing we're going to Athens today."

"Today?" Sara broke in. "I thought we were going to postpone the trip. We won't see who picks up the gold from the cave."

"The police will inform us." His tone was remote. "I'll make inquiries about Andreas when we get to Athens. If he's innocent, as I'm sure he is, he need never know."

"How do I know you and he aren't working together?" Sara said coldly. "Maybe that's why you're helping with the dig, to steal artifacts if they're found. You've never really explained what you do for a living."

Nick felt he was losing ground at every step. "I don't deal in stolen goods. I don't have to. The company that financed the dig belongs to me. I don't need to steal to make money."

This information only slowed Sara for an instant. "Maybe you want the artifacts for yourself if not to sell. Or maybe Andreas does. He's a greedy man."

"Now you're really getting fanciful, Sara," Nick said, holding a tight rein on his anger. She was the most pig-headed woman he'd ever met and he felt like shaking her. "Anyway, you don't have to take my word for it. You can check my credentials when we get to Athens." He took a deep breath, frustrated by the stubborn look on her face. Gesturing toward the bed behind him, he asked, "Didn't last night mean anything to you? You said you loved me—"

"Not last night, I didn't," she interrupted, eyes flashing.

"That night at the camp you did, and last night you showed it. I'm sure you were never like that with anyone else. Can you throw that away?"

Sara didn't want to be reminded of her uninhibited behavior. It was piling humiliation on top of hurt and disillusionment. "Yes, I can. You talked about partnership but you haven't treated me as an equal partner."

A muscle tightened in Nick's jaw until she could see the bone through the darkly tanned skin. "Sara, is that what you think? Or is it what you want to believe? Do you want to know what I think? I think you're scared to give yourself to anyone. Last night proved how involved you are with me and it scared you. So this morning you grabbed the first excuse to put a distance between us. Well, it won't work. We have to work together until this is solved. We have to find Daniel and catch whoever is after the gold. So we're in this together, like it or not."

He got up with the air of a man who has taken command of a situation that was getting out of control. "Get dressed and packed and we'll get started."

A half hour later, showered and dressed in a cotton skirt and blouse, Sara waited for Nick by the front door. His car stood on the drive, the trunk open. Obviously he had been loading his things into it.

Dr. Stamoulis came into the hall from the living room and she eyed him with barely concealed distaste. "I'm sorry things worked out like this, Sara," he said in a voice that sounded insincere.

Mentally she shook herself. She was probably imagining things. "Yes," she said crisply. "I'm going to turn the whole situation over to the police and let them handle it."

"I'm sure they'll find Daniel," Dr. Stamoulis said smoothly. He put out his hand and she shook it. "Goodbye, Sara."

"Goodbye," Sara said, relieved that Nick was coming down the hall. Surreptitiously she wiped her hand on the back of her skirt. Andreas's hand had been awfully warm and sweaty for such a cool morning.

Nick nodded to her and she preceded him to the car. He slammed the trunk lid shut and, after calling a farewell to Andreas, got behind the wheel.

Their first stop was the village to pick up Sara's car. Nick waited outside while she collected her keys. The sun had become hot, chasing away the coolness of the night. He frowned, his thoughts dark and confused as he mulled over Sara's arguments about Andreas. Was it possible that he was wrong in suspecting Daniel? Was Andreas guilty? Sara was so adamant about her father and, after all, she was the one who knew him best. Maybe she was right.

But Andreas had always been like an uncle to him....

His eyes were on her as she unlocked her car and placed her purse inside. In her blue skirt and white sleeveless blouse she looked utterly feminine and desirable. A fierce urge to protect her and to believe in her raced through him. *Sara, I love you, trust me,* he wanted to shout. Instead he did the civilized thing. He held the car door for her and asked if she wanted to transfer her luggage from his car.

"We'll have to stop overnight somewhere along the way," he added. "So we might as well leave it where it is. We could even leave your car here and have the rental agency pick it up."

"I may need it in Athens," she said coolly. "Besides, they'll charge me an extra week's rental if they have to pick it up here."

"I'll pay it," Nick offered, wanting her in his car. The enforced togetherness would compel her to drop the impersonal aloofness she had maintained since leaving Andreas' house.

"I wouldn't dream of letting you," she said with dignity. "But yes, we can arrange the luggage this evening." She got into the Renault and rolled down the window. "What's the first stop?"

Nick ground his teeth in frustration. "Sparta—the police station. Andreas says they have the car and they've recovered some of Daniel's belongings."

Her golden eyes clouded over. "Okay," she said in a quiet, subdued tone. "I'll follow you."

He was about to turn away when she called, "Wait. Are we going past the place where the car was found?"

Nick looked at her, his eyes dark with sympathy. "No, Sara. We're going through Gythion and from there to Sparta. That's an easier and shorter route."

Sara nodded. "All right. I'll see you there."

Chapter Twelve

Sara gazed in horror at the twisted metal that had once been a car. No one could have survived inside it. She closed her eyes, fighting nausea.

Nick put his hands on her shoulders, steadying her. For a moment she forgot that he might be her enemy and buried her face against the clean-smelling front of his shirt.

Nick patted her head, smoothing her hair with gentle hands. "Sara, there's no sign that anyone was inside when it went off the mountain. Either he was thrown clear when he crashed or he wasn't in the car at all. There are no bloodstains."

Sara shuddered. "Then where is he?" she asked forlornly.

"I don't know," he said. "But the police are working on it. Come, let's see what they've recovered from the car."

The police had released the wreck, and it had been towed to the back of the rental agency's office in Sparta, a branch of the same firm Sara had rented her car from. She knew there would be papers to sign although the insurance would cover the damage. With a heavy heart she pulled away from Nick's embrace and entered the office.

Inside pandemonium raged. Two elderly American couples were shouting in English at the rental agent, who was rapidly losing any command he'd ever had of their language.

Nick stepped into the fray and in short order had straightened matters out. Not to Sara's satisfaction, however. When the dust settled she found that he'd traded her car to the travelers whose vehicle had broken down. "After all," he said blandly, "it's the same agency, so you get rid of your car and they can continue their trip."

"I've only had the car for ten days," Sara retorted.

Nick shrugged, maddeningly complacent. He could afford to be; he'd found a way to get her into his car for the long drive north. Now all he needed to do was break through Sara's renewed reserve.

With swift efficiency he transferred the few items she still had in her car, ignoring the black scowls she gave him. He waved cheerfully as the two couples, good spirits restored, drove off in the little Renault.

"Greece's honor is safe," Sara said sarcastically as she watched them go.

Nick raised his eyebrows, his expression amused and questioning. "What's that?"

"You've upheld the spirit of hospitality," she informed him caustically.

"Oh." He studied her angry face for a moment. "But it's been lacking where you're concerned, is that what you're saying?"

"Yes!" She stamped to the passenger side of the Citroën. "Shall we go? The sooner we get there, the sooner I'll be able to get away from you."

Nick reached her in two strides. "Slow down, Sara. We'll eat first. Then you'll feel better. Neither of us has eaten since yesterday so it's no wonder we're snapping at each other."

She was about to argue but her stomach had the last word. It growled, loudly and unmistakably. Nick gave it a poke with one finger. "See? Your stomach says you're hungry so forget what your mouth was about to say."

Sara let a reluctant smile lift the corner of her mouth. "Okay, Nick, let's go."

Nick was more than satisfied. He had some time to regain her trust. Even if they parted when all this was over, she would remember him with affection rather than with mistrust. And if he played skillfully maybe they wouldn't have to part. He had the rest of today and part of tomorrow to work on her. They would have to spend the night in Tripolis or Navplion. He would also have the evening. Dinner together, a walk afterward perhaps. Dark doorways and soft moonlight. If he could engineer a shared room for the night, it would be perfect. But no, better not tempt destiny. She would resent him more if he made love to her after this morning's accusations. Friends, that was what he would work toward.

"We'll have to stop at the police station to pick up Daniel's things," he said. "Then we'll eat."

The Sparta police, while sympathetic, had little to report on the accident. Only Daniel's suitcase had been in the car. Sara wasn't sure what else he'd had with him but he must have carried a briefcase for his notes and books. There was no sign of it, nor of his passport.

She mulled over possibilities during their rather silent lunch. Was it possible that Nick had grounds for his suspicions? Impatiently she rejected the idea with a stab of guilt at her disloyalty. Her father was not a thief. There had to be another explanation.

"Sara, I've been thinking," Nick said the next morning as they got back into the car after stopping for coffee in the pretty town of Navplion. "Maybe I did jump to conclusions about your father. He either had a simple accident or was forced off the road. You may be right that he's been abducted in order to keep him away until the gold is moved again."

"What about Dr. Stamoulis? Do you think he's involved now that you've considered the possibilities?" Sara's intuition that Andreas was hiding something was still very strong.

Nick took her cheeks between his palms, his thumbs gliding over her mouth. "I promise I'll keep an open mind and not let my friendship with Andreas color my conclusions. I'll check on his activities when we got to Athens and phone him to ask him more about those hikers the morning of the slide. Although I can't imagine how they could have found that other entrance to the caves." He paused, dropping a light kiss on her lips. "But I want a promise from you as well. Will you stay at my apartment until this is settled, just in case you're in danger since you also knew about the gold?"

Sara tried to pull away, and Nick's hands, which had slipped down to her shoulders, tightened fractionally. "Danger, Nick? You haven't done anything to me so far and you've had plenty of chances."

Nick let go of her. "Surely you don't still suspect me?"

Relenting, Sara shook her head. "No, I guess not. Do you really think anyone will try to get to me?"

"I don't know, Sara. I hope not. However, if they got to Daniel—it's better not to take any chances."

But to stay in his apartment where they would be together day and night? No, she couldn't. She was getting deeper and deeper into a web of love, and soon she wouldn't be able to extricate herself without mortal wounds to her heart.

"I can't, Nick," she said. "I need time and space to myself."

"I won't pressure you, Sara," he said tensely. "Actually, aside from the possible danger, I could use your help in following up leads to try to find Daniel." His voice became pleading. "Please, Sara, trust me."

Her chin lifted, her expression reflecting the stubborn determination he'd learned to recognize. He sighed in exasperation. "Sara, don't be childish. I've never jumped on you, have I? Surely two reasonable adults can share an apartment that has three bedrooms and three baths. You'll even have a choice."

Sara looked at him, amusement sneaking into her eyes almost against her will. "My own bedroom? You mean no sex?"

Nick raised his eyes to the dusty ceiling of the car. "No sex, if that's the way you want it. Haven't I been the perfect gentleman the past couple of days?"

She allowed herself a smile. "Only because you thought I was angry with you."

He snorted derisively. "So you think I'm scared of you, do you? I'll show you how scared I am." He reached for her and she ducked. Instead of bringing his mouth down on hers as she'd expected, he took her hand and pressed the palm against his chest. "See how my heart is pounding? That's how scared I am."

The crisp black curls were pleasantly resilient under her fingers as she slipped them between the buttons. The rate of his heart sped up even more, becoming as erratic as his suddenly accelerated respiration. She raised deliberately grave eyes to his. "Are you sure that's fright?"

He jerked her against him. "I'm afraid you won't be warm toward me again. Sara," he groaned against her mouth. "Don't be cold. I won't hurt you. It would be easier to hurt myself."

His desire not to hurt her had caused the rift between them but even that vagrant thought burned away as he kissed her, his mouth consuming hers, his tongue thrusting against her lips, banishing every coherent reason why she shouldn't be letting him do this.

He was panting like a marathon runner when he lifted his head. "There, now you look like my Sara," he said thickly. He released her. She might be willing at this moment, and he knew he could subdue her fears and doubts with sex, but he had no wish to open himself to more accusations that he was using her. More than anything, he wanted their relationship to be honest and open. Besides, he realized ruefully, he was getting too old to make love in a car.

Sara stared out of the window as he restarted the vehicle and drove onto the highway. Her thoughts were in a turmoil. She'd accused him yesterday morning of treating her as less than an equal. Her fierce independence had fueled this conviction. Now she wasn't so sure. Maybe he had been motivated by compassion, by his love for her.

Up until now she hadn't really faced the fact that his love might be deep and sincere, not just a phrase used during the heat of the moment. He'd mentioned marriage. Suddenly she had a strange feeling he'd meant every word he'd spoken. He hadn't argued very strenuously when she'd turned him down, but that didn't mean he was only going through the motions. His restraint since their argument yesterday morning showed he could use patience, waiting while she thought matters out.

Well, she would wait also, and see what he did next. And what they could turn up on her father's disappearance. It would be foolish to refuse Nick's help simply to prove a principle she wasn't very sure applied in his case.

"Nick," she said as he maneuvered through the frenetic streams of automobiles on the Corinth-Athens expressway. "I'd be happy to stay with you."

He threw her a quick, dazzling smile before swinging the steering wheel to avoid a taxi cutting into their lane. "Stupid idiot," he muttered.

Sara raised her brows in amusement. "If that's how you feel—"

"Not you, Sara," Nick said impatiently. "That nincompoop ahead of us who got his licence by bribery."

"Is that how you'll get the police to concentrate on finding my father?" Sara asked, a new anxiety surfacing. She did need him, more than she'd realized. What did she know of laws or customs here? Or even the language.

"Of course not, Sara," Nick said, cursing again as a truck skimmed his left fender. "The police are as honest here as they are most places, maybe even more so. We won't need to resort to bribery. That was just an obscure Greek joke."

"Oh," said Sara in relief. "How long do you think it'll take before we know anything?"

"Probably a few days. The thieves won't risk leaving the gold in the cave for long. About your father—well, it's impossible to say. Naturally, I hope it won't be too long."

In Athens, the building before which Nick parked the car took Sara by surprise. New, with modern clean lines that still blended harmoniously with its older neighbors, its distinctive design seemed to embody Greece's past and future. The structure was clever and practical, giving all the tenants a spectacular view of the city. A large forecourt had grass where children could play.

Its symmetrical contours reminded Sara of Dr. Stamoulis's house. "This is another of your designs, isn't it?" The same sense of amity with its site that distinguished the house in the Peloponnesus also made this building beautiful and unique, fitting without intruding on the austere landscape.

"Yes." Nick frowned, his expression puzzling her. Didn't he think he had a right to feel proud of his accomplishments? "Sara," he said, looking straight through the dusty windshield. "There's something I have to tell you. Remember I told you I helped finance the dig?"

"Yes, the company you own," Sara said, wondering what he was getting at. "You must do pretty well if you design buildings like this."

Nick exhaled gustily. "What I'm saying is that architecture is only one branch of the company. We also build buildings like this and we have branches in other countries, including some minor interests in the United States."

Sara laughed, relieved that he hadn't confessed to a propensity for bank robbing or bigamy or something equally bizarre. "So you're rich. I think I can forgive that. Why the big secret?"

Nick fidgeted uncomfortably. "Force of habit, partly. I've always kept a low profile. And I wanted you to judge me for myself. I was afraid you might suddenly change when you found out I'm not what you thought."

"Since we're only going to be together for a few days more, it doesn't matter." Her amusement at Nick's discomfort fled as dejection took over. She didn't want to leave him, yet she could see no way out of her own responsibilities and—yes, she might as well admit it—ambition.

His apartment was in the penthouse, high above the noise of the street and the film of smog the traffic generated. A faint hope she'd nurtured almost subconsciously that Nick could leave his business to live with her died as soon as she walked in the door. No man who owned this magnificence would give it up for a simple life in a university town. His business must be enormously successful to allow him to own paintings and sculpture such as those she saw displayed around the elegantly furnished rooms.

With the departure of her last foolish dream came the realization that Nick could very well be the buyer of artifacts like those they'd found, a buyer who didn't inquire too closely into the provenance of the objects offered for sale.

But this thought was only a fleeting one as Sara faced the glaring difference between her life-style and Nick's. This was jet-set living at its best; how could he leave it to follow her?

Knowing she was behaving irrationally, striking out at the man she loved because her dreams were so different from the reality of the situation, she erupted in anger. "Where did you get all this? A lot of it should be in a museum where everyone can enjoy it. It's a crime to hide these treasures."

Thrown off balance by her sudden attack just when he'd thought their closeness had returned, Nick lashed back. "Some of it *is* in museums." He picked up a statue of a rearing horse similar to those Sara had seen in the archaeological museum her first day in Athens. Holding it in one hand he fondled it, rubbing a finger over the rough spot where a leg had been broken off, passing his palm over the earless head.

Then, to her complete horror, he opened his fingers and dropped the little horse, smashing it on the dark marble floor. "That was a reproduction, Sara," he snarled. He took a step toward her, halting when she shrank back from the fury in his eyes. "Most of these are reproductions. And the others were obtained legitimately." He closed his eyes and Sara thought she saw pain in them before they were hidden by his lashes. The anger drained out of him as quickly as it had appeared. "Sara, when will you trust me?" he whispered.

Confused by the mixture of emotions she saw on his face, Sara opened her mouth to speak. Before she could collect her scattered thoughts, he added, "Forget it. I'll show you to your room."

True to his word, there was plenty of room for both of them in the spacious apartment. Nick went to his office every day, so Sara saw little of him. They met for meals prepared by Penelope, his housekeeper, but conversation was restricted to the weather and reports on Sara's frustrating lack of progress in her search for her father.

She'd filled out numerous forms in quadruplicate at the police station and contacted the American embassy. No one had seen a man of Daniel Morgan's description. It was as if he'd vanished off the face of the earth.

However, worrying over her father was not her only heartache. She missed Nick, pure and simple. Even though she saw him regularly, it was as if, in spirit, he'd already removed himself from her life. She wished she'd never blown up at him the day they'd arrived in Athens. It had been a stupid overreaction, the first weapon that came to hand to prevent her from falling even deeper in love with him.

It hadn't worked. Every night she fought against going to him. Every night she burned with a heat that blazed out of control the moment she closed her eyes and dreamed he was loving her.

The physical ache was the least of it; that she could take care of, if need be. It was the emotional hunger that grew stronger every day and every velvet night, the need for the unique oneness they'd shared so briefly. All the cold showers in the world couldn't extinguish that.

He called her into his study one evening when he'd come home late and missed dinner. He was holding a letter in his hand as he let her in. Going over to the desk, he sat with his hip on the edge of it, one leg braced, the other swinging free. Sara tried to keep the hunger from her eyes as she gazed at the glossy toe of his shoe swinging gently to and fro.

"I had a letter from Andreas today," Nick said in a voice that sounded tense, as though he were having difficulty controlling some emotion. "He says he's resigning from the university and is going away, perhaps to England or the States. He wants me to buy back the house."

Sara waited, sensing there was more.

Nick leaned over and picked up another paper from the desk. "You were right to insist that I check him out. His family fortune is depleted and he's in debt."

Sara was sure that Nick must be saddened by this potentially damning news about his friend. Her voice was rough with compassion as she asked, "Is that why he wants to sell the house?"

Nick glanced at her face, then his eyes slid away to fix on the wall behind her. "Not gloating, Sara?"

"Don't be stupid, Nick," Sara retorted. "I know what it's like to feel someone close to you has betrayed you."

He regarded her closely once again, seeing the rise of color in her cheeks. "I suppose you do. I'd forgotten." He hitched himself farther onto the desk, fingering the crease at the knee of his pants. "Being in debt doesn't make a man a criminal."

"But it makes him more susceptible if he thinks he can make some easy money and not get caught."

"Yes, I realize that." He sounded moody and disillusioned. "Especially if the money is owed mainly to a loan shark."

"A loan shark?" Sara echoed in disbelief.

"Yes, Vergis of the red Pontiac. It seems Andreas has been gambling. He borrowed from Vergis to pay off his gambling debts."

"Why didn't he sell his house to pay them?"

"Because, my dear Sara, he'd already mortgaged it to the hilt. Which raises another question—what's he going to live on if he leaves Greece?"

"The proceeds from the sale of the art treasures and the gold," Sara said flatly. "I think that's enough proof, Nick. Andreas has to be the thief."

Nick slammed the folded paper rhythmically against his palm. "It doesn't prove anything, Sara. But the next couple of days should. The gold is now in Athens in a warehouse. It was moved there by a couple of locals from the village who weren't told what the crates contained. The police are watching the warehouse to see who shows up to collect the gold. So we'll soon know who the culprit is." Nick was sick at the thought that Andreas or Daniel might be involved in the crime. The noose was tightening, but whose neck would be in it?

The wait was shorter than they expected. "It's over, Sara," Nick announced the following evening as he came in the door.

Her heart jumped into her throat as she took in his pallor and slumped shoulders. "Have they found him?" she whispered with dread in her voice.

He seemed to shake himself. "You mean Daniel? No, they haven't. They've arrested Andreas and Vergis for conspiring to steal artifacts and smuggle them out of the country. It seems Vergis was willing to take the gold in lieu of payment of Andreas's debt. "

Sara sank into a chair. "What about my father?"

He shook his head. "We still don't know if there's any connection. Andreas and Vergis were caught at the warehouse trying to retrieve the gold, and they're now showing signs of singing like canaries, each blaming the other. We'll know something soon."

"And if they don't know anything?"

Nick patted her shoulder. "Worry about that when it happens, Sara." He jerked away from her, pounding his fist into the palm of his other hand. "There has to be a connection, Sara. They'll find him."

Sara slept badly and woke early in the morning, logy and unrefreshed. She scowled at the rainbow that rollicked about the room as it reflected from the prism wind chimes at the window. Any satisfaction she might have felt for being proved right about Stamoulis was annihilated by Nick's devastation at his friend's duplicity. One way or another, Andreas had betrayed them all.

But where was her father?

She got up, and with a resolute set to her shoulders, washed and donned clothes for the day.

In the living room she stopped dead in her tracks, her heart plummeting. Nick lay on the sofa, one arm draped over his eyes, the other hand holding a large glass, which at intervals he raised to his lips. Her nostrils twitched as she smelled the sweet aroma of licorice in the ouzo.

"Nick, what's wrong?" Her voice was a hoarse whisper. "Something's happened to Father, hasn't it?"

No response. She knelt beside him, tugging at his clothes. "Nick, tell me. Tell me!"

Nick sat up, taking another long swallow before he spoke. "They found him," he said flatly.

Fear stole her breath. "And—"

"He's okay. Sedated but okay."

Her shoulders sagged and she rested her head on Nick's thigh. He stroked his hand lightly over her hair, then took another drink. "It's okay, Sara. It's really over now."

She lifted her head. "Where is he? And when can I see him?"

"Later today. He's in hospital."

Alarm again sped through her. "In a hospital? How badly hurt is he?"

"He's not really hurt. They kept him sedated so the hospital wants to check him out to make sure he's all right."

"How did they find him?" Sara asked, frustrated by his short answers. She frowned as Nick refilled his glass from a bottle on the table. "Should you be drinking so much?" She took in the haggard lines that cut into his face, the dark smudges under his eyes. "You haven't slept at all, have you?"

"Did you think I would?" he asked, fixing her with a bleary, bloodshot stare. "No, I've been out all night, first to the police station where Andreas finally spilled his guts when he saw they weren't about to bargain. Then we went to the flat where Daniel was being held and from there to the hospital. They'll let him have visitors later this afternoon."

Relief flooded her. "And he's not hurt? You're not just sparing me?"

Nick slid his arm around her waist and pulled her close to his side. "No, he's really all right." He took another swallow, his hand shaking on the glass so that it clicked against his teeth.

"But you're not," Sara said. "Shouldn't you be in bed, Nick?"

His arms fell away from her. "Don't mother me, Sara," he said, his voice taking on a tone she'd never heard from him before. He slammed the glass down on the table with frightening force. A long crack zipped up its side and the ouzo slowly seeped onto the table, falling in glistening drops to the floor. "Damn it to hell! Andreas was like an uncle to me and he used me. He used all of us, just for greed. He wanted money. He didn't care that we were his friends. He cold-bloodedly planned the heist and used us all as pawns."

His voice broke and he covered his face with his hands. Sara dropped to her knees, threw her arms around him and held him tightly. His shoulders heaved under her touch. "Nick, oh, Nick," she murmured, aching for him as his tears soaked into her hair.

"Sara," he gulped hoarsely after a moment. His hands left his face to tangle in her hair. The salty heat of his mouth engulfed hers. "Sara, sweet Sara." Frantically he kissed her face, his tongue licking up the wetness of her own tears. Sara clung to him, returning his kisses with all the ardent feeling in her. He needed her; she would give of herself until she had nothing left to give.

The intensity of their passion could not sustain itself forever and gradually the searching kisses and caresses cooled, became comforting and soothing. Nick lay against Sara's breast, eyes closed. He felt empty, as if all emotion had drained out of him.

Sara's fingers played in his dark, silky hair. "Do you think you can sleep now?" she asked quietly. Her mind was full of questions, but they could wait. The important thing was Nick.

He moved his head, his mouth nuzzling a wet spot on her dress. "Will you come with me, Sara?"

She nodded. Holding each other, they got up and made their way to Nick's room. Sara turned down the bed and Nick lay down without removing his clothes, snuggling her against him.

She lay in his arms, her heart filled with tenderness. Softly she kissed his parted mouth. "Sleep, Nick."

He exhaled a long sigh, letting his body go limp. "Call me if the phone rings. The police said they might need me to answer some questions."

"Yes, I will." With a gentle hand she smoothed the tumbled curls from his forehead, listening to his deep breathing until she was sure he slept. Only then did she move quietly away, leaving him in the bed with a sheet tucked over him.

The day passed with leaden slowness. Sara paced around the apartment, doing little odd jobs that didn't need doing. It was Sunday, the housekeeper's day off, so there was no one to talk to. She tried reading, but the words didn't make sense. Even the telephone was stubbornly silent and a couple of times she lifted the receiver to make sure it was working.

She checked on Nick at lunchtime to see if he wanted something. He was sleeping peacefully. Obviously he'd been up sometime during the morning for he was naked, the thin sheets faithfully outlining and emphasizing the long lines of his body. She gazed at him for a moment, then turned away before she could give in to the urge to touch him.

By midafternoon, feeling that the walls were closing in on her, she knew she had to do something. Purposefully clearing her mind of everything that had happened in the past week, she unearthed a cookbook in the kitchen and prepared a batch of muffins.

When they were out of the oven, filling the kitchen with their rich fragrance, she went back to Nick's room to wake him. The bed was rumpled but empty. Through the open bathroom door she could hear the shower running. She clenched her fingers into her palms. For a crazy moment she debated joining him, seeking the same comfort she had given him that morning.

No. No, not while so many questions remained unanswered. Not while her father lay ill in a hospital. Whirling, she sped down the hall as if fleeing from temptation.

Back in the kitchen she made tea. She had never seen Nick drinking tea but she found a packet of Twining's Earl Grey in the cupboard so someone must drink it.

"The best of England and America?" Nick said as he came into the living room and saw cups and plates set out on the coffee table. He looked rested, his eyes clear, his face smooth and closely shaved. Sara found it hard to believe that this was the man who had been crying in her arms just this morning.

"I had to do something," she said. "And you're probably hungry."

"I am," Nick agreed, helping himself to a muffin.

Sara poured tea into their cups. "No one's phoned. Is that good or bad?"

Nick shrugged. "Maybe neither. It just means they didn't need my testimony, at least for now."

"When can I see my father?" Sara asked. "Wouldn't the hospital have called me?"

"I don't know but I'll check for you right now." He looked up a number and dialed it. Sara listened to the incomprehensible Greek that rattled like machine-gun fire. When he put the phone down, he was smiling. "He's awake and we can see him any time."

Sara let out the breath she'd been holding and clasped her hands in her lap. "Oh, good. Then we'll find out what really happened to him."

Nick buttered half of his muffin. "I can tell you most of that, Sara," he said quietly. "Andreas really talked last night and it's not a pretty story."

Theft, abduction, possible attempted murder, betrayal—no, it wouldn't be. She waited for Nick to go on, her appetite fleeing.

Nick finished his muffin and washed it down with a cup of tea. Then he leaned back on the sofa. "As I told you before, Andreas was deep in debt. What you didn't know was that the hikers who came to the camp the morning of the rock slide were Vergis and a friend. They'd come to *remind* Andreas about payment. Andreas had no choice but to tell them about the gold. They said they'd be back for it after they arranged a little diversion. We'll never know if they meant to trap Daniel and Paul in the cave with the slide, or if they intended to kill them in order to reduce the number of witnesses. Nobody's admitting anything."

"But we found the gold in the cave. How did it get there? Vergis couldn't have known about the second entrance."

Nick smiled faintly. "He didn't. They were supposed to take the gold when we were all away from the camp. But city-slicker Vergis and his friend wandered a little too far afield after engineering the slide. They got lost. By the time they relocated the camp, the gold was gone. My guess is that Daniel moved the gold because he was concerned about security at the camp."

Sara nodded. "And since he didn't trust Andreas, he didn't tell him."

Nick's brows lifted. "Daniel didn't trust Andreas? I thought they got along very well."

"Not according to the last two letters I received from my father before I came here. It seems that strangers had come to the camp before and talked with Andreas. Since Andreas always seemed upset afterward, Father wondered what was going on."

Nick shook his head. "Paul didn't say anything."

"Maybe Paul didn't know. According to Father's letters, he and Andreas spent a good deal of time going over notes and cataloguing the items they'd found while Paul supervised the students' digging. Andreas must have been staking his whole future on that dig."

Nick's mouth turned down. "Yeah." He got to his feet and picked up the tray. "Shall we put this in the kitchen and go and see Daniel?"

Although Daniel looked pale and thin lying in the narrow hospital bed, he managed a smile when Sara and Nick came into the room. She ran to him, throwing her arms around his neck. Awkwardly he patted her shoulder. "I'm all right, child. I'm all right."

She smiled through her tears. "I can see that. We talked to the doctor and he says you'll probably be out of here tomorrow."

"Before you know it," Daniel assured her.

Sara gave a shaky laugh. "And you haven't done anything wrong. Everyone suspected you."

"Except Sara," Nick interjected. "She never lost faith for one minute."

"But why were you abducted?" Sara asked.

"Because I'd moved the gold," Daniel said. "Andreas was right. He knew I was the only one who could have. So they kidnapped me to force me to tell them where it was."

"But you didn't tell them, did you?"

Daniel shook his head. "No, the second day after I woke up in that flat they stopped asking."

"That's because we found the other entrance and told Andreas the gold was there." Sara shuddered. "We played right into his hands."

"Yes," said Nick, "but that probably kept them from hurting Daniel. They must have been pretty desperate. It was only by chance that the car was found. They hadn't expected us to be on to them so soon."

"But Andreas told us about the car," Sara said, a look of puzzlement in her eyes.

"To throw us off his track," Nick said. "The car by itself didn't tell us anything." He turned to Daniel. "How did they get you to stop?"

"That road's pretty quiet. As I was driving, I noticed a car pulled off to the side. It looked like someone with car trouble. When I stopped to see if I could help, they must have drugged me and driven me to Athens, pushing my car off the road to make it look like an accident." Daniel shook his head sadly. "It's hard to believe that Andreas was involved in a crime this serious."

"Believe it," Nick said bitterly.

"What about Paul?" Daniel asked. "Is he making a good recovery?"

The mood lightened. "Yes," Nick said, his face relaxing into a smile. "He's getting around on crutches. He'll be in to see you later, no doubt."

Sara noticed how tired Daniel was looking. She kissed him gently. "You need to rest, Father. We'll be here tomorrow to take you home. Is there anything we can bring you?"

A smile flickered in Daniel's eyes. "Some clothes. Mine got rather beaten up and I can't walk out of here in a hospital gown."

Nick and Sara laughed. "That we can do." Sara kissed her father again, and Nick shook his hand. "Tomorrow then."

As they drove home Sara couldn't help feeling some compassion for Andreas, misguided victim of his own greed that he was. Fortunately, her father was none the worse for his experience, so she was inclined to be generous. "What will happen to Andreas now?" she asked.

Nick drew in a rough breath. "I don't know. It will depend on the judge. They'll probably call it a first offense and be lenient on him, especially considering his age."

"What about his house, Nick? Will you still buy it?"

"Yes, I want to. And Andreas will need the money more than ever now to pay for his defense."

There went any hope that Nick might cut his ties here and accompany her to America, Sara thought with a sigh. She pushed the thought to the back of her mind. They still had a few days together. A miracle might happen.

Chapter Thirteen

That evening, Nick and Sara sat at the kitchen table after sharing a light supper that Sara had prepared in the absence of Penelope, the housekeeper. They lingered over coffee, not talking much, each aware of all that was unspoken between them.

"We'll bring Daniel here tomorrow after they release him," Nick said. "He'll want a couple of days to recuperate further."

Restlessly Sara cleared the table and began to rinse off the dishes in the sink before stacking them in the dishwasher. "We could go to a hotel, Nick. I don't like to impose on you."

He snorted. "What's to impose? This place is big enough." He got up and poured himself some more coffee, then sat down again, staring into his cup. The silence, punctuated only by the clink of cutlery on china, stretched until it became nearly intolerable. "How soon will you leave, Sara?" Nick asked at last.

She closed the dishwasher, setting its dial. "As soon as we can arrange a flight. I'm sure Father is anxious to get home."

"And you?" Nick asked tensely. "Are you anxious to get home as well?"

She wiped a cloth around the already clean sink. "I have to, Nick. I have to go back to the life I know, to my work."

"Your life." Nick clenched his fist around his cup, wanting to hurl it across the room just for the satisfaction of smashing something. Two or three days and she would be gone, leaving without another thought of him. She would remember him only as a light summer romance, soon forgotten as the cool winds of autumn brought work and responsibilities. Like the sweetness of summer wine, summer love was transient, without lasting qualities. It didn't travel well. In the autumn it lost its flavor, turning bitter on the tongue. He could taste the bitterness already.

"A Greek woman would follow her man." He knew it was a dumb thing to say, but he said it anyway.

Her chin lifted. "I'm not a Greek woman. I'm me."

He sighed. "Yes, I know. And it's you I love."

Even though his remark cut deeply, she refused to yield to the urge to throw herself into his arms, into oblivion.

Nick stared at her but she couldn't tell what he was thinking. "Sara, are you pregnant?"

Startled, she searched his face. Not a trace of emotion. "No. No, I'm not."

Nick looked at her a moment longer, then abruptly got to his feet, his chair scraping harshly over the tile floor. "I'm going out, Sara. Good night."

He was gone before she could utter a word. Sara stared at the closed door, a sense of irretrievable loss beating at her. A tear crept down her cheek. She squeezed her eyes shut. No, she wouldn't cry. She'd known from the beginning that she couldn't stay and had warned herself not to feel too much for Nick. She had only herself to blame for the pain she now felt. If only things were different; if only he would meet her halfway, compromise.

She scrubbed at the wet spot on her cheek. There was nothing to cry about except her own foolish weakness. Her father was safe, no longer under suspicion as a thief. In a few days they would be home, he in the familiar house where she'd grown up, she in her own apartment within comfortable driving distance of some of the best beaches on the eastern seaboard. In the fall she would take over her exciting new position.

She almost succeeded in convincing herself it was enough.

Daniel recovered quickly under the motherly ministrations of Penelope, who seemed oblivious to the fact that he was older than she and didn't need coddling. His restored health left Sara on her own during the day, since he spent most of his time meeting with colleagues at the museum and university. At this time of year, the height of the tourist season, flights were booked solid. To Sara's chagrin they had to wait nearly a week for airline seats to become available. She had no doubt that Nick had connections that would have facilitated their departure, but he was remote and uncommunicative these days and she didn't want to bother him.

It was for the best, she mused, tossing fitfully in bed on her last night in Athens. His kindness would have made the parting even more difficult.

Her packed suitcases stood at the end of the bed, her traveling clothes laid out on a chair. She and Daniel weren't leaving until after lunch the next day, but she'd been at loose ends during the evening with both Nick and Daniel out after dinner. She'd spent the time sorting and packing her clothes, fighting back tears at the thought that she might never come here again.

Restlessly she shifted in the bed. It was hot, typical of July in the sweltering city, with little relief after dark. She knew she should turn on the air-conditioning but that meant she had to close the window. The thought made her claustrophobic. Even the heat was better than the staleness of recycled air from a machine.

Her mind went back over the past three weeks. She supposed she should be grateful that she'd taken part in the kind of adventure she'd dreamed of as a harum-scarum child. In spite of the tight spots they'd been in, it had all turned out well. Stamoulis would even get his share of the credit for the discovery of the gold mask. It was quite a spectacular find, even if it didn't further their knowledge of the people who'd fashioned it. Andreas's reputation would not be totally tarnished. She was glad about that, for Daniel had paid a brief visit to him and returned with the report that the little professor was a broken man. Greed had blinded him to the treachery of his unprincipled associates, driven him to crime and deceit.

Nick was seeing to it that his former friend had the best lawyer available, and Sara admired him for the extent of his forgiveness. She knew from his reactions on the morning after the arrest that it hadn't been easy for him, and she understood enough of the Greek character to know that not everyone would have had his generosity.

Nick. Would he miss her? Or would he forget her as soon as she got on the plane, forget her in the arms of the next woman who came into his life?

The image of him with someone else made goose bumps rise on her skin in spite of the heat. "Oh, Nick," she groaned. "I wish things could be different."

She stared at the ceiling where the soft lights from the terrace outside her window made a shimmering pattern. Was he sleeping? Or was he awake and restless as she was, as she had been for days? Now that she thought of it, his eyes had been filled with the same unhappy shadows as hers, especially when he didn't know she was looking. Whenever their eyes did meet, his had a hard glitter to them, as if he hated her. Was sleep an elusive stranger to him also?

Another shiver passed through her. This was her last night. After tonight she would never see him again. His sister lived in New Hampshire, but that was far from Boston. It was unlikely that they'd even meet.

Suddenly she knew what she had to do—the need to love him one last time burned inside her. Did she dare?

Without giving herself a chance to weigh the reasons against this insane idea, she threw back the sheet and got up. She caught a glimpse of her slender nudity in the mirror and knew that Nick would never be able to deny her. Pulling on her thin silk wrapper, she stepped out of the French doors onto the terrace.

The city lay below her, a grid of streets outlined in lights. The ever-present roar of traffic was subdued compared to its angry daytime snarl. In the distance the lights bathing the Acropolis silhouetted the ancient structure against the amber sky.

She knew Nick was in his room. It was next to hers and she had heard him come in earlier. Would he send her away if she invaded his privacy? No, she couldn't let the thought take shape lest she lose her courage. He would welcome her.

His window stood open to the night air. She hesitated, biting her lip, then resolutely crossed the sill, her wrapper billowing around her.

The room was only partly in darkness. A light outside spread its soft radiance on the bed. Nick lay on his back, half under a sheet, his arms crossed beneath his head.

He was awake; she saw his eyes flash as he turned his head toward her. "Sara," he said, and his voice was deep and husky, filled with a boundless longing that reached out to her.

Sara drew in a long breath. Her heart was deafening in her ears. "Nick, I want to be with you." She tugged the tie belt and let the wrapper slide to the floor.

Nick threw back the sheet and she slid in beside him. He folded her tightly to the length of his body, stroking his hand up and down her spine. "Sara, oh, Sara," he murmured over and over, as if her name were an incantation that would keep her with him forever.

Charges of electricity flowed between them, sensitizing every nerve and sinew in their bodies. Nick's hand moved down to Sara's hips and pressed her against him. She felt his throbbing readiness and her senses leaped. Pushing one hand between them she touched him, giving a soft exultant laugh at the gasp of pleasure that escaped his lips. She would never let him forget this night. He would always remember the sweet wine of loving that he'd tasted this summer.

He pulled away from her to give her more room to touch and fondle him. And to give himself more space to touch her. Her nipples were swollen and hard and he sucked on them, first one, then the other, all the while caressing the sweet mounds of her breasts.

He tracked a searing path back to her mouth, teasing her lips with tiny kisses that only incited a need for more. His hand trailed down her body, softly, softly, on her waist, her satin-smooth stomach, lower until his fingers probed the hidden warmth of her. She arched her body toward him, her nails digging into his shoulders as she strained to get closer.

She couldn't think. She could only feel. She lifted her head, attempting to deepen the tormenting kisses.

"No, Sara," he whispered with a husky laugh. "Not yet."

She couldn't wait, she couldn't. The ultimate explosion was so close, a need that consumed her, and she couldn't reach it. But at the same time she couldn't wait, she had to reach for it.

She twisted in his arms, her body jerking, straining, seeking the elusive pleasure that lay just beyond her. The moan coming from her throat didn't seem like her own. She wasn't herself. She was a creature made only for sensation, a creature of sensation.

Nick suddenly thrust his tongue into her mouth, at the same time closing his fingers over the center of her. She cried out, her body arching, hanging there for endless time, as the great waves stormed over her, through her, finally releasing her. She collapsed in his arms, her body liquid and formless.

Nick let her rest, eyes closed. She was almost asleep when he slid his hand over her hipbone. Sara felt as if all her nerves lay on the surface of her skin, and she shivered. *No more,* she thought drowsily, *I can't—*. The idea was barely formed when she found she not only could, but she wanted to.

Sleep fled before the renewed fire his fingers ignited. He rolled over on his back and brought her with him. The intimate position made it clear to her that he was still aroused. She had been so far from reality that she'd barely noticed he hadn't entered her, that with awesome control he'd postponed his own climax.

She ducked her head, letting her long hair caress him. The tips of her breasts brushed his chest with molten heat. Her tongue dipped into his mouth and he laughed, trying to capture it with his teeth. She gave a throaty chuckle and let it tangle with his for a moment before licking her way down his body.

She moved to lie beside him, nipping first at the flat male nipples hidden in dense curls, then tracing the thin line of hair down his belly. Where the forest thickened again she hesitated, then went further, the tip of her tongue hot on his tense skin. The sweet-salty taste, the slickness of his skin, the faintly musky fragrance of him all combined into a powerful stimulant that sent her senses soaring again. This time she would not leave him behind when she reached that elusive apex of pleasure.

Nick suddenly grabbed her hair and brought her back up to his mouth, devouring her ravenously. He flipped her on her back and poised over her.

Sara's breath was trapped in her throat as she waited for that rapturous moment when she would feel him slide silkily into her, filling her, completing her. Nick paused, gulping a steadying breath into his lungs. He was on the point of exploding but he remembered what he had to do. He reached toward the drawer of the bedside table.

Sara divined his intention at the same instant. She laid her hand on his, her eyes pleading as she looked at him. "Don't, please, Nick. I want to feel just you inside me, just you."

Nick was shaking, barely in control of his raging need. "But what if—"

She put her hand on him, helping him to come to her. "Not likely. It's the wrong time." She wasn't lying, but deep inside her she nurtured a hope that by some quirk of nature she would conceive. She would have his child to remember him by, to forge a lasting link between them.

With an anguished groan, Nick entered her, plunging deeply as if he could reach her soul. The heated thrust sent her soaring into space, a space filled with wild, singing music.

Nick relinquished the tight reins of control he'd had on his body and let himself fly with her, carried to a place he'd never dreamed, where they were joined in a mystical, perfect communication, bodies and souls forged into one.

Again and again throughout the night they reached for each other. Sometimes they slept a little but one or the other would wake and begin the cycle of love over again, as if they could store up ecstasy against the empty years ahead when they would no longer know each other. In the morning they were exhausted, but Sara knew she would never regret this night.

As if in a trance she went to her own room at dawn. She slept for a couple of hours, then awoke listless and heavy-eyed, a far cry from the euphoria she'd felt on other mornings after they'd spent the night together. Strange, it seemed as if she and Nick had loved forever, yet they'd slept together only four nights and during some of those conditions had been less than romantic. But he was part of her, would be part of her forever. As she would be part of him.

Lunch was casual, served on the terrace off the dining room, but only Daniel did justice to the food. Both Sara and Nick picked at theirs, hearts heavy at the impending separation.

Their pain was not lost on Daniel. "You could stay longer if you want, Sara. There's no hurry for you to go back until September. Why don't you stay?"

"No!" Both Nick and Sara spoke at once, then Nick passed his hand over his eyes and gestured for her to go on.

"It's best this way, Father," she said. "Now that the dig is closed there's nothing to keep me here." She dared not look at Nick but she knew his face was grim and pale.

At the Olympic terminal there was a minimum of formality. Sara let Daniel go ahead of her to board the little shuttle bus.

She turned to Nick, putting out her hand. "It's been fun," she said with false brightness. "I saw a lot of the real Greece that tourists usually don't see. I broadened my horizons." Inside she was weeping, dying. Could a person be dead and still stand on her feet?

"What?" He looked blank.

"When we were stuck at the camp in the storm." She hoped her smile fooled him. It felt as if it were glued on her face and the glue was coming undone.

Nick searched her face, his eyes dark and somber. "Sara, I wish—" He broke off, jerking her into his arms. Oblivious to the stares of onlookers he kissed her with a passion that turned her bones to water. When he lifted his head at last, his eyes were wet and his breathing ragged. "*Adio,* Sara," he whispered. "Take care."

"Goodbye, Nick," Sara choked through the tightness in her throat. Blinded by tears she hurried to the bus. She didn't look back.

"I wonder if I'll ever get another chance to go on an archaeological dig," Sara mused several days later. She and Daniel were sitting in the back garden of his house, drinking lemonade and soaking up sunshine. An unexpected heat wave that rivaled the weather they'd had in Greece had turned Boston and its suburbs into a furnace. Sara had gratefully accepted her father's invitation to spend a couple of weeks at his house, especially since he was planning to take over a lecture tour that a colleague had been forced to cancel.

The air was heavy with the scent of roses, honeysuckle, cut grass and summer. A cloud of tiny midges danced over the center of the beautifully kept lawn.

Daniel opened one eye and looked at her. "I don't know, Sara. There are plenty of sites that seem promising, but money is always a problem. Unless they get a generous sponsor like Nick."

Sara had initially tried to suppress any thought of Nick, eventually declaring an uneasy truce with her feelings for him. She was surprised to discover, though, that just the mention of his name could stir her blood. She hoped this heart-wrenching awareness would soon pass as she resigned herself to living without him. "Is he that wealthy?" she asked, keeping her voice neutral. The sumptuous appointments of his apartment indicated that he was very well-to-do, even though he had told her that his family had collected art for generations. Much of what she'd seen had been inherited. Even now a rueful smile broke out on her lips as she remembered how she had accused him of stealing works of art. Nothing could have been further from the truth.

"He has a lot of assets," Daniel said slowly. "But it's difficult to say how wealthy he is. He's not one to advertise his life-style."

"Then architecture is only a sideline."

Daniel reached over to fill his pipe. "No, I believe architecture is his real love. The construction business, the interests in shipping, his connection with Greek archae-

ology, all of those came from various branches of his
family. They haven't been notably prolific in recent generations, so the task of running the family conglomerate
has fallen largely on Nick.'' He put the filled pipe between his teeth and puffed until he had it going, pale
smoke wreathing his head. ''One of Nick's professors in
college is a friend of mine, and he gave me something of
his background before I went on the dig. Of course I'd
met Nick years ago when he was a student in one of my
classes.'' He looked shrewdly at Sara, squinting slightly
against the smoke. ''You probably don't remember.''

Sara gave an awkward and slightly embarrassed laugh.
''Nick mentioned it but I still don't recall it myself. I felt
it gave him some kind of advantage over me that he remembered our first meeting and I didn't.'' She toyed with
her lemonade glass, making wet rings on the yellow
plastic tabletop.

Daniel's shaggy brows lifted. ''Advantage, Sara? Is
that what you thought? Or is it just an excuse to explain
why he could touch you when no one else has been able
to? I may be your old father, but even I could see the
electricity between you and Nick.''

Sara traced the wet rings on the table with her fingertip, surprised and a little embarrassed at her father's unexpected frankness. Then she leaned back and ran her
fingers through her hair, closing her eyes. ''There's no
use making a big thing of it. There was no future for us,
no possible way we could be together.''

Daniel made no reply, puffing in silence and filling the
still summer air with intricate smoke rings. His lack of
reaction irritated her and she sat up abruptly, swinging
her legs to the ground and glaring at him. ''Damn it, Father, he could have given a little, too. He expected me to
give up my career just when I've become a success.''

"There are many definitions of success," Daniel said, without taking his eyes from a study of the leaf patterns in the tree over their heads.

"Maybe, but what about him? Why couldn't he give up his career? Is it so much more important than mine?"

Daniel shifted in his seat. "From an economic point of view, yes," he said a touch acerbically. "A great many people depend on him. It's a romantic myth that a person will just drop everything that's important to him and give it all up for love. If you think that, Sara, you're not living in the real world. You're still believing fairy tales."

Sara said nothing and after a moment Daniel added in a gentler tone, "Listen to your heart, Sara. Happiness is also a form of success. Like most strong women you've been looking at only the practicalities and doing what your head tells you is the right thing. Don't forget men get hurt, too, when they fall in love."

"Oh, Father, you're wrong," Sara said with faint exasperation. "Women are the ones who suffer. Men just keep sailing blithely along without giving women a thought until they need them again."

"Is that right?" Daniel sat up, training his gaze on her. He took his pipe from his mouth and set it in an ashtray at his elbow. Leaning forward he took Sara's two hands in his. "Sara, maybe I tried too hard to protect you when you were growing up, and maybe I put too much emphasis on studying and making something of yourself—"

"I wanted to make something of myself, to be independent," Sara interrupted. "You didn't have to push me."

"Perhaps not, but I still should have taught you more about life, taught you to be softer when the situation warrants it. When I hear you say men don't have the same feelings women do, I know I've failed somewhere.

No—" he lifted his hand to stop the words that tumbled to her lips "—no, let me finish. You have to realize that men suffer just as much over love, maybe more because we're taught to hide our emotions and that makes the pain greater. When we fall in love, it's often deeply and sometimes hopelessly. We have no more control over it than your sex."

Sara realized he must be referring to her mother, the only woman he'd ever married and thus, in Sara's mind, the only woman he had loved. "Did you feel like you were dying when Mother left?" she asked slowly. "I did, and again when I left Nick at the airport." She laughed humorlessly. "We both seem to be unlucky in our relationships."

"It's not too late for you, Sara," Daniel told her, his voice becoming contemplative. "Yes, I missed your mother. But I was lucky to have her as long as I did. It was probably harder on you. Children always seem to blame themselves when a marriage breaks up but usually the seeds of failure were there long before. Our marriage was bound to fail from the first day. She was a butterfly. She couldn't be caged. I was wrong to try."

"Then why does she keep marrying, if she wants freedom?" Sara asked bitterly.

"Because basically she's a conventional person. She can't settle down and yet she abhors promiscuity, especially since it's so common among her friends. So she marries."

"She's shallow," Sara said, and in the inflexibility of her tone she heard the child abandoned by her mother.

Daniel sighed. "Yes, she is. But none of her husbands hate her. I know I don't."

The echo of that long-ago argument drifted through Sara's mind like an ephemeral ghost. "Didn't you then, Father, when she left?"

"Perhaps for a week or two," Daniel admitted. "But I couldn't keep hating someone so effervescent, so full of life. The world needs some butterflies."

But Sara was an ant, toiling to prepare for winter, practically an immutable part of her nature. She remembered something Nick had said to her early in their relationship, which she had fiercely resented at the time: *Don't be so uptight, Sara. The world isn't going to fall apart if you have fun once in a while.*

The world hadn't. It had taken on new light, new life. She'd allowed him into herself in much more than a physical sense, and her life had been enriched.

But now she had to put that behind her, store it away like the photographs of a vacation, brought out only occasionally to be viewed with bittersweet nostalgia.

Three weeks, such a tiny portion of an entire life span. Yet those three weeks had the bright magic to color all the years ahead of her.

Chapter Fourteen

Nick sat in his office on the top floor of one of Athens's most striking new buildings. His chair was turned away from his desk, and he idly rolled a pencil between his fingers as he gazed out of the window. The day was bright, high summer, and the brilliant cobalt sky was only slightly dulled by a haze of smog. Traffic blared in the hot streets below, attesting to the annual tourist invasion, that essential backbone of the Greek economy. He saw and heard none of it.

His mind was on Sara and how forlorn she'd looked a week ago as she'd walked away from him at the airport. He had hoped, up until the last minute, that she would change her mind and stay. He knew he'd had no right to think that, but the human mind and heart are strange, never giving up until all hope dies. His fingers tightened and with a sharp crack the pencil snapped. He had not been able to hold Sara; she had gone, walked away without looking back.

And his love, his passionately real love, had been shoved into the background of her life.

Then why hadn't he been able to get her out of his head? It was obvious that she hadn't really loved him. If a woman loved a man, she stayed with him. Women were willing to sacrifice, at least he'd always believed that until now.

But not Sara. Sara had her career, her precious independence, which was more important to her than he was. She probably hadn't given him more than a fleeting thought since she'd left. If she'd thought of him at all.

While his mind was filled with her, until he couldn't eat or sleep or concentrate on his work.

He closed his eyes, reliving for the thousandth time their last night and that final scene at the airport. That night he had hoped. She had come to him, and their unity had been so flawless, so deep and perfect, that he had been sure of her love. Yet, in the morning, she'd left.

How could she? Hadn't the going torn a wound in her as it had in him? He pounded his fist on the arm of the chair, wincing as pain wrenched up to his shoulder, but the physical pain was nothing compared to the bleeding emptiness inside him.

He swiveled the chair to face the desk, and his eyes fell on the pen stand with its discreetly embossed gold plaque. The highest award for architecture in Europe last year for a building he'd designed and his company had built.

With an oath he swung one arm and swept a stack of papers to the floor. What good was all this—success, riches, acclaim—without Sara?

The intercom chirped once, startling him. He depressed the Talk button. "Mrs. Carydis, didn't I make it clear I don't want to be disturbed?"

"I'm sorry, Mr. Angelopoulos," his staid, middle-aged secretary said apologetically. "But this man says you gave him an appointment a month ago. That was just before your trip to the Peloponnesus. He's on a tight schedule."

On the point of telling her what the visitor could do with his tight schedule, Nick stopped, a memory surfacing. "What does he want?" he asked wearily.

"He says he's in computers," came her reply.

Nick sighed. "Let him in."

Two hours later Nick and the computer salesman were having a drink in the bar of the Grande Bretagne. A weight seemed to have fallen from Nick's shoulders since the man's arrival.

Nick raised his glass in an exultant salute, somewhat to the man's bewilderment. He had the answer to all his problems.

Now if only he could persuade Sara.

The country restaurant Sara entered later that week had an old-fashioned ambience that appealed to her at once. Bright sunlight followed her in, easing the depression that dogged her days since she'd left Greece, and erasing the misgivings she'd had about keeping this appointment.

The woman who rose from a seat just inside the door was nearly as tall as Sara. The friendly manner with which she offered her hand, and her warm smile so like Nick's, put Sara instantly at ease. "Hello, I'm Stephanie Johnson. You must be Sara. You're exactly like Nick described you."

"I'm so happy to meet you," Sara said. After Stephanie's unexpected phone call two days ago, Sara had anticipated this meeting with a certain apprehension. Would seeing Nick's sister revive all the pain she'd managed to subdue since leaving Greece, the pain that only came back to haunt her in the dark reaches of the night?

But now, she knew she'd done the right thing. Stephanie, with her firm handshake and warm brown eyes, was everything Nick had indicated in words and by implication—kind, understanding, charming.

A waiter led them to a table and took their orders. While he was consulting Stephanie about an appropriate wine, Sara studied her. A slender woman with curling dark hair and a handsome rather than pretty face, she looked much younger than the forty or forty-one Sara knew her to be. Both her unabashed zest for life and her smooth unlined skin made her appear youthful.

Sara came out of her brief reverie with the realization that the waiter had left them and Stephanie was scrutinizing her with equal interest. For a moment they were silent, each woman a little unsure of what to say to the other. Sunshine streamed through the small-paned window next to them, creating patterns of light in the crystal glasses and dancing sunspots on the immaculate table linen. Sara's spirits lifted. Yes, Stephanie had been right to instigate this meeting and it wasn't painful as she'd feared.

At first they chatted about neutral topics, laying the foundations for a friendship they both knew was possible. Stephanie had three children, a boy—a man really, she laughed—of twenty, and two girls aged fifteen and eleven. Her husband was the manager of a large shopping center near their home outside of Manchester, a city with an active Greek community. In turn Sara told her of her new position teaching history, and her voice was filled with pride as she thanked Stephanie for her congratulations.

"Quite a plum job, isn't it?" Stephanie said in sincere admiration. "I'll be at school in the fall. My last year of law."

Sara lifted surprised brows. "That's a tough course of study."

"You mean for an old lady with almost grown children?" Stephanie asked with an infectious laugh.

"Of course not," Sara protested, laughing.

Stephanie waved aside her attempted apology. "Never mind. Tell me what you thought of Nick."

Sara couldn't hide the ache inside her as her golden eyes grew misty. "I love him," she said simply, surprising herself that she could so readily admit this to Stephanie an hour after they'd met. She'd never had close women friends in whom to confide, but with Stephanie she felt she could say anything. Kindred souls, she thought in astonishment. She'd never believe that clichéd term, never thought it would apply to her.

"He loves you too, you know," Stephanie said, touching the back of Sara's hand.

Sara's eyes blurred with tears and she swallowed to keep them from falling. Her throat was tight. "It was impossible," she blurted out. "I couldn't stay there and he couldn't come here. Sometimes I wish I could wipe out all memory of him, it hurts so much."

Stephanie held her hand for a moment. "Don't Sara," she said gently. "Things have a way of working out when you least expect it. When I met Adam we thought we'd never be free to marry, either. He was a tour director in Greece for the summer, and I didn't see any possibility of coming here."

"You didn't have a job, though, a career you'd worked all your life for," Sara said. "It wasn't the same."

"I was studying law at Athens University," Stephanie said. "I could have transferred to a college here but my father was ill and I couldn't leave him. When my father died unexpectedly, Adam persuaded me to marry him and emigrate. He was so kind, even taking in Nick, who was only a child and bewildered that the father he'd adored had left him. Adam was wonderful. What man would marry a woman who had to bring up a younger brother?"

"A man who loved you," Sara said.

"Yes, a man who loves me," Stephanie said seriously. "As I'm sure Nick loves you."

"Perhaps not enough," Sara said with a trace of bitterness.

Stephanie stirred sugar and cream into her coffee. "You can't measure love, Sara. You can't put conditions on it, the kind of conditions that say if you loved me you'd sacrifice for me. Compromise is what brings people together, not sacrifice. You and Nick will have to find the right compromise."

Sara sighed. "I know. That's what my mind tells me, yet my heart wishes it were simpler. I guess I'm looking for a knight on a white horse who'll carry me away. Instead I fell in love with a real man. Anyway, the knight idea offends everything about independence I've ever believed. I don't want to need a man to solve all my problems."

"But they're nice to lean on when you need a friend, if you find a man like that," Stephanie said astutely. "I've always wondered how women can marry men who aren't their friends first of all."

"That's how I felt about Nick from the beginning," Sara said. "And it came to nothing."

"Don't give up and join a nunnery, Sara," Stephanie said with a smile. "I'm sure Nick is working on something right now. Don't forget I was practically his mother and I know him. He never gives up when he sets his mind on something. And he works fast to get what he wants. No patience at all. You should have seen him at Christmas, feeling all the presents until the wrappings were decidedly shabby. It will work out and you'll really be my sister.''

So Stephanie had felt the instant kinship between them as well. "I wish it could," Sara said. "I'd be proud to be your sister."

"As for your career, Sara, you don't have to worry about Nick interfering in that. He would want you to have it, if it makes you happy. He would encourage you in your work."

The waiter brought their check on a small tray. "I'll get it this time, since I invited you," Stephanie said. She laid a bill on the tray and smiled at the young man. "Keep the change."

"We must do this again," she added as they walked toward the door.

Sara smiled. "The next one will be my treat."

"Just make it soon," Stephanie said, giving her a warm hug. "We'll keep in touch. Before the summer is over you must come to our house and meet Adam and the children." She gave Sara one last squeeze. "Remember, Sara, look at what's in your heart and meet Nick halfway. He's worth it."

Tears pricked Sara's eyes although a smile came over her face. "Goodbye, Stephanie."

She was still smiling as she drove down the highway toward home.

Her talk with Nick's sister gave Sara a lot to think about during the next several days, but no solution. Stephanie had not hesitated to give up her own ambitions for Adam, but Sara wasn't Stephanie, neither were their situations exactly parallel.

And if she did give up her career, would Nick take her back after she'd left him with the impression she'd only been having a summer fling?

One night she had a dream in which she saw his face as plainly as if he had been standing in front of her. He appeared as he had been that last moment at the airport, when he'd kissed her so desperately. At the time her vision had been blurred by her own tears. In her dream, her memory made her see clearly. His dark eyes had also been filled with tears, and the love in them was unmistakable, love and the agony of seeing her walk out of his life.

She woke in a golden summer dawn, her mind lucid and made up. Jumping out of bed, she yanked on a robe and hurried to the desk in her father's study. There she typed two letters and their envelopes, sealing them carefully and affixing the correct postage, as well as an airmail sticker to the fatter of the two.

This done, she went back to bed and slept until noon, the most restful sleep she'd had in weeks.

In the afternoon she tackled work in the garden that she'd been postponing. She had promised Daniel she would look after the house and she'd barely kept up the essentials. It was too beautiful a day to spend indoors anyway, especially with the new buoyancy her decision had made in her spirits.

Dressed in an old shrunken T-shirt and faded, raggedly cut-off jeans she was reaching up to clip dead blossoms off a tall Queen Elizabeth rose when two warm hands grasped her waist from behind. "I always knew it—you have the cutest behind I've ever seen."

Her heart stopped, then raced ahead at an alarming pace. "Nick," she mouthed silently without turning around. She would know those hands if she were separated from him for a thousand years.

Dropping her clippers she whirled to face him. "Nick, how did you know? I wrote you. You couldn't have received my letter. I only mailed it today." The words tumbled over one another, losing coherence with every beat of her heart.

Nick laughed, lifting her off her feet and swinging her around. "Sara, you're babbling. Does that mean you're glad to see me?"

"Glad?" She hid her face in the hollow of his neck, breathing in the tangy male fragrance of him as if it gave her life. "Oh, Nick, I missed you so."

His laughter vanished. He buried his face in the sweet, silken mass of her hair. "And I nearly died without you." He kissed her, his mouth hard and passionate, hurting her with its intensity, a sweet pain that sent joy singing through her.

She kissed him back, rapturous tears flooding from her eyes. Although she couldn't recapture the kisses she'd missed during the weeks they'd been apart, she tried to recoup their loss the first minute they were together.

He pulled them both down on the resilient grass, his legs twining with hers. Sara couldn't get enough of the delicious feel of him and writhed voluptuously under him. The clothes that kept them from really touching were driving her mad. She tore at his shirt buttons, finally baring his chest. Her T-shirt had ridden up and when her bare breasts came into contact with his skin she groaned and arched closer.

"Sara, Sara," Nick moaned into the open, receptive heat of her mouth. "Sara, I love, I want you, I need you...."

His gasped words were accompanied by subtle thrusts of his body against her, driving her to a frenzy. Her hands were at his waist, struggling with the intricacies of his zipper when he stopped her.

"Sara, not here, in full view of the whole world." Tenderly he brushed the damp hair from her forehead, drawing her to her feet.

Her legs were shaking, but she was calm again, conscious of the warmth of his bare skin against hers, and even more conscious of the love emanating from him. She looked up at him, their eyes meeting in a communication as profound as the deepest lovemaking.

Wordlessly he held her, his hands clasping her head. She pressed her face against him, breathing in the wonderful, real essence of him. How could she ever have contemplated a life without him? Great silent tears slid down her cheeks and Nick kissed them away.

"Sara, I love you."

Much later they lay together on Sara's bed in the languorous contentment of love fulfilled. Sunlight from the open window bathed their entwined bodies in a shimmer of gold permeated with the scent of roses. Early-evening birdsong drifted around them like a benediction.

Nick ran a tender finger down Sara's nose and traced her lips, warm and pink from his kiss. She playfully bit his fingertip, then rolled it over her tongue, savoring the salty-sweet flavor of him—loving him.

Nick sighed, his eyelids drooping in lazy tranquillity. Sara saw the dark circles under his eyes and knew he'd suffered in the same way she had. Her gaze caressed the long lines of his body and she saw that his ribs were more prominent than they had been, as if he hadn't been eating enough. Did he see the same changes in her?

Suddenly she shivered, a cold fear gripping her stomach. They had just made love as if they'd never been apart, but what if he hadn't come to stay? She'd been so happy to see him she hadn't given it a thought. Now she realized he hadn't said a word about the future.

Nick felt the tremor that shook her and held her closer, inhaling the gardenia scent of her skin. "Sara, are you cold?" he asked drowsily. "Oh, it feels good to hold you like this. We'll never be apart again. Every night I found myself thinking that just to hold you one more time would be a luxury I'd give everything for. And now I can hold you every night."

Sara relaxed, curling herself into his body. His muscles, so tense and hard earlier, were at rest, pliant against her. She sighed in pleasure; she had brought this peace to him.

After a moment he spoke again. "I found a way to solve the problem of our career conflict, Sara. We're going to buy a house here and get married."

A house? Married? Was it possible? She'd been willing to settle for less. Her lassitude fled and she raised herself on one elbow and looked down at him, her mouth curving with mischief. "Shouldn't you ask me first, Nick?"

His eyes opened, blue as the midnight sky, shadowed with sensuality and satisfied love. "I didn't have to, Sara. I read your mind."

"And what else do you read, Nick?"

"That you love me. That you need me."

Sara sighed gently and stretched herself next to him. "Yes, I need you," she said quietly, no longer ashamed of feeling this way. "I'm only half alive without you." There was a moment of silence, then she asked, "What about your business, Nick?"

A hint of laughter played around his magical mouth. "That's what I was trying to tell you, Sara," he said with mock severity. "But you distracted me."

Sara tangled her fingers in his hair and playfully tugged. "So tell me now."

He looked at her, humor crinkling his eyes so endearingly she was tempted to forget the whole thing and make love to him again. "Computers, my darling. They're going to solve all the problems. With a computer hookup I can run my business from anywhere in the world, from a South Sea island, from my Athens office or from here. Of course I may have to fly to Athens once a month or so, but it would only be for a couple of days at a time. And once I get more people trained, even that shouldn't be necessary. I can concentrate on architecture, which I've had too little time for lately. I can do that anywhere."

Sara watched him, bemused, lost in the dark sea of his eyes. So it was really true. He had compromised so that she could pursue her own career.

Nick shook her a little, laughing. "Don't go to sleep on me, Sara. Aren't you going to say anything?"

Sara gave a shaky laugh, staggered by the unexpectedness and efficiency of his solution. Stephanie hadn't lied about his propensity for getting what he wanted. "We can live in Greece if you have to," she said at last. "I wrote you a letter, telling you I'm going to take a leave of absence. I was coming to Greece, to live there for a while so we could see each other under ordinary circumstances, to see if I *could* live there."

Nick stared at her, an incredulous smile spreading over his face. "You'd do that for me, Sara?" he asked. "Give up everything you've worked for?"

"Not give up. Just to give us a chance to work something out. I did a lot of thinking, and I had a talk with Stephanie."

"My sister Stephanie?" Nick hit his forehead with a clenched fist. "Oh no, now it's all over. If she talked about me, you won't want me. I won't have a secret left." He collapsed on his back, pretending to be mortally wounded.

Sara nearly choked in her laughter. "Nick, you idiot. She didn't tell me anything about you except that you were stubborn, impatient, ripped up presents before Christmas—"

Nick's hand shot out to cover her mouth. "Enough, Sara. I can't stand it."

When she began to kiss and nuzzle his palm he removed it, his face becoming serious. "What did she say, Sara?"

Sara looked at him, her beautiful eyes golden and transparent. "She told me to stop listening to my head and look at what was in my heart. When I did, I found you. I need you. My career would never be enough by itself."

"You can still have it, Sara," Nick said gently, his hand threading through her hair.

"I know. You're wonderful, just as Stephanie said. But I think I'll take some time off when we have our children."

Nick gave her a hard, smacking kiss. "Yes, our children. Do you want to start on them right away?"

Sara pretended to consider. "Well, not right away unless we've started one now. Maybe in a year or two when we're more settled." She poked her fingers into his ribs. "I want to enjoy you first."

Nick grinned. "Do you? You'll have your chance now. I won't let us be apart again. We'll get married as soon as we can arrange it. We'll buy a house and I'll get the computer connections installed so I can run my business. You can keep working as long as you want. In fact, since your school year usually ends in April we can still spend part of each year in Greece if we want to. How does that sound? Oh, you will marry me, won't you?"

Sara's eyes were filled with golden light as she gazed into his earnest face. This moment must be the happiest of her life. She had it all, more than she'd ever dared to dream. With an impulsiveness she would not have recognized in herself two months ago, she flung her arms around his neck, bearing him down to the mattress. "Yes, Nick, yes!" Then she stopped kissing him as she raised her head, a horrified look on her face. "The letter to the university—I mailed it. Oh no!"

Nick laughed, tumbling her across the bed. "Never mind. We'll phone them and ask them not to open it." His mouth began to trail a path of fire down her cheek and over her lips. "Later, though. Much later."

AMERICAN TRIBUTE

Where a man's dreams count for more than his parentage...

Look for these upcoming titles under the Special Edition American Tribute banner.

LOVE'S HAUNTING REFRAIN
Ada Steward #289—February 1986
For thirty years a deep dark secret kept them apart—King Stockton made his millions while his wife, Amelia, held everything together. Now could they tell their secret, could they admit their love?

THIS LONG WINTER PAST
Jeanne Stephens #295—March 1986
Detective Cody Wakefield checked out Assistant District Attorney Liann McDowell, but only in his leisure time. For it was the danger of Cody's job that caused Liann to shy away.

AM-TRIB-1

AMERICAN
TRIBUTE

RIGHT BEHIND THE RAIN
Elaine Camp #301—April 1986
The difficulty of coping with her brother's
death brought reporter Raleigh Torrence
to the office of Evan Younger, a police
psychologist. He helped her to deal with
her feelings and emotions, including love.

CHEROKEE FIRE
Gena Dalton #307—May 1986
It was Sabrina Dante's silver spoon that
Cherokee cowboy Jarod Redfeather couldn't
trust. The two lovers came from opposite
worlds, but Jarod's Indian heritage taught
them to overcome their differences.

NOBODY'S FOOL
Renee Roszel #313—June 1986
Everyone bet that Martin Dante and Cara
Torrence would get together. But Martin
wasn't putting any money down, and Cara
was out to prove that she was nobody's fool.

MISTY MORNINGS, MAGIC NIGHTS
Ada Steward #319—July 1986
The last thing Carole Stockton wanted was to
fall in love with another politician, especially
Donnelly Wakefield. But under a blanket of
secrecy, far from the campaign spotlights,
their love became a powerful force.

Silhouette Special Edition

COMING NEXT MONTH

LOVE'S HAUNTING REFRAIN—Ada Steward
Amelia had left the East Coast to join King on his Oklahoma ranch.
Theirs was a marriage of love and passion, yet it was threatened by
the secret that King dared not reveal.

MY HEART'S UNDOING—Phyllis Halldorson
Colleen's love for Erik had grown from a schoolgirl crush into the
passions of a woman. Erik had loved before.... Could he forget the
woman who'd broken his heart, or would she haunt their future?

SURPRISE OFFENSE—Carole Halston
Football superstar Rocky Players had a reputation as a womanizer,
so why was he treating Dana like one of the boys? Dana was
definitely a woman, as Rocky was soon to find out.

BIRD IN FLIGHT—Sondra Stanford
When Andie and Bill met by chance in London, they were each
flooded with memories. Had a three-year separation taught them
enough to overcome their differences and rediscover their love?

TRANSFER OF LOYALTIES—Roslyn MacDonald
Adrienne was a dedicated employee who thought of little but her
career, until Jared Hawks came along and showed her the truth in the
old adage "all work and no play..."

AS TIME GOES BY—Brooke Hastings
Sarah needed the funds that Jonathan Hailey controlled in order to
continue her underwater exploration, but slowly her need for funds
was overridden by her need for Jonathan.

AVAILABLE NOW: